P9-CQK-218

SOME REASON IN MADNESS

Also by Cathy Vasas-Brown

Every Wickedness

SOME REASON IN MADNESS

CATHY VASAS-BROWN

DOUBLEDAY CANADA

National Library of Canada Cataloguing in Publication

Vasas-Brown, Cathy
Some reason in madness / Cathy Vasas-Brown.

ISBN 0-385-65999-7

I. Title.

PS8593.A77S65 2004 C813'.6 C2003-904995-7

Jacket image: Hans Neleman/Getty Images
Jacket design: Leah Springate
Printed and bound in the USA

Published in Canada by
Doubleday Canada, a division of
Random House of Canada Limited

Visit Random House of Canada Limited's website: www.randomhouse.ca

BVG 10 9 8 7 6 5 4 3 2 1

In loving memory of
Chester Geza Vasas
who loved music,
dancing,
telling stories,
laughing,
bike riding,
jigsaw puzzles,
crossword puzzles . . .
apparently, I didn't get it off the trees.
Thank you, Daddy, for the many gifts you've given me.

There is always some madness in love,
but there is also always
some reason in madness.

Friedrich Nietzsche
Thus Spoke Zarathustra

SOME REASON IN MADNESS

1

"NO MORE FUCK-UPS, okay, Ventresca? Here's your stuff."
The matron shoved a pile across the counter. Frank caught a look at her badge. Her name was Becky. He almost laughed. She was at least six feet tall, with boobs big enough to support a set of Britannicas, and her name was not Helga, not Bertha, but Becky.

He examined his pile, one item at a time.

A black comb, two teeth missing. He ran his thumb down the teeth and listened to the plinking sound. A white T-shirt, a pair of black sneakers with laces knotted in several places where they'd broken, and a pair of Levi's, still grease-stained and smelling of 10W30.

One cassette: Carlos Santana. He turned the plastic case over and scanned the list of tunes. Almost immediately, he began to sing softly. *Got a black magic woman.* He looked up to find the matron staring at him. He stopped singing and focused once again on the pile, trying to ignore the cords of pain at the back of his neck.

One ballpoint pen. And his wallet. Still in pretty good shape, the black leather molded comfortably by the curve of his ass. He opened it. Two credit cards, both expired in 1987. His driver's license, car ownership, and the picture. The one he'd traded for.

Sure you can drive my car, if I can have a picture of you.

She was kind of half-smiling, her long brown hair in a single braid to one side, stray wisps floating around her face. He pulled the picture from the wallet and held it, stroking its surface with a dirty index finger.

The matron cleared her throat.

When Frank glanced up again, she was staring at the photograph. Then she looked him square in the eye and repeated, "No more fu—"

"Hey, don't you worry 'bout me, Becky. I'm not coming back to Sunnybrook Farm."

His things were packaged. The State of Massachusetts gave him a suit he would never wear, along with some cash. He counted it. Enough here to set up a small lemonade stand in a good neighborhood. Knowing he'd have to get a job, and fast, he grabbed his gear and felt himself being hustled to the door, Becky's long strides proof of her eagerness to get rid of him.

He wasn't quite prepared for the shock of late-autumn air that hit his face when he got outside. He inhaled deeply, waiting for a whiff of cafeteria food. Or stale urine.

But the air was fresh, and the sky was full of huge billowy clouds rolling eastward. At least he thought it was east.

When he reached the gate, he saw a bus pulling away and broke into a run to catch it. Then he stopped himself. He didn't even know what bus fare cost these days. He wasn't about to look stupid in front of anybody.

So he walked, following the direction of the clouds. He pulled the picture from his wallet once again. With the cool, clean air working its way into his pores and her pretty face in front of him, the knot in his neck began to loosen. Within minutes, he felt great.

2

"SO YOU WANT TO hurt Jenny?"

"Yeah."

"Why is that, Derek?"

Samantha Quinlan looked at the boy's clenched fists, his tight jaw, the muscles in his neck straining against his black T-shirt.

He's afraid if he loosens up, he'll unravel.

"Because she hurt me . . . she hurt me so bad." His shoulders slumped, his head dropped, and the tears came, the genuine sorrow that had been hidden beneath his armor of anger. She let him cry for a while, remembering her own pain of a lost first love.

Eventually, she asked, "Do you really want to hurt Jenny, Derek? Deep down?"

He shook his head miserably. "No."

She waited.

"I still love her, Mrs. Q." His voice broke, and he began sobbing again, his fists grinding away tears from bloodshot eyes.

Part of her wanted to cradle the youth in her arms, tell him there would be other Jennys, a lifetime of magic ahead of him. A trained counselor, she knew better, and she kept her mouth shut.

Derek talked about the good times with Jenny and the bad times. Samantha listened.

Derek was the fifth student she'd seen this morning. He sat in a moss green chair, picking at the stuffing, rolling the pale yellow fluff between his thumb and index finger.

Only fifteen, Derek was built like a battering ram. His head was half a size too large for his body, and he was clumsy. He moved slowly, like a geriatric wildebeest, his bulk not enough on its own to get him on the football team. But when puberty had run its trying course, Derek would be a handsome boy. Right now he had the look of a tough young prizefighter who had gone a few rounds and lost. He spoke in a deep, garbled drawl, which made him sound a lot dumber than he was.

But he had a big heart. "That Derek is the *nicest* guy," Samantha often heard girls whisper as they gathered by their lockers. But right now, his big heart was broken.

Samantha persuaded Derek to list all of Jenny's positive qualities.

"She's pretty," he said after a while. "Fun to be with . . . uh, has nice clothes . . . uh . . ."

Samantha paused long enough to give him a fair chance to add to the list, but it came as no surprise to her the list was so short. She thought of Jenny, whose nice clothes were widely rumored to have been flung about the back seat of more than one make of automobile during the past year. Samantha knew Derek would be hard-pressed to make Jenny sound like Joan of Arc.

"I'm sure Jenny was very special to you, Derek."

"Yeah, she was. But I shoulda listened to my buddies. They said I was too far gone, that Jenny'd just end up hurting me."

"Can you count on those friends now? To help you through this?"

Derek nodded. "They want me to go to a party on Saturday."

"Sounds like a plan. How do you feel about it?"

"I guess it'd be all right. Maybe I'd meet a few people." Derek scratched his large head with chewed-off fingernails.

"Beats sitting around moping, doesn't it?"

"That won't bring Jenny back, will it." Then he attempted a cautious smile, which broadened slowly to a grin. "Know what? I'm starting to feel a little better. Say," he said, tossing his hair out of his eyes, "maybe I'm too good for Jenny. Whadya think?"

Samantha smiled. "Derek, I think there are a lot of nice girls out there just waiting for someone like you to come along."

"Yeah? Hey, Mrs. Q., you won't tell anyone about . . . you know . . . the crying and stuff?"

She stood, walked around her desk, and patted him on the shoulder. "Your secret's safe with me. Drop by soon and let me know how things are going." She initialed the bottom of a yellow slip of paper and handed it to him.

Derek ducked as he went through the door. Though he was in no danger of hitting his head, Samantha knew he was self-conscious about his size.

Once Samantha had removed the pile of stuffing from the linoleum beneath the chair, she had a chance to survey her office. *God, what an awful place to be miserable.* Hardly an office at all, really. More like a cubbyhole, about the size of a celebrity's shoe closet. An old gray metal desk with one stuck drawer, a swivel chair that tipped over if you leaned back too far, and tubes of fluorescent lighting that flickered and hummed. In front of her desk were two mismatched armchairs, the green one now beyond salvation. All in all, not an inviting place for students to come and talk about their problems. But they came anyway.

Being the guidance counselor didn't make her popular with the high-school staff. Her peers knew she listened to complaints about them and they cold-shouldered her whenever she went to bat for one of the students. In spite of that, she loved her job.

At thirty-four, Samantha was the school's youngest counselor. She dressed as fashionably as her budget would allow. She spoke the kids' language. It wasn't forced and she made no concerted effort to be cool. The school had fifteen hundred students, and Samantha knew a good number of them by name. She knew, too, that there was something about her that drew the students to her office while the other counselors twiddled their thumbs and made coffee. Several of her colleagues were put off by her way with the kids, which they thought too casual for a teacher. Samantha knew better.

The kids came in confused, troubled, and hurting. They left as friends. After school, while the rest of her colleagues stampeded to the parking lot and hightailed it home, Samantha enjoyed lingering at the corner doughnut shop, sharing coffee and conversation with one or more of the kids. Students seemed to cluster about wherever she went.

On her bulletin board, she'd pinned a poster of a marmalade kitten clinging to a tree trunk. *Hang in there, Baby!* Plain and simple.

Samantha looked at her date book. *Faculty meeting—4:00.* Had she told Matthew? Yes. Her son would be downstairs keeping their landlady company until Samantha got home.

Tom Lundstrom poked his head through the half-open door and waved a brown paper bag. "Lunch, anyone? I've got extra."

"Not going to the staff lounge?"

"Are you kidding? And eat with the barracudas? My ulcer's just nicely under control, thanks." Laughing, Tom plunked down in the chair Derek had just vacated and set half a roast beef sandwich in front of Samantha. "Looks like I got here just in time."

"What do you mean?"

"This chair. Were you so hungry you took a bite out of it?"

"Very funny."

Tom chuckled "Thought you might be trying to kick your

chocolate addiction by adding a little fiber to your diet."

Samantha and Tom had known each other since high school. They'd had one date, doubling with another girl and Tom's constant companion, Scott. When Samantha fell for Scott, there were no hard feelings. Tom was a devoted friend, and together, they'd paddled through adolescent white water. They enjoyed the thrills of the ride and bailed each other out during more perilous legs of the journey. And it was the same today.

Tom, like Scott, had been an excellent athlete. He was tall and muscled, and still retained his Malibu beach-bum looks along with a boyish smile that many women found irresistible. Samantha was drawn to him more because he could make her laugh, even on days when there was precious little to laugh about.

"So eat, *eat*," Tom said, nudging the half-sandwich toward her. "Listen, if you get to the faculty meeting first, save me a seat, will you? The last two times I got stuck next to dumbass Halloran. Let someone else have the privilege for a change."

Neither Tom nor Samantha were fans of the principal, a man they suspected must have a calloused behind from sitting on so many fences.

"Yep," Tom continued. "Our Peter Principal. Bert Halloran's proof that if you stick around long enough, someone'll be stupid enough to promote you. Anyway, no more about that jerkoff. He gives me indigestion. What'll it be tonight? Bowling? Pizza and a video?"

"Sorry, I can't. I'm catching a movie with Chris. He just got back from his conference. We haven't seen each other in over a week. I hope you're not disappointed."

"Not to worry. Is Matthew still on?"

Samantha shrugged. "He said something about studying for a test. You'd better check with him." She took a healthy chomp out of the sandwich.

Samantha, her son, and Tom had had a standing Wednesday-night date for as long as she could remember. When Matthew was younger, it was outings at the local park or tossing a Nerf ball around the tiny back yard, occasionally a spirited game of miniature golf. Samantha thought the male companionship did Matthew good. Once in a while, they would go for Saturday drives—antiquing in Essex, lunching at a lobster shack in Rockport, visiting the Salem Witch Museum. It had been nearly a year since their last all-day excursion and now "Hump Nights" seemed to be going the way of the pterodactyl, too. The threesome was lucky to get out together every other week.

"I'm sure if Matthew's busy, you'll be able to occupy yourself with some willing female," Samantha said, looking at Tom's new sweater. "Someone who'll tell you that shade brings out the blue in your eyes, that sort of thing."

Tom grinned. "You know me so well."

"No one special jumping out of your little black book?"

"Come on, Samantha. You know they're all special. Banana? Or a Mars bar."

"Ass. You already know the answer." Samantha snatched the candy bar from Tom's grasp, tore the wrapper off, and bit into it before Tom could rescind the offer. "Boy, did I ever need this."

"Hard day at the salt mines?" Tom aimed the banana peel at the wastebasket, where it dangled, half in, half out.

Samantha nodded again. "One modest success, though."

"Modest? Somehow I don't think so. You're the best counselor this dump's seen in years."

"Why, thank you, kind sir." Samantha clasped her hands behind her head and leaned back, affecting her best smug look. The rickety chair went *sproing,* and Samantha had to hook her foot into the bottom of her desk to keep from falling over.

Tom convulsed with laughter. "Counselor, schmounselor.

You're the one who's unstable around here. You should have seen your face!"

Samantha steadied herself. "Damn," she said, rubbing her foot. "I've ruined another pair of panty hose. Halloran owes me." She licked traces of melted chocolate from her fingertips.

There was a firm knock at the office door and Bert Halloran walked in, carrying an arrangement of flowers. He glanced at Tom, cleared his throat, and scowled. "These just came. Got your name on them." He handed the flowers to Samantha.

Samantha took the bouquet and placed it on her desk. It was an odd mix—purple mums, purple daisies, carnations dyed purple. The flowers were arranged in an old-fashioned china cup and saucer. "I wonder who sent them."

"Read the card," Halloran said. "I've got better things to do than run around delivering flowers. This is a school, after all." He shot them both his best threatening look, scowled again, then left, closing the door loudly after him.

"Great," Samantha muttered as the footsteps retreated down the corridor. "We're in here with the door shut having lunch. How long do you think it'll take before the rumors of our alleged affair resurface?"

"Let's see." Tom checked his watch. "Halloran's probably on his way to tell Petrella right now, and once Jim gets hold of the news, I'd say . . . half an hour at the outside. Anyway, my boxers aren't in a twist about it. We've laughed it all off before, we can do it again. Now forget about it. What's with the flowers?"

Samantha plucked the small mauve envelope from the center of the bouquet. The name Sam on the outside of the envelope was printed in a cramped, irregular backhand. "Only one way to find out."

The message inside was brief and cryptic. *Can't wait to see you again.* There was no signature.

"Well?" Tom asked.

"Damned if I know."

"Must be your rich boyfriend."

Samantha read the message again. "I guess so." She recalled the dozen cream-colored roses Chris had sent her after their first date. Simple. Beautiful. She looked down at the gaudy arrangement.

"They sure are purple," Tom said.

"You've got that right. Somehow, I credited Chris with having better taste. Oh well, I'll be gracious and enthusiastic when I thank him tonight."

She rose and set the hideous bouquet on top of her filing cabinet, unable to relax the stiff frown that had settled on her face.

3

SAMANTHA SNAGGED AN AVAILABLE seat at the end of a long laminate table. A mere ten minutes in the staff lounge reminded her of the reason she rarely graced the place. The room was a hive of gossip, the more malicious and difficult to prove, the better it was received. Much of it buzzed from the mouth of Hank Ehrhart, senior phys. ed., who was holding court on the sofa.

"Hear some of the city schools are having trouble with Satanism. Found a few dead animals, some pentagrams . . ."

Ehrhart's fan club leaned closer for more dirt. Among them was science teacher Rudolf Stanfield, still clad in the same tired tweed blazer and bow tie he'd worn for the staff photo in '78. Stanfield had to lean closer than the rest; on a good day, he was merely hard of hearing, but most days he was deaf as a post. Frequently he asked Ehrhart to repeat some juicy tidbit he'd only caught half of. The coach was eager to oblige.

"Any devil worship around here and you know who'll be at the root of it," Jim Petrella, the shop teacher, said. "Jonny Nesmith."

Grunts of agreement erupted from the chorus.

"Always dresses in black. Can't look you in the eye. That kid gives me the creeps."

"Don't even talk to me about him," Ehrhart chimed in. "And what about Pete Sinclair? Kid's been acting funny ever since he came back to school."

Samantha seethed. Pete Sinclair had been to see her. His alcoholic, abusive father had returned home, and his mother had taken him back. Again. And Jonny Nesmith was pathologically shy, an easy target for gossip among those who couldn't understand him. He was also one of the few regular churchgoers Samantha knew.

She inhaled deeply and forced herself to face the group. "Hey, come on, gang. We don't even know if we've got this problem yet." She tried to keep her voice light, but Petrella and Ehrhart were glaring at her. "No sense jumping to conclusions, is there?"

"Oh, here we go again with the bleeding-heart routine." Petrella played an air violin.

"Pete and Jonny are good kids."

Ehrhart rolled his eyes and smirked. "Did you ever stop to think maybe some of us are tired of your self-righteous attitude, *Counselor* Quinlan? This is our time, our room. We deserve to let off a little steam."

Samantha felt warmth rush to her face. She turned away and wished she had a cup of coffee, tea, arsenic, anything to occupy her mouth so she wouldn't blurt out what she was really thinking. Behind her, she heard Stanfield's voice.

"What'd she say, Hank? Come again, Jim?"

The first-year teacher on Samantha's right gave her arm a light tap. "Went over like a lead balloon, didn't it," she whispered. "Ten points for trying, though."

Samantha braved a smile and looked at the clock, wondering when this day would end and why Halloran could never be on time for his own meetings.

Tom came in, grabbed a cup of coffee, and sat down on Samantha's left. A few knowing glances were exchanged among members of the rumor mill. "Caught Matt before he left. He's studying tonight, so it looks like it's me and my little black book. Well, actually, it's blue."

"Where were you when I needed you?"

"What happened?"

She briefed Tom.

"So that explains that huge black spot on the back of your head."

"What?"

"Ehrhart. He's burning a hole with those beady eyes of his. Can't you feel it?"

The gym teacher clung ferociously to his pessimism. "There are some people out there who are just plain bad," he said, in a deliberately loud voice. "You can analyze 'em and discuss their feelings till the cows come home, but one day they're still gonna go out and take an ax to the whole family. If *some people* wanna save 'em, they can damn well go ahead and try. But leave the rest of us out of it."

Samantha whirled around. "I'd love to leave you out of something, Hank. The trouble is, you keep showing up."

It was a good line, and mildly satisfying, though Samantha knew that the stunned look on Ehrhart's face was temporary. He wouldn't forget this episode and, sooner or later, he would find a way to rub her face in it.

"Nice going, my friend," Tom whispered to Samantha. "You've really got him wound up. This should be a great meeting. And here comes old Hee Haw now."

By the time Samantha climbed the rear stairs to her second-floor apartment, she was certain her head would crack wide open. The staff meeting didn't have the fireworks and bloodshed Tom had predicted. Instead, Halloran had delivered his usual hour-and-a-half monologue in his one-note, one-rhythm voice that drove Samantha mad. During the first fifteen minutes, while Tom sketched pictures of jackasses, Samantha balanced her checkbook and made a grocery list, then spent the rest of the time thinking of countless other things she could be doing. Nothing gave her a headache quicker than one of Halloran's meetings, and this one was a killer. She hoped a few aspirin would chase the pain away so she could enjoy her evening with Chris.

When she unlocked the kitchen door, Matthew was staring into the open refrigerator, gyrating to an old Aerosmith song, and emitting a pretty convincing Steve Tyler scream. Thankfully, Beatrice, who owned the house and lived downstairs, was nearly as challenged as Rudolf Stanfield in the hearing department.

"Matthew!" Samantha shouted. "Headache! Off! Mercy!" She pointed frantically at the archaic tape deck in the living room.

Matthew slammed the fridge door, which sent another stabbing pain directly to her temples, and hurried toward the offending noise. "Sorry, Mom," he said sheepishly when the room was quiet. "I should have known listening to Halloran would make you sick. What should we do about supper?"

Samantha glanced at the clock.

"Wait, let me guess," he said. "You want to shower and get ready for your date, so no fuss, no muss. Am I right?"

"On the money, Swami Matthew."

"There's a pizza in the freezer. Be ready in twenty minutes."

"Sold."

"I'll do chef duty, you hit the shower."

"Aye-aye," she retorted.

She'd done all right raising her son on her own, Samantha thought as she headed toward the bathroom. In fact, it was the accomplishment she was proudest of. Matthew was a dream kid.

There were times when Samantha still wondered how she'd rated such a son while other parents couldn't wait until their teens were old enough to move out. Samantha used to joke that her son became a man in kindergarten. Lately, the only flaw she could pick on was Matthew's habit of playing his music too loud. Even when he raided her collection of '70s and '80s ballads, the acoustic guitar reverberated through their tiny apartment. No reason to wish him off to college, though. They were a team, and a tight one.

When she and Matthew had moved to the upstairs floor of Beatrice's house, neither woman was sure the arrangement would work out. Beatrice Hazelton, then fifty-six and a widow, was glad of the company, a friendly footfall overhead, but she hadn't been so certain about having six-month-old Matthew aboard.

"Are you a smoker?" she'd asked.

"No."

"Lots of boyfriends?"

"Furthest thing from my mind."

"Steady income?"

"I'm a waitress, studying to be a teacher."

"If you look after my laundry, I'll reduce your rent."

"If you'll baby-sit my son, we've got a deal."

"Let's try it."

So they tried it. It had been working ever since. Luckily, Matthew was well behaved and quickly endeared himself to Beatrice, becoming her loyal companion. Beatrice was happy, and Matthew was happy. Samantha got to know the neighbors when they hung their clothes on the lines in the spring and summer, preferring this "just folks" environment to impersonal high-rise living. No elevators and underground parking to contend with. No rape traps.

Though her apartment might not make the pages of *Better Homes & Gardens,* it was cozy and warm. She had scoured, papered, sanded, and painted, turning the once neglected quarters into a comfortable retreat. Matthew got the only bedroom, which she'd outfitted with a wall of shelves for his collection of books. A bulletin board, screw-nailed to the wall behind his headboard, was a yardstick for his growth. His posters had progressed from Barney the Dinosaur to Luke Skywalker to Michael Jordan. Now supermodel Gisele Bündchen hovered over him at night.

Samantha's sanctuary was their living room, its pleasant floral sofa opening into a double bed. The rest of the furniture had been purchased at secondhand shops masquerading as antique stores. Samantha took pity on the scarred, eroded finishes of others' castoffs. If a piece had a gouged surface or a missing knob, she bought it.

Matthew had taken one look at the ratty pieces with Colonial paint flecks dotting the wood and had called the stuff crap. He later refined his vocabulary and christened it *junque.* But almost overnight, primitive became the thing. Magazines were full of pictures featuring the look Samantha had thrown together.

When she returned to the kitchen wearing clean clothes with her hair blown partially dry, Matthew had the meal prepared. The pizza was steaming hot. He'd even thrown together a salad.

"I don't know about the tomatoes, Mom. They got shoved to the back of the fridge and were half frozen when I pulled them out. But you know what they say. Presentation is everything. How come your meeting went on so long?"

Samantha sat down at the table, then rolled her eyes, remembering the session at school. "Someone mentioned something about an outbreak of devil worship at one of the downtown high schools. Can you believe it?"

"Well, nothing like that's gonna happen at our school. They won't be able to find a virgin to sacrifice."

Samantha laughed. "Tom says you're studying tonight, but now that I think of it, didn't you write your history test this morning?"

There was another sheepish look. "Guilty. I just didn't feel like hanging out with Mr. L. tonight. Are you gonna whup me, Ma?"

"If anyone deserves a whuppin, boy, it'd be you. Any particular reason you don't want to see Tom?"

"Nah. It's just that I knew you were going out with Chris, and, well . . . Let's face it, Mom. This tradition's getting a little old."

"Oops. Sounds like you're growing up. Tom's been awfully good to us, Matthew."

"I know, and I'm not saying I want to dump him cold, but maybe seeing a little less of him would be okay?"

"I just don't want to be unkind, that's all. Tom has no family around here, and I really think he enjoys his times with us."

"Okay, Mom. I won't be a jerk about it."

"Didn't think so for a second." Samantha carried the dirty plates to the kitchen sink.

"I stopped by your office today on my way to Spanish class."

"What for?"

"Money, what else? Who sent you those purple flowers?"

"Chris, I think."

"Gee, after dating you for almost a year, you'd think he'd know you hate purple."

"Maybe he just forgot." *And he forgot to sign the card, too.*

"I betcha they're not from Chris at all," Matthew said. "Probably some lovesick student sent them."

"Why do you say that?" He avoided her gaze. "Matthew?"

"Ah, Mom. You know, it's just that some of the guys at school, well . . . they think you're a real babe."

Samantha bit her lip, rinsed a plate and set it on the drainer. "I'd rather they were from Chris and that the florist had only purple flowers left. The idea of some mystery admirer out there is creepy."

"Well, you'll find out soon enough. Chris oughta be here any time and you can ask him."

The phone rang. "Can you get that, Matthew? I'm up to my elbows in suds."

A minute later, Matthew was back in the kitchen picking up a tea towel. "Wrong number, I guess. Nobody there. Just like last night. Tell you what. You go comb your hair or put on some lipstick or do whatever it is women do. Remember, the better you look, the more money he'll spend on you. It's a well-known fact."

"Babes like me don't need to concern ourselves with that." Samantha whipped a rubber glove at her son's backside. He dodged too late, and the sodden rubber smacked loudly against his blue jeans. While Matthew hurled mock accusations of child abuse, Samantha went to the bathroom to touch up her lipstick.

She smiled as she thought again about the poster kitten dangling from the tree branch. It really was true. If you just hung in long enough, things would work out. Until she'd met Chris, she'd dated only sporadically, cautiously. But Chris turned out to be several cuts above the rest, charming without being slick, attractive without too much flash. He placed no conditions on his kindness. He hadn't pressured her for sex, didn't try to convince her how good they'd be together, or use any of the smooth lines women's magazines listed as "The Ten Favorite Come-ons of North American Men." When they'd finally made love, she was relaxed and it was terrific. Chris had a counselor's attention span and could listen at length to her complaints about the infamous teachers at Somerville Central. Plus, he got along well with Matthew.

She looked closely at herself in the mirror. The lipstick was fine. She smoothed her hair back into a ponytail and secured it with a scarf. Seconds later, she yanked the scarf out, and her hair tumbled loose. She piled it into a knot on her head and examined the effect. Frowning, she let the hair fall. She tried dividing it into sections for a braid, but nixed that idea, too. Finally, fluffing the still-damp hair with her fingers, she allowed it to fall onto her shoulders in gentle waves. Still fussing, she tugged at her stiff upturned collar, then undid another button on her blouse, exposing the top of her lightly freckled chest.

"Going down to Beatrice's?" Samantha asked her son when she returned to the living room.

"Nah, I visited her after school. Think I'll stay up here tonight and watch some TV."

"Beatrice might be lonely, Matthew."

"Or I might be too young to stay here alone? Mom, I'm almost *fifteen.* Give me a break. No dark mysterious stranger is gonna kidnap me while you're at the movies. Besides, Beatrice is just downstairs. I'll be fine."

Footsteps sounded on the rear stairs, and Matthew stepped across the room and opened the kitchen door. Chris stood on the rear balcony.

Quickly, Samantha fastened the button on her blouse and went to greet him.

4

THE FILM'S TITLE BLAZED across the screen as Chris and Samantha entered the theater. They followed the path of tiny lightbulbs until they spied two vacant seats along the aisle, about halfway down, not in the last row, as Matthew had slyly suggested to Samantha.

The movie was good, a taut thriller, just like the newspaper review said, and when the onscreen couple began making love on the hood of a black Corvette, Samantha felt a momentary glitch in her stomach. Months ago, she would have averted her eyes, muttered an excuse and bolted for the ladies' room. If Chris tried to reach for her hand, she would have fumbled instead for a tissue to wipe a nose that didn't need wiping.

Now as the couple writhed on the screen, Samantha's fingers were securely and comfortably laced with Chris's strong ones. He leaned toward her and whispered, "I know what you're thinking, and forget it."

"What?"

"It's too cold outside."

"You're awful," Samantha replied, pretending to be aghast. "I wasn't thinking anything like that."

"Liar." He gave her hand a squeeze.

Chris was right. Her thoughts strayed to the two of them often, en route to work in the morning, between appointments during the day, and in the quiet hours of night. In her frequent reveries, Chris wasn't always wearing clothes.

After the movie, they went to their favorite Back Bay café for dessert and coffee. To Samantha's amusement, the waiters, all in black berets, sprinkled their vocabulary with the prerequisite *mercis* and *s'il vous plaits.* French with a Boston accent.

Samantha followed Chris from the back counter to an upholstered booth near the front of the restaurant and sidled in. Shirred Austrian curtains were festooned across the large front windows, shielding their view of the traffic rushing by on Arlington. As she sipped her cappuccino, Samantha asked Chris about the flowers.

"I didn't send you any," he replied. "Must be from one of your other boyfriends." He cut into his napoleon, watching as the custard slid out from the center. "There's just no delicate way to eat these things, is there. So who's my competition?"

"I have no idea. The card wasn't signed. Matthew thinks it might be a student with a crush."

"Probably right. Can't say I blame him, whoever he is. If you were my teacher, I'd be chasing you around the desk every chance I got."

"And I'd let you catch me."

"Every time?"

She paused to consider the question, then said, "Pretty much."

Chris leveled his gaze at her and grinned. "Tramp."

It all felt so good, Samantha thought, this kidding around, especially about things that for years weren't funny. Countless therapy sessions and a string of insensitive men had produced a two-sided Samantha, with half of her yearning for affection while the other half cringed at the mere thought of intimacy. Now, with Chris, she was glued together in one piece, as if awakened from an evil spell and ready to experience pleasure.

"Anyway," Chris continued, "have you got any suspects on this flower caper?"

"Nope. I asked the secretaries if there'd been a delivery or if they'd seen the name of the florist on a van, but they said Bert Halloran found the flowers on the floor outside his office."

"Hmm, that's weird, all right. But listen, don't lose any sleep over it. Sooner or later, lovesick teenagers either come forward or move on to another fantasy."

"Well, I'd sure like this one to move on. I find it kind of unsettling."

Chris put his fork down and snarled at his dessert. "I give up." The pastry crust was all over the plate. There were crumbs on the table. "I should have had an éclair."

"Subtle, Dr. Paxton. Very subtle." Samantha held up her éclair and Chris took a bite. For an instant, his lips brushed her fingertips. There was a trace of whipped cream at the corner of his mouth. She wiped it away with her finger, feeling the soft warmth of his skin.

"We could get ourselves some more whipped cream," Chris said, grinning again, "go to my place . . ."

Samantha reached across the table for his hand. "As tempting and as fattening as that sounds, not tonight, Chris."

"I know, I know. Matthew's home alone, you've got to get up early tomorrow . . . Can't blame a guy for trying, though. That sound you hear is my heart breaking, but don't you worry about it. I'll still introduce you to my mother, God help you."

"Your mother? She knows about us?"

"She does now. After another of her unsuccessful attempts to set me up with a society bimbo she thinks is perfect for me, I finally had to tell her I was seeing someone. You should have been there for the third degree. I could have used some advice."

Samantha peered closely at him. "You seem to have survived. I don't see any bruises. What did you tell her about me?"

"Basic stuff. What you do for a living, that you have a son, you're okay to look at, terrific in the sack . . ."

Samantha laughed and raised her coffee cup to her lips. "That must have gone over big."

In the year Samantha had known Chris, she had heard many stories about the battle of wills waged between him and his mother. Chris, one of Boston's finest oral surgeons, was widely published in dental journals. Before setting up practice in the city two years before, he'd done a stint in the army, traveling around the world to wherever his services were required. In that time, he'd learned the importance of ministering to others; he'd removed bullets from more jaws than he cared to count. Now, many of Chris's patients were battered women, their jaws broken by abusive partners. Despite his label, "the dentist with a heart," Chris's mother, Meredith, seemed embarrassed by the nature of his work.

"Looking into people's mouths all day is so undignified," she'd said to him frequently. Meredith yearned for the day when Chris would leave all his altruistic nonsense behind and take over the reins at Paxton Pharmaceuticals, the company founded by Chris's late father.

Samantha knew it would never happen. Chris immersed himself in his work, devoted long hours to it, sometimes at the expense of romance. Samantha had fielded many last-minute calls, canceling dinner plans because an emergency had arisen. She had to remind herself that Chris was doing what he loved and that he was happy, but there were times when she felt the jealous pangs of having to accept second-place status. Still, the thought of Chris as a corporate man kowtowing to his mother was worse, so the battle of wills between the two Paxtons continued, with Samantha keeping score.

"I hate to foist my mother on anyone, Samantha. You know that. She's an incurable snob with grandiose plans for me, but she's still my mother and you'll have to meet her someday. Especially now that I've fallen in love with you."

Samantha lowered her cup. "You what?"

"Yep," Chris said matter-of-factly. "I tried to talk myself out of it. Told myself there were better-looking women out there. Smarter ones, too. But there's no getting around it. You're the one, all right. Dammit."

She looked at his handsome face, the longish sandy hair curling over his shirt collar, his hazel eyes with the golden flecks. This man could have his pick of women.

"And don't even bother trying to talk me out of it or I'll slap you silly. Now, if you won't let me carry you off for a night of unbridled lust, then I guess I'd better get you home. Come on."

The ride back to Somerville was quiet. Samantha picked at her nail polish, brushing the clear peelings from her lap onto the deep blue carpet of Chris's car. He appeared not to notice. From time to time, he hummed along to the radio, leaving Samantha to her private thoughts.

Chris Paxton loves me. Baggage and all.

As the car pulled up in front of Beatrice's, Samantha saw all the ground-floor lights on. Matthew and Beatrice must be watching scary movies again. She preceded Chris through the chain-link gate and around the side of the house. Beatrice's jalousie windows were cranked partway open to admit a crisp breeze. Sheer priscilla curtains swayed their seductive dance. Samantha resisted the impulse to rise up on tiptoe, lean in, and holler, "Boo!" Instead she knocked—three short, then four short—on Beatrice's kitchen door, a signal to Matthew that she was home. Then she and Chris went up the wooden staircase to the second-floor landing.

After an awkward pause, Chris said, "Dinner Saturday night?"

She heard the question, just barely. Her mind was still on what he'd said earlier. And she was sorry they hadn't gone back to his place.

"Samantha?"

"Dinner? That sounds wonderful."

He laughed softly. "Then get your best dress ready. We'll do it up right, okay?"

She nodded.

Their kiss began as sweet, teasing, like teenagers experimenting on a first date, then desire overcame them and their contact became urgent, deep, full of yearning. Chris pressed against her, and Samantha felt the delicious pain of the porch railing on her spine.

There was a telltale squeak from one of the steps. "Caught ya!" Matthew hollered. "Shame on you two! Making out where everyone in the neighborhood can see you! Don't suppose you've thought about *my* reputation?"

It seemed as if her dreams had texture that night. There was the smoothness of skin, the bulky, coarse warmth of Chris's thick sweater. The dreams had color, too—sandy hair, hazel eyes with little gold flecks. And hideous purple flowers. In a lilac-patterned teacup.

5

HE PARKED ACROSS the street and waited.

It was a so-so neighborhood, many of the houses covered with yellow, green, or blue siding, but the once cheery pastels had faded over the years, and now the whole street looked neglected and sad. It was as though the homeowners had worked hard enough over the years and had finally given up. Even the Pepsi sign outside the corner mom-and-pop store dangled lopsided, broken. He wondered if anyone noticed.

He'd spent days looking up S. Dubecki in every phone directory in and around Boston. Revere, Charleston, Dedham, Brookline, Quincy—he'd tried them all. But each time he dialed, he hit a dead end. Then he got smart. He remembered the hotshot jock and began again, searching under the new surname.

On his fifth try, he hit pay dirt. The minute she'd said hello, he knew. Her voice was the same, husky like a smoker's. When he heard it, a lazy blue heat washed over him. He hung up. He had a hard-on. In the limited privacy of the telephone booth, he laughed good and long. Some things never changed.

It was twilight before he finally saw some action from the

house across the street. The front door opened, and an old lady came out to sweep the concrete stoop. Skinny little thing. Not much wider than her broom. Who the hell was she?

Soon, a kid came out, took the broom from the woman, and swooshed it across the porch and down the front walk. The old gal went inside. The kid was tall, a little thin, but he was sweeping that sidewalk to beat sixty. Dirt and leaves flew. He was bent over the broom, his face half-hidden in the evening shadows.

Then, there she was, coming from the back of the place. He sat up behind the wheel, blinked, then blinked again.

Yeah, it was her. The same, but different.

He'd only caught a glimpse of her last week, when she had run to her car the morning it was so cold. But she sure wasn't wearing schoolteacher clothes now.

He couldn't get over the way she looked. She was maybe a little thinner than he remembered and her hair was still long—brown and wavy like before, but instead of it being tied in a girlish braid or ponytail, she was wearing it loose, blown high off her forehead. Kind of . . . reckless. Her dress was black, or maybe navy blue, with a double row of buttons. The hem stopped above her knees. The straight cut of the dress and the dark stockings made her legs look endless. The neckline of the dress formed a deep V. In the fading light, he couldn't see the misting of freckles across her nose and cheeks, or the deep green of her eyes.

But he remembered.

Again, he felt a stirring in his groin, and he smiled. The object of every guy's wet dreams. Right here. All his.

Another person came into the front yard. A guy, maybe late thirties, a smooth aftershave-ad type. He hurried to catch up with her, then draped a trench coat over her shoulders, kept his arm around her for a few seconds, gave her shoulder a squeeze. The guy was dressed pretty sharp—dark suit, white shirt, boldly patterned tie. His jacket flapped open.

One thing was for sure—this wasn't the jock. He'd had black hair. This guy's hair was dirty blond.

They weren't holding hands, just walking kind of brother-sisterly toward the kid. And they weren't kissing either, not the way he'd kiss her when they were together.

She planted one on the kid, though, and messed up his hair. Laughing, the kid waved at the couple, then walked, broom in hand, toward the old lady, who had come back out on the porch.

The couple was getting into a car now, a white foreign job, with a license plate that read: I TEETH. And they were off.

He puzzled at the scene for a moment, watching the kid follow the old lady into the house. He didn't understand the whole picture yet, but he would.

Soon.

6

SAMANTHA THOUGHT THE RESTAURANT was handsome. A gallery of nineteenth-century theater posters adorned darkly paneled walls. Candles gleamed in hurricane lamps, their tiny flames repeating their flickering dance throughout the room. She was already light-headed after a glass of wine on an empty stomach, or perhaps her giddiness came from the delicious feeling of Chris's lingering glances, his gaze traveling over her as though seeing her for the first time. With a single look, a whispered word, a mischievous grin, Chris could engage her in the most exquisite, prolonged foreplay and not lay a hand anywhere near her. The silky lingerie she'd splurged on brushed smooth and cool against her skin, and she wasn't certain she could make it through dinner without begging him to remove it.

"Two can play at this game, you know," she told him.

"Game? What game?"

"Maybe I should describe what I'm wearing under this dress."

"You mean, aside from your perfume?" He grinned. "Now stop being such a wicked woman and make up your mind about dinner."

She ordered an appetizer, then savored her entrée of grilled shrimp, the pungent sage sharp on her palate. Dessert, a liqueur, and strong coffee finished off the meal that had stretched to nearly three hours. "I'm afraid I *have* been very wicked," she said when she was done eating. "This meal will cost a fortune, Chris."

"Yeah," he responded, smiling. "What do you suppose I'll want in return?"

"A hamburger could have bought you that. Really, Chris, why the royal treatment? You've still got your office equipment to pay for."

"I know. Up to my eyeballs in debt. If I were you, I wouldn't marry me either."

"I beg your pardon?"

"Here you go, princess," he said, sliding a closed fist across the table. "A little something to start off your collection of crown jewels." Chris uncurled his fingers. On his flat palm lay a gold band with three large oval diamonds.

She gasped.

"Shh," he warned. "Keep it down or everyone will want one."

"I don't know what to say."

"Something along the lines of 'Yes, Chris, you wonderful guy, of course I'll marry you' would work."

She felt her throat constrict, and her eyes began to well up. All she could manage was a nod.

"Maybe we should leave before the floodgates open." When they were outside, Chris said, "Where to, your majesty?"

"Your castle, where else?"

Chris took her hand and led her down the steps, away from the restaurant. His car was parked a few blocks away, so they strolled along, aware of only each other. Samantha nuzzled against him, reveled in the feel of his skin, the faint smell of his cologne, the way his voice sounded, low and close to her ear as he told her again how much he loved her.

"I love you too," she murmured. "I didn't think I could—"

"It's okay, Samantha."

The street was nearly deserted, save for a single vehicle, a dark van, parked under a spectral wash of lamplight. A man, his face lost in the shadows, leaned casually against the hood, arms folded in front, legs spread-eagled. In spite of the cool October temperature, he wore a white T-shirt, the short sleeves rolled up. Even from a distance, Samantha could see the cocky look as he watched them draw nearer. Black hair swept across his forehead. She squeezed Chris's hand. Hard.

"What is it? That guy? We'll be all right."

The stranger reached into his pocket, and Samantha froze.

For a split second, the flame of a cigarette lighter illuminated the man's face. He was Asian.

Samantha exhaled and loosened her grip on Chris's hand.

"What was that about?" he asked when they got into his car. "Are you okay?"

"He just . . . reminded me of someone. Sorry. I didn't mean to startle you."

"I've never seen you so scared. You sure you're all right?"

She nodded and they drove off.

From its parking space a block down, a black Trans Am also pulled away from the curb, sticking close to the taillights of the Saab.

7

IT WAS AFTER 2 A.M. BY the time Samantha arrived home, but Matthew was still awake. He had opened up her sofa bed and was sprawled across the blanket watching television.

"How was the big date?" he asked, handing her a bag of ripple chips.

She took one and crunched. "Big." She held out her hand. The ring sparkled. "Really big. What do you think?"

"Wow! Look at the size of that thing!"

"How do you feel about it?"

"How about you? Are you happy?"

"Yes. Very."

"Then I'm happy. Chris is a great guy. He's nuts about you—anyone can see that. And he likes me, too. Of course, who wouldn't?"

"So you're really okay with this?"

"Sure. Best part is maybe when I get my driver's license, Chris'll let me borrow his car. Just think of all the girls I'll be able to impress, cruising around in a Saab."

"Matthew Quinlan, you're such a brat. So it's all systems go?"

"You bet. Hey, after all these years, I'm really going to have a father. How about that!"

"Yeah, how about that." She punched him playfully on the shoulder and was certain he would get up and head for his room, but instead, he turned to her and asked, "Mom, do I look like Dad at all?"

"What brought this on?"

"Just asking."

She averted her eyes, just for a moment, and thought about Scott, her high-school sweetheart, with his rugged outdoorsy complexion, and wide, friendly smile. Sometimes she felt as though she could reach out and Scott would still be there, ready to gather her into an embrace. She looked at Matthew's delicate features, his dark brown hair, the shower of freckles across his nose. "No, Matthew. I'm afraid you inherited my looks. Your dad's hair was black and his eyes were blue, not green like ours." She stared at her son's thin lips.

"What about that funny bump on your nose? How come I don't have one?"

Samantha touched the spot self-consciously. "Just lucky, I guess."

"You still think about him once in a while?"

She fingered the wedding ring that still hung from a gold chain around her neck and nodded. Matthew, satisfied and wide-awake, picked up the TV guide and scanned the listings. After fiddling with the remote, he settled down to watch *Platoon*. Samantha, not sleepy either, settled into a corner easy chair and picked up a magazine from the end table.

You still think about him once in a while? Not a day went by, she had wanted to say, but the words had gotten stuck.

She began dating Scott Quinlan during their freshman year of high school, casually, between studying and part-time jobs. During their final year, their friendly relationship turned serious, and Scott proposed during spring break. Everyone said they were right for one another. They married on one of those cloudless days at the end of May, repeating their vows before a kindly minister in a whiter-than-white church. There'd been dancing till dawn under a rented canopy in the Quinlans' back yard, and the next morning she and Scott poured themselves into his secondhand van, Scott's hang glider on the roof. Carloads of their friends followed them to the outskirts of town, honking horns and shouting best wishes.

They took turns driving. Scott sang badly along with the radio, each sour note eliciting her laughter. According to Scott, he wasn't off-key at all—he was *harmonizing.* They made the three-thousand-mile trip in five days and celebrated their late-night arrival in San Diego by hurling themselves, fully clothed, into the Pacific. It was the first time either of them had been away from home, and they treated each day like the endorphin rush of freedom it was. They strolled along the beaches, drank Singapore slings by the motel pool, hiked and picnicked in nearby parks, mingled with the locals in the restaurants and bars at night. Their lovemaking was hesitant, in part because of inexperience, but also because of the terrible sunburns they had. They touched one another carefully, but when it came to actual sex, Samantha wondered what all the fuss was about. She loved Scott, loved to kiss and cuddle, but no amount of foreplay or K-Y jelly was enough to make sex pleasurable. Scott promised her it would get better. She wanted to believe him.

Each day without fail, Scott would set off in the van, sometimes with Samantha, sometimes not. He would take his brand-new double-surface Vision, launch into space, and try to glide to a smooth landing within feet of his target. Then, like Sisyphus, he would make the climb again. Even on flights that lasted only minutes, he claimed to feel a peace that eluded him on land. From an early age, he had been a champion athlete, mastering complex dives from the high board, carving turns on double black diamond ski slopes. Now there was only the sky to conquer. Samantha could hear the glee in his voice as he spoke of soaring into thermals with the wind swooshing past his ears. She had read somewhere that husbands and wives needed separate interests. Well, he could have this one, she thought, content to watch from a safe place on land.

So they had driven to California, not only for sea and sun and sex but to fulfill one of Scott's dreams: hang gliding at Torrey Pines, the mecca for anyone interested in the sport. When would he get a chance like this again, with four years of college looming ahead?

On their last day before heading north to Los Angeles, they drove to Torrey. Low-level cumulus clouds hung in the sky and the winds were gustier than they had been all week. A few sailplanes were in the area, but other than these, there were only two pilots at the top of the slope, both flying HPs. Experienced pilots. Samantha watched as Scott performed his pre-flight check, then she hopped in the van and drove to her place on the beach, where she would be in a prime position to get some great pictures for the photo album. She was following California rules: if there are no pictures, then it didn't happen. The kids back home, especially Tom, would be green.

As she made her way through the hot sand, she stifled a laugh. The sunbathers were completely nude, an item Scott had neglected to mention. She snapped the zoom lens on the camera they'd borrowed from the Quinlans and forced herself to look up.

Scott planned to launch from the ridge three hundred and fifty feet above the beach, soar along the ridge, then land right in front of her on the sand. She wondered if he knew he'd have to scatter a few naked people in the process, then thought, of course he did. She smiled.

Through the zoom she recognized Scott, his brightly colored

sail unfurled atop the cliff, the glider's nose facing into the wind. His launch was quick and confident. Even though she had watched a dozen of his flights, there was always that fraction of a second when her breath caught, knowing Scott's feet were no longer on the ground. Right now, he was so far away, so small, and the cliffs were so high.

From this distance, she knew her view was distorted, but it looked like the glider's nose was too high. There was a brief moment when he seemed to catch a thermal and soar, but then the striped Dacron dipped, dipped again, and disappeared.

There seemed to be so much noise around her, people all talking at once, and yet it was as if she was in a tunnel. Everything was muffled, distorted. She raced across the sand to where the other two pilots had landed. One, a diminutive sunburned Mexican, prevented her from going farther.

"My husband!" she screamed, arms reaching forward.

"Lo siento mucho, Señora. Punto menos que imposible. Bizarro. Trágico."

She didn't know how long she sat there, a fetal ball on the scorching sand, listening to a flood of Spanish, before her eyes finally beheld the truth she already knew. On the horizon, a group of men lifted a crumpled, lifeless body from the rocks. The second pilot, who was clearly stoned, explained the whys and wherefores of what happened. He spoke a mixture of English and gliderspeak, not much easier to comprehend than the small man's Spanish. She caught bits of it. Broken-up thermals. Turbulence along the ridge. Turned too soon. Popped his nose on launch.

One sentence she understood perfectly. *The instructors at the top told him not to fly.*

In a split second, she had become a widow, and Scott wasn't Scott anymore. He had become the Body. She was flying home with the Body. The Body would be ready for viewing on Friday.

She wasn't sure she would survive the funeral, with strangers hugging and kissing her, telling her that Scott was at peace now. You idiots, she wanted to scream. He looked peaceful when he slept beside me, when we walked on the beach. He's not peaceful now—he's dead.

Older, more experienced people told her she was young and beautiful and that someone else would come along. Their insensitivity turned her stomach.

She hibernated at home, storing toasters, blenders, electric blankets, and other useless wedding gifts in her parents' basement. She moped around, refusing calls from friends, preferring to stay in her bedroom, the childish white furniture and canopy bed providing the only security she knew. For weeks, her routine was the same. She would wander down to breakfast in a daze, eat without tasting, then wander back upstairs to lie on her bed and stare at the rosebuds on the wallpaper.

What shook her out of the trance was a tiny kick, then another deep within her. She looked at her calendar.

"A honeymoon baby," her mother clucked. "Something to remember Scott by."

As if she needed any help. As her abdomen swelled, Samantha took to wearing Scott's clothes, the familiar scent of English Leather clinging to the soft cotton sweatshirts.

Then came the Lamaze classes. Husbands and wives. Samantha and her mother.

She had been cheated out of the joys of pregnancy. Baby showers, preparing the nursery, reading Dr. Spock—she wanted none of it.

And the baby came early.

Then she got angry. At Scott, who wanted so badly to fly. And at Scott's parents, too. Why had they ever given him permission to take up such a dangerous sport?

Finally, she blamed herself. She shouldn't have allowed Scott to fly so high when he wasn't ready. Maybe they would have had their first fight as a married couple, but at least they would still *be* a married couple.

" . . . know him."

"What?"

"I said it would have been nice to know Dad, even for a little while."

Samantha lowered her magazine. "Scott Quinlan was one of the good guys."

But as she spoke, she looked not at her son but at a grimy spot on the kitchen linoleum.

8

HE SAT ON A STOOL AT the counter, ordered a beer and some fries with gravy. The wooden counter formed a square, with bartender and booze in the middle. The place was a real slice of something nice and familiar—red vinyl booths, two-toned linoleum tiles, chrome and leatherette bar stools, and along one wall, posters of vintage automobiles covered the fake wood paneling. A guy could get a decent meal here without having to dip too deep into the rent money. There was also a big picture window facing the street.

"What kind?"

"Huh?"

"Beer," the bartender said. "What'll it be?"

He shrugged. "Beantown Lager, I guess."

The bartender, with the physique of a pipe cleaner, shook his head. "You been out of the country or somethin', pal? That brewery's been out of business for years. We got Sam Adams, Rolling Rock, Coors, Bud . . ."

"Yeah."

"So which one?"

"The coldest, cheapest one."

The bartender shook his skull again and turned away.

Frank pulled her picture from his wallet. Funny how what felt so right could have turned out so wrong. Wasn't there a song that went something like that? He couldn't remember who sang it. He propped the picture up against the stainless napkin container. If he tried real hard, he could almost smell her, that sweet perfume made from those purple flowers.

"She's a real looker," the bartender said, putting the beer bottle and a frosted mug in front of him. "Your girl?"

"Yep." He pushed the mug away and chugged from the bottle.

"Some guys have all the luck."

"That's me."

He guzzled the beer, ordered another, and bulldozed through the fries.

Halfway through his third beer he began to think about the other night, when he'd seen her come out of that fancy Cambridge restaurant, how he'd pulled away from the curb and followed the two of them to some uppity neighborhood in Boston. They disappeared into an old building and the upstairs lights had come on, but only for a minute, and it didn't take a high-school graduate to figure out what was going on up there. They didn't come out again until well past midnight. By that time, his imagination, fueled by several belts of rum, had run wild with thoughts of the two of them and what they'd been doing.

Several times he thought he might puke, but he fought off the bitter taste with dry crackers and more booze. The churning in his stomach reminded him of all those other times he had watched her, so many years ago.

She and the hotshot jock used to go to the park after one of their dates, sit on the same stone bench under a huge willow and smooch it up pretty good. He'd been able to see them clearly from where he'd crouched, barely ten feet away, behind a bank of soft-needled shrubs. He even remembered how he'd learned to ignore the burning pain in his stiff back and cramped legs.

He could hear what they were saying, too. The guy was saving for college, so there'd be no movies, no dancing, no bowling, not for a long time. She didn't seem to mind, just kept on kissing him, running her hands through his hair, talking about a wedding.

Their wedding.

She was wearing a ring, the diamond barely larger than a fruit fly—he'd had to squint to make it out—but she was staring at it like it cost a million bucks.

The scene, as always, got hotter, the kisses longer, and the hands moved faster as the guy eased her down onto her back. They put on quite a show, the jock's hand traveling in front to cup her breast, her hand brushing his away, but not too soon.

"Just a few more months . . .," she used to say.

"I'm not gonna make it." The jock.

It took every bit of Frank's control not to spring from his hiding place and beat the ever-livin' shit out of the guy. But he looked at loverboy again and stayed behind the bush. The guy's thighs were like tree trunks pressing against the seams of his jeans. His arms had done more than a few push-ups. It would have been a close contest, but close wouldn't have been good enough. His old man had taught him that much. Don't play the game if you're not gonna win.

Now, though, it was different. He knew he could whip this society boy with his own ass Krazy-Glued to the sidewalk. Still, he held back. He had a feeling he'd be better off learning a little more about Sam and her situation. The real fun could come later.

For the moment, there would be no more fuck-ups. He wouldn't lose it again. He raised his empty bottle and the bartender brought another.

Opening his throat, he swallowed long, draining half the bottle. Now he could really smell her, and not just the perfume. *Her.* And he remembered that night, how he'd gotten up from the ground, soaked with sweat and short of breath, smelling those smells.

She lay still on the lawn. Her legs had mean red welts all over, and a whole bunch of blood had dried underneath her nose. There were some bruises too, on her face, her arms, her chest. A different-colored one on her neck. A hickey.

And he left her there. Like that. Knowing she would be all right. He'd seen his mother in the same shape or worse hundreds of times. His old man could really tie one on. There was Mrs. Camiletti too, from down the street, who always wore deep purple lipstick way past where her lips ended. But you could still see where the lip had split wide open. Happened all the time.

He wasn't the only one who lost it, but he was the one who got burned. A five-to-fifteen sentence. Sexual assault. For trying to show her how he felt, for trying to make her see she just couldn't marry that guy.

"Hey, buddy! Easy!"

The fork was in Frank's clenched fist, the three stainless steel tines digging into the soft pine countertop. Quickly the bartender removed the fork and plate.

"Jesus. Sorry."

"You wanna settle up?"

"Better give me another."

"You're not driving, are ya?"

"Not me."

A fresh beer was set down.

Frank got up and stretched his legs, went to the can and tried to pee. Another hard-on. The guy at the next urinal moved away fast.

When he came back into the bar, he spotted the jukebox in the far corner. It was a beauty, a Wurlitzer, with bubbles going through a neon-colored tube. He scanned the list of titles, found the one he wanted, and dug in his pocket for a quarter. The record dropped into place. He hovered a bit, watched the record spin, then heard the song.

Black Magic Woman. She'd cast a spell on him, all right, and he was still hooked.

He went back to his stool and sat down, quietly singing along with Santana. He caught a glimpse of himself in the mirror behind the bar and reached for a napkin to wipe a glob of gravy from his shirt. Then he stopped singing. Her picture was gone.

"Hey, you!" he hollered at the bartender. "Where is it?"

"Where's what?"

"The picture, goddammit. Where is it?" Frank snapped to his feet, hands gripping the edge of the counter. The stool crashed against the tiled floor.

"Easy does it, pal. Here she is." The bartender bent over and picked up the photograph from the floor behind the bar. "Must have blown off the counter when the front door opened."

"Yeah. Sure it did."

"Hey, relax. Look, you pick up that stool, I'll get you a cup of coffee, then you gotta go. Deal?"

Frank tucked the picture safely back in his wallet, picked up the stool, and sat down. He forced himself to count to fifty and waited for the heat to pass through him.

No more fuck-ups, Ventresca.

It was this same stupid kind of thing that got him screwed the last time. He should have been out in three, if not for that smart-ass guard.

He'd been doing some woodworking in the prison shop, making picnic tables, when the guard happened along and picked up a library book Frank had been carrying around for weeks. *Classic Sports Cars,* with big colored pictures. There were Vettes, Spitfires, MGs. Classics, all right.

"Give it back," he'd said to the guard, who was holding it too long.

"What's it worth to ya?"

"Give it."

"How bad you want it? What do I get instead?" The guard pointed to his crotch.

Frank didn't even remember the wrench was in his hand.

Later, they told him the guard's eye would probably stay in its socket, but they'd put fifty-three stitches in what was left of his face. He still knew the number because '53 was the year the prototype of the Chevrolet Corvette Dream Car was first displayed.

The bartender brought the coffee. Frank's stomach heaved when he smelled it. He pushed the cup away, wondering what society boy would look like with fifty-three stitches in his face.

From his swivel stool, Frank could turn and look through the big window to a restaurant across the street. She was there, with the big shot again and another, older gal, but not the same one he'd seen sweeping the porch. This one was small, too, but smooth and cool, and from the looks of it, she'd never swept a porch in her life. Even from here, Frank could smell money. The three of them were sitting by the window, drinking wine and talking to beat the band.

He didn't like the way it looked, Samantha all comfortable and friendly with the fancy folks, but he hooked his feet around the bottom rungs of the stool and stayed where he was. Information was power—he'd heard on some TV show—and Frank could use an edge.

He looked toward the curb where his car was parked. His old black Trans Am, once driven by a salesman, so it had all the bells and whistles. A real beaut. There were a few rust spots around the wheel well, but the car still purred like a panther. Pretty soon, he would have *her* purring like a panther too.

There was movement in the window across the street. Society boy was pulling her chair out. She was standing up.

Well, if it was charm she was after, he could be charming, too. Real charming.

9

"Feel like a walk?" Chris asked. "Looks like you could use some air."

Samantha nodded. Chris parked on Commonwealth Avenue, and they made their way to the Public Garden. The park was still crowded with teenagers on skateboards, tourists with cameras, couples pushing sleeping children in strollers.

Samantha and Chris crossed the suspension bridge over the pond. The swan boats huddled together, bobbing in unison in the center of the lagoon. As they walked beside the formally arranged flower beds, Samantha admired the mounds of yellow marigolds bordered by purple lobelia still displaying their cheery colors in the dim light.

Eventually Chris asked, "What'd you think of Casey Jones?"

"Who?"

"Mother. The little engineer that could. Didn't I tell you you'd be inspected like a cut of USDA beef?"

Samantha resisted rolling her eyes. "She's a force to be reckoned with, I'll give you that."

"Now you see where she gets her reputation. It's no wonder the press calls her the micromanager from hell."

Samantha gave a tactful smile. "She was pretty blown away by our engagement, too. Maybe we shouldn't have sprung it on her that way. She should have gotten used to the idea of our relationship first."

Chris waved away the notion. "Wouldn't have mattered."

"So help me out here. How can I win the great lady over?"

"Don't waste your time. Mother will come around on her own, or she won't, but you'll just be spinning your wheels if you think there's something you can do to make her swing your way."

"Clearly she thinks Georgina MacPherson's a better catch for you than some semi-impoverished guidance counselor with a nearly full-grown son. Exactly who is this MacPherson woman, anyway? And you'd better tell me she's overweight, has bad skin and a few front teeth missing."

"Uh, not quite. Georgie's quite slim, her complexion's clear, and as far as I can tell, her teeth look like they'll be in place for a few years yet. But she's a classic society blonde, Samantha. Not one idea in her pretty little head, and she could put frost on a stove."

"If you recall, I was rather an Ice Maiden not so long ago."

"You were never icy," Chris said, wrapping an arm around her. "Just . . . cautious. And don't give Georgie another thought." He led her beneath the canopy of a tree and pinned her against the rough bark, trapping her there with the weight of his body. "Besides," he murmured between short kisses, "you know I prefer the dark, sultry type."

Their kisses lengthened, deepened, then a faint throat-clearing noise made them break the embrace.

"What was that?" Samantha whispered.

"Beats me," Chris said, peering into the darkness. "I don't see anybody."

"Maybe there's a homeless person sleeping behind those bushes. Anyway, let's get out of here. There are better places to respond to libido's call. You *are* going to ask me back to your place, aren't you?"

"I am indeed," Chris admitted, "though you know, perhaps my mother has a point. You'd never catch Georgie suggesting anything so brazen." He feigned shock, then grinned. "That's one of the things I love about you."

Arms around each other, they headed back through the park toward Chris's bow-front limestone on Commonwealth. As they climbed the wide staircase to his second-floor apartment, Samantha said, "You don't think your mother will . . . how do I say this—make trouble for us?"

"What's she going to do, threaten to cut me out of her will? I'd marry you anyway, and she knows it."

"I don't want to cause problems, Chris. This seems like such an adversarial way to begin our life together—"

"That's Mother's choosing, not ours. And if it's a battle she wants, so be it. She can pull whatever she wants from her repertoire of tricks. Lord knows, she's had years of practice. We're still gonna win. Right?"

"You bet."

As Chris inserted the key, he said, "Don't suppose I can talk you into staying the night?"

"Oh, Chris, you know how I feel about leaving Matthew by himself—"

He put a finger to her lips. "I know. But maybe a weekend away? Soon? I'd like to find out whether my fiancée snores or hogs the blankets."

"A weekend away would be terrific," Samantha answered, already wondering whether Tom would mind Matthew staying with him. "And yes—soon."

Samantha loved coming to Chris's place. Had a magazine done a photo layout entitled "Boston Bachelors' Apartments," she would have picked out Chris's immediately. The living room was large and clubby in décor, its color scheme revolving around dark green, navy, and deep gold. A marble fireplace accented one wall; oak bookcases flanked it. The shelves were filled with leather-bound volumes, onyx obelisks, an assortment of bronze bookends, and a collection of English countryside prints.

Chris slid her coat from her shoulders, hung it in a hallway closet, then ushered her to a low leather sofa. "Sit. I'll bring something to warm you up." He disappeared through an ornate archway.

Would they live here when they got married? Samantha wondered. Where would Matthew go to school?

Chris re-entered the room carrying two snifters partially filled with amber liquid, the glasses foggy with condensation. "Grand Marnier," he announced. "Fifteen seconds in the microwave. Guaranteed to take the chill off."

"Why, sir," Samantha said, patting the vacant space beside her, "I believe you're trying to take advantage of me." She batted her eyelashes. "There. Was that more Georgina-like?"

"Very," Chris said, sitting next to her, "and don't do it again. Speaking of creepy people, have you heard any more from your phantom admirer?"

"No more flowers, at least." Samantha nestled in the comfortable crook of Chris's arm and took a sip of the steamy liqueur. "Mmm. That is good. There've been a few strange phone calls . . ."

"Strange? How so? You mean obscene?"

"No. Nothing like that. But when Matthew answers the phone, whoever's on the other end hangs up. When I answer, I get a breather—nothing heavy, just enough so that I know there's someone on the other end. Sometimes there's a lot of background noise. Something like machine-gun fire. It's weird."

"How often has this happened?"

"Five or six times in the last week or so."

Chris tilted her face toward his. "I don't like the sound of that. Maybe you should think about getting an unlisted number. After all, you've got fifteen hundred potential suspects right where you work."

Samantha promised to consider it, but was already fairly certain she would leave things as they were. There'd been a few occasions in the past when one of her students had been desperate for someone to talk to, and she'd been glad she was able to help over the phone.

She took another drink, then looked at her watch. "Chris, I'd like to be home by eleven tonight—"

"So?"

"So . . ."

The snifters, still both half full, were set on the coffee table. Their lovemaking was both silly and wonderful, with Samantha letting loose a fit of carefree giggles as Chris emitted mock-Neanderthal growls in her ear. After a time, the laughter subsided, replaced by cautious tenderness. Carefully, he eased her back onto the sofa. She felt her blouse being slid from her shoulders, Chris's lips teasing along her throat, feathering softly against her skin. There was a sharp, delicious sting as he pressed his teeth to the taut muscle at the side of her neck. As his mouth covered hers, Chris grasped her wrists, stretching her arms overhead. She was ready for his strength, his desire, but he became gentle again, his warm tongue tracing a dotted line along the soft flesh of her inner arm. She was sure she would go mad from it all, so excruciating was the waiting, but in the throes of exquisite anticipation, there came an angry knock at the door.

"You must be kidding," Chris muttered, pulling slightly away from her. "Be quiet and maybe they'll go away."

But the knock came again, this time louder, more insistent.

"You'd better get it," Samantha said, wriggling out from under him and groping for her blouse. "It might be an emergency."

He groaned and rose to his feet. "Who is it?" he called out, tucking his shirt into his pants as he padded across the carpet.

There was no answer.

"What the—?" When Chris opened the door, there was no one in the hallway. Samantha, her blouse partially buttoned, peered over his shoulder. They looked both ways along the corridor, then down the staircase, but the entry below was deserted.

"Well, I'll be damned. What the hell do you suppose that was all about?" Chris scratched his head and closed the door with a thud. "I'll say one thing. Someone's got lousy timing."

"Speaking of time, it is getting late, Chris." Samantha stroked his cheek. "Maybe you should just take me home."

He nodded, looking both resigned and disappointed, and went to the closet for her coat. "Samantha?"

"Yes?"

"I'll get working on those weekend plans. Right away."

10

MOST DAYS, SAMANTHA'S OFFICE would have benefited from a revolving door, and Mondays were the worst. Problems that festered at home during the week exploded on weekends, and often kids came in first thing Monday morning for a pep talk to help them cope with another five days of school and studies on top of their other woes. Already the staff-room hoopla surrounding her engagement seemed far away as Samantha handed out Kleenex, sharpened her listening skills, and patched up shattered self-esteem. It was only 10:30.

The buzzer sounded for the commencement of the next period, and in marched Derek Townsend looking pretty pleased with himself.

"Well, look at you!" Samantha said. "This is quite a change from last time."

"Been around some, Mrs. Q. Keeping busy, you know."

"Keeping busy with anyone special?"

"Nah. It's too soon for me. Still got a thing for Jenny. But," he said with a grin, "you never know what'll happen. Halloween Dance coming up this Friday. I got a great costume."

It was good to see Derek so hopeful. "Keep me posted, will you?" she told him.

As he was leaving, he mumbled, "You're terrific, Mrs. Q."

Moments after he ducked out the door Samantha frowned at the prospect that he might be the mysterious sender of the flowers. She could see him doing it, being too shy to sign his name, yet somehow she didn't picture Derek as the type to call her and then hang up. Still, as she'd learned on the job so often, anything was possible.

She luxuriated in the few uninterrupted minutes she had, allowing herself yet another glance at her engagement ring. "What a rock!" Hank Ehrhart had said at the coffee machine. "What's this guy do for a living, sell dope?"

"What's going on?" As usual, Stanfield had missed the announcement.

"She's engaged," repeated Yvonne, head of the English department. "Isn't it wonderful?"

"Her and Lundstrom?" asked Stanfield.

Tom, standing nearby, gave a hearty laugh.

"Don't be silly," Samantha replied. "Tom is like my twin brother. Right, Tom?"

"You betcha. Congratulations, Sis," he said and gave her a big hug.

Her swirling happy thoughts were cut off by the appearance of Bobbie Donaldson and Maria Rodriguez at her office door. The two girls plunked themselves down and immediately burst into tears. Petrella, their auto mechanics teacher, had been, among other things, looking down their tops again.

Petrella was the school's industrial arts teacher, a short man with a wrestler's build and a bow-legged swagger. Because of declining numbers in some of the tech courses, Petrella had to wear two hats and add second-year auto mechanics to his list of responsibilities. Bobbie and Maria were the only girls in the class.

Samantha listened to the girls' story and nudged the box of tissues closer to Bobbie.

Great, she thought after they'd left. Petrella was at it again. The last time, Halloran had given the shop teacher a slap on the wrist and issued a half-hearted threat that his job would be in jeopardy should there be any repeat offenses. Then they'd gone off to play golf. This time the principal would not be able to straddle the fence, regardless of how comfortably one of the posts was inserted up his ass.

Samantha pulled a pad of paper from her desk drawer and began a sketchy list of ways in which she could deal with the problem. Writing things down sometimes clarified issues for her, but today she wasn't meeting with success. Regardless of how she handled Petrella's situation, the fallout would be ugly.

"Pssst!"

This time she was grateful for the interruption. It was Tom, his overcoat slung over one arm. "Come on!" he whispered conspiratorially. "The inmates have banded together. We're breaking out."

"Where to?"

"Who cares? Let's just run for it."

Samantha looked at the clock. It was lunchtime. "You're on," she said, reaching for her camelhair coat.

There was a chill in the air, and the stiff autumn breeze eddied fallen leaves at their feet as they walked along.

"You looked pretty serious in there," Tom said. "Anything wrong?"

"It'll pass."

"Well, let's hope so. This is a happy time for you. You're engaged, remember? How does Matthew feel about it?"

"He's happy. He and Chris get along so well."

"I remember when my mom remarried. I was pretty shaken up. Kept it all inside, though."

"Matthew's not like that. He tells me everything. And he's excited about this."

"Terrific. Got a date for the wedding?"

"Early spring. No definite date, though."

"Still riding high on the romance, huh?"

Samantha smiled. "Something like that."

"And speaking of riding high, have you taken a good look at Ehrhart today?"

"I try to avoid it. Why?"

"He's cranky as sin. Really wired. I wish he'd start smoking again. And I don't think Petrella took news of your engagement too well."

"Why should he care? Jim can't stand me."

"Yeah, he makes it look that way, doesn't he. But I still think he wants your body."

"Oh, please, don't even go there. Is it any wonder that I haven't been to a staff party since Black Christmas?"

She hadn't thought twice about accepting a lift home from Jim Petrella after a particularly raucous party at Halloran's house a few years before. Petrella was sober, very married, and eager to get home to tend to his wife, who had the flu. So he said. Petrella had always been polite, at times even protective toward Samantha, but it wasn't protection he offered her that night. Luckily, during the scuffle in his cramped Alfa Romeo, Samantha was able to shove her fist squarely at his scrotum.

"Right up inside you, Jim. That's where your balls will be unless you back off. I mean it."

She didn't know where the words had come from, but they had worked. Petrella backed way off, and neither mentioned the episode again, though the lingering slimy residue always oozed around Samantha when Petrella entered a room. The shop teacher retaliated in the best, most infantile way he knew how—by making Samantha's life at school miserable, and he recruited aid from his co-musketeers, Ehrhart and Halloran.

Tom pulled a granola bar and a package of Glosettes raisins from his coat pocket and handed the chocolate to Samantha. "Let's change the subject, or I won't be able to digest this."

"Sure. I met Chris's mother last night."

"And?"

"Much as she tried to hide it, there was an undertone of N.O.C.D."

"*Pardonnez-moi?*"

"Not Our Class, Dear. She was kind of like Mrs. Howell on *Gilligan's Island.* All pastels and pearls, you know the type. Salon hairdo, carefully arranged and sprayed in place. I'm not what she expected for a future daughter-in-law, that was pretty clear, but she did her best to be gracious. Good breeding and all that."

"Too bad when you marry somebody, the relatives come along, too. Your future mother-in-law's got quite the reputation. To put it kindly, democracy is not her middle name."

"I'm starting to pick up on that."

"She sits on a lot of boards, likes to pass herself off as philanthropic, but every endowment she signs her name to comes with a shitload of conditions. She's issued more ultimatums than the world's worst dictators. From what I've heard, the phrase 'my way or the highway' was invented for her."

Samantha sighed. "Chris said his mother always plays to win."

"And this is the woman you'll be sitting down to Christmas dinners with? Family birthdays? See why I'm a confirmed bachelor?"

True enough. Tom had plenty of dates, but there was never anyone long-term. Samantha wondered if that contributed to his occasional complaints of boredom and bouts with depression.

They reached the halfway point of their walk; they needed to turn back to arrive at school for the afternoon's first period. A convenience store with a prominent KitKat sign beckoned, but Samantha resisted, and they crossed the street. Samantha froze.

On centipede legs, fear skittered up her back. "Tom," she said, her voice tremulous. "That noise." They were outside a service station.

"What? It's just a mechanic riveting wheel nuts back on. No big deal."

"That's the sound I was trying to describe to you. Chris couldn't explain it either. But now I know."

"Sam, you've lost me."

"The phone calls. That machine-gun sound. It's a riveter. The purple flowers should have tipped me off."

"To what?"

"To Frank."

"Ventresca? Oh, shit."

Samantha examined each parked car they passed, checked narrow alleys between houses, and repeatedly glanced behind her. She couldn't see him, but it didn't matter. She could feel his presence bearing down upon her. She could smell his sweat, the noxious odor of gasoline. Frank had dropped flowers off at school; he'd phoned her at home.

He knew where she lived, where she worked. What else did he know?

When she and Tom reached the school, Halloran was standing on the front steps monitoring the students smoking at the edge of the property. When he saw the two of them, he scowled. Then Samantha realized the reason for the grimace—at some point, she had taken hold of Tom's arm for support or he had offered it, she wasn't sure which, but she knew how it looked. She released her grip, trying her best not to appear guilty, but she knew Halloran was already imagining students' whispers, parents' phone calls.

Somehow she managed to inhale one shaky breath and brush past the principal, head held so high she feared her neck might snap.

The corridors were still a flurry of activity, with kids scrambling to class, slamming lockers, and jockeying through doorways. The hall smelled of rancid food and unwashed socks. By the time Samantha reached the tech wing, her heartbeat had almost returned to normal. Tom, his face full of concern, still mustered up one of his barbed comments, this time about the size of Halloran's penis, which provided a modicum of comic relief. Samantha was glad of that; she needed to force both Halloran and Frank Ventresca to some nether region of her mind. Ahead of her loomed the industrial arts room and the problem of Jim Petrella.

Class was already in progress. Randy Dennis was sanding the hell off a two-by-four. Skip Bemelman was putting the router to a curved table leg. Sawdust flew everywhere. A bandsaw screamed through a sheet of plywood.

Jim Petrella came right over, a work apron around his waist loaded down with tools. Keeping her voice low and even, Samantha explained Maria and Bobbie's concerns, but all her private rehearsing had been for nothing. Petrella blew. "What the hell is going on here, some kind of feminist vigilante bullshit?"

The bandsaw squealed to a stop.

He lowered his voice to a hiss. "What are you trying to pull, Quinlan?"

"Jim," she said, forcing calmness she did not feel, "I'm not trying to pull anything. I'm here on behalf of two girls who are upset. I thought you should know before I take this to Halloran. I'm sure you'd like to tell your side of the story."

"Sure, I'll tell my side. It didn't happen. And Bert'll believe me."

"Those girls were really upset, Jim. They're uncomfortable in your class."

"So you think it's true?" The saw started up again. "Think I need to go looking down goddamn blouses for a peek at some spoiled brat's training bra? Don't insult me. Besides," he said, his eyes burning into hers, "I like my women more mature."

Samantha ignored the innuendo but it wasn't easy. "I just wanted you to know what's going on, that's all."

"Gee, thanks for the heads-up, Counselor, but I'll be just fine." Petrella's hand sank into the pocket of his apron. "Now if there's nothing else—" His last statement was punctuated by the repeated pounding of a claw hammer on his open palm.

11

THIS WORK RELEASE DETAIL wasn't so bad. He knew the score. Obey the parole officer and report when instructed. Notify change in residence. No criminal conduct. No possession of weapons. Watch his *associations* with women. In short, he had to keep his nose clean.

For starters, he'd landed a job. Lou's Service Center had four automotive bays and enough business to keep cars up on the hoist pretty steady, and some fancy ones, too. He'd love to be able to tinker with a few of them, but Lou said he would need his class "A" mechanics papers, and that meant going to school. For now, Frank was satisfied pumping gas, topping up oil, and cleaning windshields like the good old days.

He'd found a furnished apartment, too—nothing special, but it was the first place he'd ever had to himself. It was one big room above a greeting card store, with a pull-out couch at one end and a kitchenette at the other. He had a card table and two folding chairs that he never sat in, and the stove had never been turned on. He ate most of his suppers, either bologna sandwiches or pork and beans out of a can, hunched over the kitchen sink or spread out in front of the television. He got five channels on his fourteen-inch TV, but the reception was fuzzy on three of them. The set rested on a metal stand, its rear casters seized up. Car magazines piled on the rusted grid shelf below. He also had a radio, a stainless steel coat rack, and a framed picture of some snow-capped mountains.

His bathroom was small, wedged into the corner, but the way he figured it, for the three S's—shave, shit, and shampoo—he didn't need much space.

Maybe once he got a little more money in his pocket, he would think about jazzing the place up a little. It could use a coat of paint, and a rug would be nice. He grinned. Hell, he was already starting to sound like one of those responsible tenants.

Next paycheck, he would get a phone installed. Then he wouldn't have to keep calling her from Lou's. Besides, some things were better said in private, and soon, he would be phoning her plenty, just to hear that low, raspy voice. They would talk for hours, just like they used to. About everything.

Pretty soon she'd see the wimp she was with just couldn't go the distance. The guy reminded Frank of those snot-nosed kids in high school, cruising around in Daddy's car, going on ski weekends, joining tennis clubs. During so many sleepless nights in his cell, he could still hear their laughter, the way they used to mock the tech boys, like getting a little grease on your hands was some kind of crime. Sam deserved better than that kind of uppity crowd.

He sat up in his car and rubbed his neck. He took a swig of whiskey, then replaced the stopper on his thermos. The tension in his neck eased a little. He clicked the key in the ignition and smiled. Time to step up the action.

The couple was on the move.

12

THE NIGHT AIR WAS CRISP, the mercury plunging as it always seemed to just before Halloween, eliciting groans from children forced to wear coats over their costumes. Samantha and Chris made their way from the parking lot near the harbor toward Quincy Market in search of a drink and warmth.

A trendy collection of shops, restaurants, and bars flanked the central market building with its market-stall layout and its classic dome and rotunda. While some locals sniffed at the overtly commercial feel of the place, Samantha, like the tourists, loved it.

She stepped gingerly on the cobblestone walk, her heels finding more than their share of ruts and cracks. She clung to Chris, not for fear of falling but for affection, marveling at how her body curved so comfortably into his. She curled in closer.

At the end of the pedestrian mall, a lone cellist, scarcely older than sixteen, was packing up, her solo concert unable to compete with the rowdy strains of "Jack Was Every Inch a Sailor" wafting through the windows of the Irish singalong pub behind her. The open instrument case on the ground didn't have much change in it, and the girl's overcoat was several sizes too large. A familiar expression crossed Chris's face, and Samantha knew what would happen next. Chris strode over to the girl and, without having heard whether she could play a note, deposited a ten-dollar bill into the case.

He didn't wait for an acknowledgment or even a smile, just clasped Samantha's hand again and led her into an upscale brasserie, where they sat at a wrought-iron table near the greenhouse window. They blew on their hands and ordered Spanish coffees.

"You're quite a guy, you know that?" Samantha said once their waiter disappeared.

"Yep. You don't deserve me."

"Well, I wouldn't go that far . . ."

Chris asked her what she thought of the play; he had taken her to see "Shear Madness." The comedy whodunit, after a nearly two-decade run, was still drawing sellout crowds into the basement of the Charles Playhouse. One of the main characters, a wealthy dowager, reminded Chris of his mother.

Samantha smiled. "A few similarities, perhaps, but honestly, Chris, maybe we should give your mother more credit. She is offering to host an engagement party. She even wants to come shopping with me for a new dress."

"That's so you don't screw up and wear something completely inappropriate."

"I really don't mind her input. Besides, it'll give us a chance to get to know each other."

"Just watch it," Chris cautioned. "Remember the story of Jonah?"

"Yes. And?"

"Give Mother a chance and she'll swallow you whole."

Samantha let the comment lie. The not-so-friendly fire between Chris and his mother had gone on too long to be appeased by a few words from her. At the same time, Samantha had seen a different side of Meredith when they'd met for lunch earlier in the week. Though still reserved and formal, Chris's mother expressed an interest in hearing all about Matthew, the kind of student he was, his hobbies, his friends. She was also eager to assist with the school's major fundraiser and was planning to set up an appointment with Bert Halloran to discuss it. What the woman lacked in warmth she made up for with generosity.

The coffee came, and Samantha spooned the maraschino cherry into her mouth. Smiling, Chris pulled his from the whipped cream and fed it to her. She felt her face go hot, the touch of Chris's fingers against her tongue erotic.

Words tumbled out. Samantha talked about Jim Petrella, off on "compassionate leave" until the school board could figure out what to do with him. "He was really angry with me. The way he was pounding that hammer—"

Samantha followed Chris's gaze to the spot outside where the young cellist had stood. "Chris, what is it?"

"Nothing," he said. "I'm sorry. You have my undivided attention."

But she didn't. She asked him about work, tried to press him to plan their weekend getaway, but throughout the mostly one-sided conversation, Chris's glance continued to flicker between Samantha and the open courtyard.

"Chris, what are you looking at? Is that girl still out there?"

"No. Some guy. Sitting on that bench over there, shivering. Underdressed for the weather. He's gone now."

Samantha looked out at the vacant bench anyway. She thought briefly about Chris's years in the army and how he still couldn't pass a street beggar without hustling him into Au Bon Pain for a coffee. The trunk of his car was filled with extra blankets, scarves, and gloves. "The city's homeless problem really gets to you, doesn't it."

"This guy wasn't dressed like he needed a handout. And he seemed to be staring at us." Once more, Chris scanned the nearly black space beyond the window, then shrugged. "Too many Ludlum novels." He reached across the table for her hand. "Now what were we talking about?"

"Hiya, girl."

Samantha froze.

"How ya been?"

She looked up, and there he was. The face from so many icy nightmares. He was grinning at her, his thin lips nearly disappearing as his mouth widened.

His eyebrows were thicker now, unruly and wiry, giving his face a hooded look. His nose was wide at the base, the pores huge. An ugly mole had sprouted to one side of his mouth. He was wearing a denim jacket two sizes too small, Levi's, and a T-shirt.

"How ya been?" he repeated.

"Please." Her voice came out a whisper. "Go away."

"I just asked a question, Sammy girl. No harm done."

Chris tightened his grip on her hand. "I don't think she wants to talk to you, friend."

"Well, I don't remember askin' you," he said, still staring at her, "and I sure as hell ain't no friend of yours."

"Go away," Samantha said again.

"Take it easy, girl. I don't want no trouble. We'll do this another time." He glared at Chris. "When we won't be interrupted."

His voice made her skin alive with insects. She quelled a shudder and forced herself to look straight up at him. "You sent me flowers."

Frank smiled.

"And you've been phoning me."

The smile broadened.

"Maybe you'd better leave," Chris said. "There are laws in this state against harassment."

"There's laws against bein' an asshole, too. Least there should be."

Chris started to stand up, but Samantha shook her head furiously. Once more, she looked straight at Frank. "I want you to go away," she said firmly, loudly. "No more flowers, no phone calls, nothing. Get it?"

Frank sneered at her. "You'll come around. Just wait."

Her insides churned, the onslaught of memories hitting her full force. She fought them off long enough to gasp, "Go away."

For a moment, Frank looked ready to say something but then he shot Chris a full-body appraising glance and with a final smirk he walked away, hands shoved deep into his pockets.

Chris stared at his own hands, to where four blood-red arcs were marring the soft flesh where Samantha's nails had dug in.

13

SAMANTHA MADE CERTAIN THAT Matthew's bedroom door was tightly shut, and then she called the Victim Services Unit at the Department of Correction and informed the woman who answered of her unwanted contact with Frank. She was advised again to get an unlisted number, to ask friends and neighbors to keep an eye out for Ventresca, to lock her car at all times, and to avoid isolated locations even during daylight.

"And make sure you have a deadbolt lock on your door."

From where she huddled on the couch, Samantha could see the kitchen door, its flimsy chain lock little more of an impediment to an intruder than a child's bracelet. The sympathetic woman at Correction also thought it might be wise to keep a written record of each encounter she had with Frank, including the time, date, words spoken, names of witnesses, and action taken after the event.

Beyond that there was little to be done. Frank hadn't uttered a threat, hadn't admitted to sending the flowers or making the calls, and he definitely hadn't touched her. His appearance at the restaurant had been unsettling, ill advised to be sure, but not illegal.

Frustrated and wide-awake, Samantha checked her watch. Seeing it was still before midnight, she called Tom.

"Jesus, Samantha, are you all right? Want me to come over?"

No, she assured him, she was fine. She just needed to talk. Forty minutes later, though the presence of Frank still haunted the shadowy corners of her mind, she felt some of the weight removed from her shoulders. But, despite Tom's reassurances that Frank wouldn't dare try anything, Samantha found herself wedging a kitchen chair against the back door before retiring.

That week, she did her best to keep busy and tried to forget the scene at the restaurant. On Friday night, she and Matthew went down to Beatrice's to shell out candy for the parade of trick-or-treaters roaming the streets of Somerville. She even managed a laugh at the toddler dressed in black-and-white-striped prison garb, ball and chain dragging along behind. Samantha thought briefly of Derek Townsend and hoped he was having a good time at the dance.

Saturday she spent doing laundry, groceries, and scrubbing mold from the bathroom tiles. On Sunday, she and Matthew bundled up for a last bike ride of the year along the Charles River, giving up early when stiff winds made their pedaling nearly impossible. Then it was a Papa Gino's pizza for supper and their traditional game of Scrabble to banish the Sunday-night blues. It wasn't until Samantha said good night to her son and got one of his I-love-you smiles that she remembered Frank's thin horrible lips and the way his stare bore through her.

Frank Ventresca.

She couldn't imagine what Chris must be thinking. "He was someone I knew in high school," she'd explained. "A piece of my past. Best forgotten."

He didn't press, but his expression registered both concern and disappointment.

She wasn't ready to tell him. There had been hundreds of

rehearsals in her mind, but the right words did not materialize. Perhaps in time, if Frank made no further appearances, Chris might come to forget he had ever seen him.

Samantha wished she could do the same.

"Hiya, girl."

It was the same phrase he'd used that night.

She recalled removing the key from the front door and turning around. She'd scanned the darkness in the direction of the voice. Across the lawn a lone figure stood beside her parents' garage. "What are you doing here?" she said, her own voice hushed.

"I gotta talk to you," he said. "I was waitin' for your boyfriend to leave."

She remembered getting a funny feeling in her stomach, wondering whether he had witnessed Scott's fervent good-night just minutes before. "How long have you been standing there?"

"Coupla minutes. Say, can you come over here and talk a sec?" He glanced up at the darkened windows of the house. "I don't wanna wake your folks."

She hesitated. "It's late."

"I know, but I—I got a problem."

Even in the deep murk of night she could see he was troubled. His feet, in white high-top sneakers, shuffled nervously on the lawn. There was something pathetic about him. She saw his faded jeans, snug and torn at one knee, not to make a fashion statement but because they were his only pair. His yellowed T-shirt, white years ago, was stained and crepe-paper-thin. He looked everywhere but at her.

It was his father again, she thought, and stepped off the porch.

The closer she came to the garage, the farther he retreated into the shadows, until they both stood under the lilac tree at the edge of the lot. Wind chimes tinkled from a lower bough. "How come you don't come around no more? I been waitin'."

"I—I've been busy, I guess."

"Yeah, so I see." The voice took on an edge, just for an instant, then it was gone. "I tried to call you. Thought we could maybe take in a show, but your folks' number's not in the book."

"It's unlisted." Samantha's father had little patience with his teenage daughter's friends telephoning at all hours. The new number, along with strict orders not to give it out, had put a stop to that.

At once, Samantha wanted to be rid of Frank, finding his presence under her favorite tree an eerie intrusion. She thought of childhood puzzle magazines: *what was wrong with this picture?* This time, the answer was simple. Frank Ventresca. He didn't belong here. In the dark. With her. She wondered what her parents would say if they saw her talking to this boy, half shielded from the street by the curtain of branches.

Though the night was fairly warm, she shivered. "You said you had a problem?"

"Oh, yeah. Well, it's like this." He fumbled for the words. "I miss ya. We had good times." More shuffling of feet.

She tried to recall what he was talking about. "Hey, sure we did," she said, touching him briefly on the arm. In truth, she had only a vague memory of a short ride in his Trans Am, a few hellos on the street. One crazy night she taught him a few dance steps in a vacant bay at Miller's Service Station. That was the night he first told her about his father. She had tried to cheer him up.

"Real good times," he repeated. "The best. So where ya been?"

She concealed her irritation. She was engaged, she loved Scott, and she wanted to be upstairs, in her room, dreaming about their wedding, not stuck down here with some lovesick dropout. Another glance at Frank's face told her she would have to let him down gently. Her parents had raised her to care about the feelings of others, and besides, he looked as though she was the only friend he had. The heel of his sneaker chopped at the turf.

She reached up and stilled the wind chimes with her hand. "Listen, we had some fun, sure . . ." Her words sounded hollow even to her, and she realized there was no kind way out of this. Sometimes the plain truth was best. "You're great and everything . . . a real nice guy, but, well—I'm seeing someone else, and we're sort of engaged."

His gaze stopped flitting and he focused on her. She released the wind chimes.

Every part of him seemed to constrict—his eyes narrowed, his lips tightened into one horizontal line, his upper body went rigid. He took a step forward and smacked her hard across the face.

Her hand rose protectively to her stinging cheek. She backed away.

"Oh, hey, I'm sorry." He put his hands in the air. "I didn't mean that. Honest."

"You hit me," she said, stunned.

"I said I was sorry. I just lost it for a second. Look, we gotta talk about this."

She turned to go. "There's nothing to talk about."

"*Hey.*"

Even when he took hold of her arm, she didn't completely sense the danger. In the next instant, she was face first on the grass.

A rough hand clamped onto her shoulder, turned her over. He was on top of her then, with all his weight, his greedy mouth over hers. She tried to cry out. He jammed his tongue deep into her mouth. She bit it, tasted blood. He pulled away, howling in pain. His fist came down, smashed into her face.

She heard a sickening crunch. He hit her again. And once more. A scream died in her throat.

The struggling made him angrier. So did her tears. "Please," she cried. "I'm only seventeen."

The heady scent of lilacs perfumed the air. Wind chimes tinkled overhead. The last thing she saw was the starless sky above her as he yanked down his zipper. The last thing she felt was the cool springtime air and the wetness of the grass as her cotton panties were torn from her. And the last thing she heard him say was, "You are mine. Forever."

The memory was never really gone, but over the years, she had managed to dilute it, to immerse herself in her son or her job until the shivering subsided. She always shivered when she thought about the attack—during the bitter winters since, she had never been as cold as she was on that night in April, limping across the wet lawn, carrying her skirt and her ripped underwear into her parents' house.

Now, she was shaking again. She had thick socks on her feet, and she grabbed an extra blanket from the hall closet. But when she got into bed, she was still cold.

14

IT WAS COLD THE NEXT morning at school, the building's antiquated furnace apparently too stunned by the sudden drop in temperature to kick on. Samantha kept her coat on and hurried to the staff lounge for coffee. One of the secretaries, wrapped in a bouclé-knit cardigan, met her at the staff-room door. Through chattering teeth she said, "Mr. Halloran's been looking for you, Samantha."

"Really? I'll just grab a cup of coffee first."

"I think it's important." The secretary smiled nervously, her gaze darting everywhere.

"Okay, Janet. I won't shoot the messenger. I'm on my way."

Halloran's voice came over the P.A. system. "Mrs. Quinlan, would you please report to my office?"

Now craving both coffee and chocolate, Samantha swore under her breath, then retraced her steps down the hall.

In Bert Halloran's office, a small baseboard heater was plugged in, its bright red coils blasting warmth into the room. Halloran closed the door behind her.

The principal's office was spacious, with a pair of large

windows facing the street, but even though the modern furniture—desk, chairs, credenza—all matched, the room was ugly. There were no framed photographs, no desktop mementos, nothing to let a visitor know who the occupant was. A calendar from a local auto body shop was the only thing tacked to the bulletin board and it still showed the month of September. On the windowsill, a small dieffenbachia in a plastic pot had turned yellow.

Samantha settled into a chair and waited for whatever was about to hit the fan.

"This thing with Jim's a real mess," Halloran announced when he'd sat down again. His doughy face was molded into its customary scowl, his mouth turned down at the corners, his lower lip protruding. To Samantha, the man looked like someone had snatched his favorite toy from the sandbox. Tom could imitate the expression perfectly.

Samantha, unsure how to respond, said nothing.

"He'll probably lose his job," Halloran added. "Shouldn't have to come to this."

The principal continued to stare at her over pudgy steepled fingers, though what he expected her to say or do she still didn't know. In the uneasy silence, the man's fingertips tapped together, irritating as a leaky faucet. Samantha was gripped by the urge to crush those fat sausages under a heavy book.

"Bert, why am I here?"

Halloran heaved an exasperated sigh, then shook his head as though gazing upon the casket of a friend who had died inexplicably and too soon. "Jim Petrella is a good man. There must have been something that those girls said that struck you as—false? Contrived? Maybe even conspiratorial? Especially Bobbie Donaldson. That girl's been around."

Samantha winced and forced her words to flow evenly. "Bobbie's activities are irrelevant here. That said, she would certainly be able to accurately identify a male's erection being rubbed against her thigh."

"This could all be some kind of vendetta—"

"Why, Bert? Both girls' grades are good—"

"Teenage girls can have some wild fantasies."

"You didn't see them in my office. They were mortified. Humiliated. Inconsolable. They could barely choke out what had happened."

Halloran's scowl deepened.

"I know Jim's your friend, but there's nothing I can do for him. Face it, this isn't the first time he's gotten into trouble over something like this." Two years before, Petrella had been accused of making lewd comments to a well-endowed sophomore, and rumors circulated about him having been transferred from another school board because of a similar offense with a student teacher. "He needs help, Bert."

"None of this would have happened in the old days. Girls stuck to sewing, cooking, hairdressing. You didn't see them in machine shop and auto mechanics."

Samantha bit her lip, unable to determine whether Halloran was baiting her or if he really believed what he was saying. She rose to leave. "If there's nothing else—"

The principal gave a disgusted nod and Samantha made her exit, preferring the near-frigid temperature in the corridor to the stifling atmosphere of Halloran's office. The chill continued for much of the morning, not merely because of the malfunctioning furnace but more because of the icy stares from a few of her colleagues. In their view, she had betrayed one of their own.

Hank Ehrhart was less subtle than the rest. "Haven't got a fucking clue about loyalty, have you, Counselor?" he hissed, beady eyes black as marble bearing down upon her as she was retreating to her office.

"I'm loyal to the truth, Hank. I've got to do what's right."

"Must be a helluva thing, being perfect."

"I never said—"

"Rich boyfriend, perfect kid . . . nice cookie-cutter world, held together with enough molasses to make an ordinary person puke. Yeah, you've got it all, Counselor, and Petrella's about to lose everything. Doesn't seem fair somehow, does it?"

Outside her office she squared off to face the coach. "Ah, Hank, do everyone a favor and go to hell, would you?" She closed her door on his face.

Tom poked his head into her office between classes. "Is the scuttlebutt true? Petrella might get the ax?"

Samantha shrugged.

"He's got it coming," Tom said. "Guy's a lech. Not to mention a dork."

That got a smile out of her. So did the Three Musketeers bar Tom tossed at her before rushing off to his next class.

Somehow, even with her head about to explode, she made it through the morning. She wondered briefly if Derek Townsend would stop in to tell her about the dance, and when he didn't, she assumed all must have gone well. When the noon buzzer sounded, Samantha groaned along with it.

Monday. Cafeteria supervision. With Hank Ehrhart. She groped in her purse for some Tylenol, then she grabbed a mirror and checked her appearance. She might as well look good for the public stoning in the square.

The cafeteria was a quarter full when Samantha got there. Ehrhart entered from the opposite side, having changed from his double knits into gray sweatpants and a white polo shirt. The shirt stretched across his abdomen, denting at the navel. The miracle diet obviously hadn't yet taken effect. Ehrhart's extra thirty pounds still jiggled around his waist.

Samantha slowed her pace, waiting for Ehrhart to choose his seat so she could remain as far away as possible. Although there were scores of tables between them when they both sat down, Samantha could feel his hateful stare from across the room.

The cafeteria filled quickly, students racing to available seats, calling out, "Hi, Mrs. Q.," as they passed. A few paused to chat.

No one chatted with Hank Ehrhart, but he probably didn't care. He ruled the phys. ed. department like a mob kingpin. When his jocks did something wrong, they were dumb bastards. When they did something right, he told them it was about time. He saw no point in getting buddy-buddy with his students. "Play cutesy with these kids and you lose their respect," he'd said at more than one staff meeting, looking at Samantha each time.

Halfway across the cafeteria, Jenny Rideout sat with a muscular, redheaded youth. The new boyfriend. Older than Jenny, Bill Pankow was a hotshot basketball star recently transferred from a high school in Dorchester. He seemed fond of Jenny. They were laughing and holding hands across the table, lost in each other's eyes, like the songs said.

Donna Chetwynd sat one table over, surrounded by four boys, all staring at her ample chest, none of them the fellow she'd claimed to have been madly in love with when she'd spoken to Samantha the week before. Samantha smiled, raised her hand to wave, but Donna quickly looked away. She knew Donna's type. Befriend only those who could be of service. Service provided, you were history. Samantha lowered her hand.

Derek entered the cafeteria, an oversized jacket hanging sloppily on his bulky frame. Samantha tried to signal to him, but he was staring ahead at nothing in particular.

"Hi, Mrs. Q.! Any hope of me pulling out of that French class?" Tony Puglia plopped onto the chair opposite Samantha.

Tony, a kid who was only happy when he was miserable, began to complain about his French teacher. Louise LaPlante was one of the best teachers in the school, except in Tony's mind. Louise dared to accuse him of speaking French with an Italian accent.

"And she asked me to conjugate some irregular verb in the pluperfect tense. She was trying to make a fool outta me, Mrs. Q. I had my hand raised for three other questions, but does she call on me? No way."

Samantha wished she'd put her purse on the vacant seat, thinking it might have dissuaded Tony from sitting with her.

"A guy can only stand so much humiliation, know what I mean?"

What in the name of heaven was the boy going on about? And why couldn't she stay on track?

" . . . has favorites. Like your son."

"Pardon? You were saying, Tony?"

A shrill scream split the air.

"Uh-oh!" Tony chuckled. "Not the plastic puke again."

Samantha leaned sideways to see where the noise had come from.

Ehrhart was rushing over to Jenny's table. Even from a distance, Samantha could see his face was pasty. She stood up.

Derek hovered over Jenny's table, one arm extended toward her, the other clamped at his side.

Some of the students had scattered, running toward the nearest exits. Others stayed glued to their seats. Many dropped to the floor and crawled under tables.

Derek's outstretched hand. It held a gun.

Samantha's feet felt as if they were encased in concrete. Crucial seconds seemed to drag as she moved toward Derek, her body traveling as though in suspended animation.

Ehrhart was approaching Derek cautiously from behind.

Samantha chanced a quick glance at the coach. His soft, paunchy flab billowed over his drawstring pants. Against Derek's solid mass, Ehrhart wouldn't stand a chance. She saw nearby students, still frozen to their chairs, any of whom could end up innocent victims if the gun accidentally fired. She had to get to Derek before Ehrhart grabbed him.

As Ehrhart drew close to Derek, he glanced at Samantha. She shook her head furiously. Ehrhart stopped, confused.

Samantha spoke softly, her voice barely audible above Jenny's wailing. "Derek. Please."

The boyfriend was mute, his eyes glassy.

"You need someone to talk to, Derek," Samantha said. She stretched out her arms, motioning cautiously toward the exits at each end of the room. To those within earshot she said, "Everything's fine. Don't panic. Just leave the cafeteria. Quickly and quietly."

She riveted her gaze on Derek, hoping he would focus on her. If only Jenny would stop crying. "Derek, let me help you. There are answers. Even though you may not see them clearly right now. There's time."

"No. There isn't." His voice was harsh, the tone bitter. "There's no time at all. Not for her. Not anymore." He raised the gun. It looked foolish, almost like a toy in his hand. A feminine, pearl-handled revolver.

"Derek, listen. I promise that whatever has happened, the hurt will go away. We'll get you through this."

He shook his head, but the motion was barely there, as if he, too, was afraid to move.

"Mrs. Q. You don't understand. Your advice was good. I did exactly like you said. I got dressed up. I went to the dance. I was having a good time." His gaze was still fixed on Jenny's face. The girl whimpered. Her cheeks were blotchy. Mascara puddled under her eyes. "Then I thought I'd just go over and say hi, you know, to be friendly. To show there were no hard feelings."

"Derek, that's very mature. I—"

"But there's just no being nice to some people." His finger tapped at the trigger. Jenny's eyes bulged wider. She pushed farther back into her chair. Bill Pankow was gray.

Samantha persisted. "Derek, what happened?"

"They laughed at me." His voice broke. "I was dressed as Igor, all hunched over, with scabs and a crooked mouth, and that bastard"—he pointed to the boyfriend—"asked me where my costume was. Said it was real original to come as myself. Called me an ugly dumb fuck."

"Derek . . ."

"And she laughed. She laughed real loud." His hand tightened around the gun. The flesh beneath the chewed-off fingernails was white.

Ehrhart was moving in again, creeping slowly. He stared at the gun, edged toward it.

"No, Hank," Samantha said. "Stay where you are. Derek's not going to shoot anyone."

She saw her words take hold. Derek's face changed. Though he continued to gape at Jenny, he no longer seemed mesmerized. He appeared shaken, realizing Ehrhart was behind him. The hand holding the gun began to tremble. Derek glanced about the cafeteria. Ehrhart took a step back.

"Derek, look at me. *Look at me.*"

The boy turned only slightly toward Samantha, keeping Jenny in view, the gun still aimed squarely at Jenny Rideout's head.

"Listen to me, Derek. Hurting Jenny won't work. You know that. You've never been in trouble before. Don't blow it now. You deserve better. You're a good person."

He turned his head, focused on Samantha. For a brief moment he smiled. Then his face took on a weary, defeated look.

"You can pull through this, Derek. I know you can. And you

don't have to do it alone. No problem is so big it can't be solved. We talked about that."

His eyes seemed to brighten a little. The deep furrow on his forehead softened. He sighed, and there were traces of a smile at the corners of his mouth. "You're right, Mrs. Q. Hurting other people just isn't my style. Why stoop to their level, huh? Thanks for your help. I know you care. You're real special."

Slowly, he turned the gun away from Jenny.

It was Samantha's turn to sigh.

"Give the gun to Mr. Ehrhart, Derek. He's—"

But Derek had raised the gun again. To his own head.

He pulled the trigger.

15

SAMANTHA REMEMBERED POLICE. Everywhere. Sirens wailing. An ambulance, firefighters, the canine unit. The cafeteria was now a crime scene, the school under siege. And there was Halloran's voice over the P.A. telling everyone to remain calm, report to the auditorium, await further instructions, remain in the building. But the kids were everywhere, overflowing from classrooms into the halls and from the halls into the schoolyard. Above the din, Halloran continued to bellow his message, adding to the panic and chaos.

One of the female gym teachers brought a spare tracksuit to the lounge for Samantha. "Here. Change into this."

Tom Lundstrom, reluctant to release her from his comforting hold, gave her a reassuring squeeze and said, "Good idea, kiddo."

She hazarded a glance at her lap. Her beige corduroy skirt was smeared with a large rust-colored stain. "Tom, so much blood . . ." She felt weak, dizzy, and she leaned against him.

"You were holding Derek," Tom said gently.

She nodded, recalling the compassionate police officer who allowed her to cradle Derek for a moment longer. She remembered, too, Hank Ehrhart backing well away, as though some of Derek's blood might rub off on him.

With the tracksuit bunched under her arm, she allowed Tom to lead her from the staff lounge toward the girls' change room. She thought for a moment she was hallucinating, but when she blinked again, she realized it was indeed Meredith Paxton, clad in a mint green couturier suit, coming along the hall.

Meredith gasped. "Samantha, are you hurt?"

"I—no. What are you doing here?"

"The fundraiser, Samantha. I was in a meeting with the principal when we heard the terrible news. But never mind that now. Get out of those clothes and give them to me. I'll send them to the cleaners immediately. You simply mustn't look at them in that condition."

Samantha staggered into the change room. Derek's blood had seeped through to her panties and had left a pinkish stain on her abdomen. She used a dampened paper towel to remove the traces as best she could. She craved a shower but there wasn't time. Halloran was on the P.A. again, urging everyone to proceed in an orderly fashion to the auditorium. Samantha donned the sweatsuit, the fleece-lined outfit roomy and warm.

In the corridor, she handed her soiled clothing to Chris's mother, who rolled everything into a tight ball. Meredith muttered, "Do call if you need anything," touched Samantha awkwardly on the arm, and headed for the nearest police officer. After a brief exchange of words, the officer escorted Meredith to the door.

"So that's the dragon lady," Tom said, ushering Samantha in the direction of the auditorium.

Samantha nodded.

"Something's off about her, Sam. I can't put my finger on it. But be careful."

She could summon no words. In the main hallway, the mere

sight of the students shuffling numbly along rendered her mute. Some of them were hysterical, clinging to each other; the rest were zombies as they filed through the doors into the tiered auditorium.

Police officers stood at each entrance. Halloran, on stage, tested the microphone, tapping several times in succession, the shrill feedback mimicking Jenny Rideout's scream. Then, facing the student body, Halloran cleared his throat, yanked up his trousers, and began.

His speech was wooden, his voice stilted as he delivered the facts as he knew them. He clutched the lectern more, Samantha was sure, for his own insecurity than from any unsteadiness caused by grief. Scanning the faces of the dumbstruck teenagers, she could see the principal's words were doing little to soothe their roiling emotions or cushion the dreadful blow they had been dealt.

Throughout Halloran's awkward address, Samantha's mind was a jumble. Hundreds of unconnected thoughts rushed through her, darting and flitting like sparks. Mental overload. She wondered if this was how Derek had felt during his last moments. Too much to think about. Nowhere to run. Lost.

She wondered, too, what words she might have uttered that could have saved him.

Never, even during her blackest times, had Samantha contemplated ending it. Not in the months after the rape, not after Scott died, and not during the lonely period after she had moved out of her parents' house. No matter how bleak things had become, there was always a glimmer of hope, always one more corner to turn.

She had failed Derek. She hadn't walked him far enough around the corner, yet she had been so certain he was fine. He had plans, coping strategies, his confidence was returning. Those were good signs. Or had he just been telling her what she wanted to hear? She had missed something. She should have seen, should have known. She should have done a better job.

With haunting locomotor rhythm, Ehrhart's words echoed in her mind, the words he'd hissed in her ear as she stroked Derek's blood-matted hair. "The kid would be alive if you'd let me move in on him. This is your fault, Counselor."

She shook the memory away and tried to focus on Halloran.

"You will be escorted to the gymnasium," the principal said. "Look for your homeroom teacher. Your parents are being notified that they may pick you up there. All staff without homeroom responsibilities will meet in the front hall to assist in a locker search."

Groans erupted in the auditorium and Samantha's heart sank further. Halloran raised his voice above the outburst, though his composure was slipping. "This search is for everyone's safety."

Two boys sitting near Samantha began whispering.

"What's the search all about?"

"Weapons, you gonad. I heard the cops talkin'. They think Townsend might have been part of some death cult or gang or something."

"Jeez. So why do we have to go to the gym?"

"So they can frisk us, I bet."

"Anyone touches me, my dad'll sue."

Samantha waited for Halloran to humanize his address, to offer words of condolence, but none were forthcoming.

Yvonne Colford slipped her arm around Samantha. "You going to be okay?"

Samantha shrugged. "It's not me I'm worried about now. Look at the faces on those kids."

Yvonne nodded. "Isn't that jerk going to say anything to make them feel better? Does he always have to be so—"

"Official? Maybe he does. But I don't."

She rushed toward the stage and motioned to Halloran, interrupting him mid-sentence. He excused himself from the microphone.

"Bert," she whispered. "This search. Is it really necessary?"

"Can't take any chances. There may be a real hard-core group out there just waiting for the police to leave."

"But the police saw the gun. So did I. It wasn't the kind of weapon a gang member would use."

"Did enough damage, didn't it? Blew the kid's brains all over the place."

Samantha winced. "Derek was distraught, Bert. What happened was an isolated event. A tragedy. There's nothing brewing out there. Those are good kids. And they're hurting."

He squared his shoulders, his face now resembling a bulldog's. "There *will* be a search, Mrs. Quinlan."

"Fine," Samantha muttered. "You do your job your way, but let me do mine." She shoved past him and stood at the lectern. Staring back at her were fifteen hundred pairs of eyes, waiting for some counsel, some sympathy, some permission to grieve. Something.

She scanned the gallery of faces, then homed in on one in particular. Matthew. Sitting in the front row.

She adjusted the microphone. The students were silent. Though her voice was deep and soft, there was a slight quiver as she spoke.

"What has happened here today is a horrible tragedy. We can't begin to understand Derek Townsend's torment, nor the reasons for his actions. Those of you who were his friends will miss him, wonder what you could have done, could have said. If you didn't know him, you might still struggle to comprehend how such a thing could have happened. At the very least, Derek's death reminds us how important it is to reach out to one another. Let's start today." She watched as Matthew and some other students openly wiped away tears.

More firmly, she said, "Be aware, too, that Derek Townsend's decision was not a courageous one and should in no way be glorified as such." Samantha was acutely aware of the contagious nature of teenage suicide. "Remember, we all grieve in our own ways. I encourage you to express your feelings—to family, friends, teachers, clergy. We will all need one another's support in the days ahead."

She left the stage on Jell-O legs. Halloran resumed control of the mike and announced, "Those seated in the last five rows will now proceed to the gymnasium."

Like robots, the students rose, turned, and left.

16

AT THE FRONT ENTRANCE a pair of police officers stood guard. Panic-stricken, irate parents pressed against the glass from the other side as the police motioned for them to go around the building to the gym doors. Samantha hurried over.

"Pardon me, officers, but do the lockers really need to be searched?"

The taller of the pair, a squarely built female with a ruddy complexion, answered, "Your principal wants to be sure there's no more guns, ma'am."

"It's just that so many of the students are upset. Enclosing this kind of hysteria could be dangerous too—"

"But guns kill."

Her companion, a double-dimpled younger man with a crosshatch of razor cuts along his jaw, offered his own wisdom. "There's a special program kids can attend if they're caught bringing weapons to school. Straightens them right out." His eager expression seemed to indicate that he wanted more weapons to turn up.

"You won't find any guns," Samantha stated firmly.

"You're being very naïve about kids today, ma'am," the policewoman said.

"I believe the term you're looking for is 'bleeding heart.'"

Samantha whirled around and slammed headlong into Hank Ehrhart.

"You're making one mistake after another today, aren't you, Counselor?" His smirk was mocking, cruel.

Why don't you just fuck off? resonated so beautifully in her mind, but aloud she said, "Take care of the kids in the gym, Hank. They need someone."

Samantha reached the bank of lockers she had been assigned to search, feeling the flush of heat that had risen to her cheeks. She was a part of the school's Crisis Response Team, but Halloran had removed her from the crisis. In her efforts to reach out to the students, she had trod heavily on the principal's feet, showing him up in the auditorium, and now he was punishing her. Relegating her to search lockers was the closest Halloran could come under the circumstances to assigning her latrine duty.

The corridor was less crowded now, most of the students having been corralled in the gym under the watchful stares of Halloran's henchmen. Samantha thought again of the sea of troubled faces in the auditorium, and she agonized once more about the vast distance between herself and the kids. Shy Suzie Yamada, who cried at the mere mention of violence—how were Halloran's disciplinarians dealing with her? Jenny Rideout, the intended victim of Derek's bullet, now being questioned by the police in Halloran's office, and Matthew . . . no, she could not think about any of them now. Her throat tightened, and her eyes stung.

As she reached for the first locker, a hand clamped on her shoulder, making her gasp.

"How you hanging in, friend-o'-mine?"

"Tom," she said, sighing with relief. "Don't ever do that."

"Sorry." He gave her arm a few firm pats. "I thought you saw me coming."

"No, I didn't. And to answer your question, by a few microscopic hairs, that's how I'm hanging in." She heard her voice crack.

"You're allowed to be human, you know. I'm here if you need to let it go."

It was tempting, and it might have made her feel better, but crying now struck her as unprofessional, weak, and she didn't want Ehrhart or his ilk to have any additional ammunition.

We were all busting our asses and she did nothing except cry like a girl.

"Now's not the time," she told Tom, her voice raised, her tone more harsh than intended. She did not apologize. During difficult days, she always welcomed anger, knowing that over time, it would diffuse. Sorrow, in her experience, grew and infected others. She could not keep company with sorrow now. She was needed by others, and she was needed intact. Anger would serve her well. It kept her strong, held her together.

Tom took a respectful step back and nodded. "Well, I've got locker detail in the tech wing. Shout if you need me."

"I've got all these lockers to go through, plus half the ones around the corner. I'll be here forever."

"Columbo's got nothing on us," Tom said. "This could be the career change we've been hoping for." He shot her an encouraging smile.

No sooner had Tom disappeared around the corner than Louise LaPlante showed up holding a mug of tea. "Drink this. I wish I could offer you something stronger."

"Me too," Samantha said, taking the cup. "Thanks." In a few gulps, the tea was gone.

"Great job you did on stage, Samantha. You should be principal instead of that twit we're stuck with."

Samantha felt an appreciative squeeze on her arm.

"Oh, I almost forgot. I passed Matthew as he was being herded to the gym."

Matthew. The fissure in her heart widened. "How did he look?"

"Same as the others—shell-shocked, but he's more worried about you."

"I'll be okay," she said. "I have to be."

"Not a doubt in my mind," Louise said. "Think you can smuggle a book down to him? He's afraid he'll go stir-crazy."

"I'll do the best I can."

Then with a thumbs-up, Louise was gone, and Samantha, grateful for the momentary distraction, inserted the master key into locker No. 100.

The inventory consisted of smelly sneakers, a rotten orange, a beige windbreaker, and some books. No guns, no knives, not even a toothpick. The next locker was sparkly clean. A suede knapsack hung from a hook. Samantha untied the drawstring. White socks, tennis shoes, talcum powder, deodorant, two tampons, and a copy of *Wuthering Heights.* The next twenty lockers were equally unremarkable, save for one, which held the notorious plastic vomit. Disgusting, but hardly a weapon.

Locker 125, however, was different. Samantha saw the handle sticking out of a pile of gym clothes. Gingerly she pulled it out. A pistol. A water pistol. She returned it to the heap and slammed the door.

She continued on, wading through more dog-eared paperbacks, malodorous athletic wear, and weeks-old lunches spotted with blue furry mold. The inanity of the search once again fueled her temper, giving rise to a mental litany of obscene nicknames for Bert Halloran.

When she opened locker 156, she was stunned. An alien lived

here. The narrow space was jammed. Contributing a well-worn dime would have risked an implosion. Rollerblades competed for space with a half dozen thick binders, a knapsack, a gym bag, two pairs of decrepit sneakers, three sweatshirts, and a familiar-looking windbreaker. On the top shelf, an assortment of mangled paperbacks and a black clarinet case perched at a precarious angle. Her son's locker.

At home, Matthew's bedroom was operating-room clean and hyper-organized, so Samantha was thunderstruck by what her eyes beheld. Perplexing, too, was the collection of wallet-sized photographs affixed to the inside of the locker door with various-sized magnets. Samantha recognized Kelly Frid, a cute ninth grader who played flute in the junior band. One photograph showed Matthew and Kelly together. When had that been taken? And where?

Days or maybe weeks from now, when things were funny again, Samantha would mention the pictures, ask her son if he needed a brush-up on the penis and vagina talk, then Matthew would open up to her about Kelly. For the moment, she needed to straighten out those books.

The instant her hand shifted the books, the clarinet case slid out and down, grazing the side of her head before crashing onto the concrete floor. The case sprung open and the disassembled instrument scattered, the cylindrical smooth neck of the clarinet rolling the farthest away.

Samantha glanced around, wondering if the noise echoing down the corridor would bring someone running, but no one came. Quickly, she stooped to pick up the contents of the case, returning each piece to its crushed-velvet niche. She retrieved the instrument's bell, a plastic container of resin, the mouthpiece, and some spare reeds, but not before hastily gathering up the ten little black pills that had rat-tat-tatted like BB pellets onto the floor.

17

IT WAS SEVEN O'CLOCK WHEN Samantha drove up in front of Beatrice's and parked her Toyota at the curb. She could see the blue light of the elderly woman's television screen, and as she passed by the living-room window, Vanna White was busy with letters on *Wheel of Fortune,* smiling as if all was right with the world.

Samantha's energies had been drawn and quartered. The police had questioned her again. Then she was assailed by students, coming at her from all flanks, clinging, weeping, asking her for answers she didn't have. Somehow, there were bits of her that managed to remain glued together and she held on tenaciously—she still had Matthew to deal with.

The back stairs took the last of Samantha's strength, and with each step, she decided, then changed her mind, then decided again what she would say to her son. The anger that had propelled her through the remainder of her day had run its course. In its stead was a limp, washed-out nothingness, an invertebrate emotion stemming from too many unanswered questions. A beloved student had died, her precious son was taking drugs, and for someone who had once prided herself on being in step with the times and people's motives, Samantha suddenly realized she was a rube—she knew nothing at all.

In the apartment, Samantha's favorite Kenny G cassette was playing, but the mellow soprano sax was anything but soothing. Matthew had made tea, and as soon as he saw her, he poured a generous amount into an oversized china mug. "Hope you don't mind," he said, "but I went ahead and ate. I didn't know if you'd feel—"

She cut off his sentence with an upheld hand, ignored the tea, and strode into the living room to turn off the music.

Matthew followed her. "You look beat." He shoved aside pillows and magazines to make room for her on the couch. "I can throw together a sandwich, open a can of soup . . ."

Samantha was past hunger. "Come. Sit." She patted the cushion beside her.

Where to begin? What tone of voice? Facial expression? None of the courses she had taken could prepare her for this. These were unfamiliar, treacherous waters, and she was sailing them alone. With a deep breath, she leaped from the gangplank. "We've always been straight with each other, right?"

Matthew shot her a quizzical glance. "Geez, Mom, you don't think I'd ever do anything like Derek—"

"No, Matthew. But—what I mean is, we get along, don't we? You'd tell me if something was bothering you?"

"Sure, Mom," he said, his look uneasy, or was it evasive? "But I'm fine. Really. What happened to Derek was pretty awful, but I never really knew the guy, and I wasn't in the cafeteria when he—well, you know."

Samantha swiped a hand across her brow. Her forehead was clammy, and a ring of moisture dampened the elasticized waist of her borrowed tracksuit.

"Maybe I've put too much pressure on you, kidding you about

being the man of the house, that sort of thing. And the high marks—it can be tough trying to stay on top. Because I counsel all day, maybe you felt you'd be burdening me by talking about your problems."

"What problems?" Matthew's voice came out a prepubescent squeak. "Mom, I'm *fine.* And believe me, if I had a problem I'd tell you."

"Then tell me about these," she said simply. She removed the ten capsules from a zippered compartment in her purse and held them cupped in her hand.

"What are those? Vitamins?"

"Nice try, Matthew. Care to go again?"

His eyes widened. "Was Townsend on drugs? Is that why he—?"

"This conversation has nothing to do with Derek! It's about you! And these!" It was inevitable that on this, the blackest of days, she would lose it. She tried to regain her composure. Her son would hardly confide in her with her shrieking at him.

Matthew had inherited her trait of wearing his emotions close to the surface. His cheeks were stained pomegranate, his breath coming in rapid huffs. He pointed at the pills. "What do those have to do with me?"

"I found them in your locker. In your clarinet case."

"But I've never seen them before!"

"They were in your locker, Matthew."

"Well, maybe they were, but I didn't put them there. Mom, those lockers can be opened by any four-year-old with a nail file."

"So you're telling me the pills aren't yours."

"Yes," he said, looking squarely at her, "that's what I'm telling you."

Samantha remained mute. She hadn't considered Matthew lying, though she should have. Many young people, when backed into a corner, would do the same. The silence dragged on,

Samantha unsure how to bridge the chasm that divided them.

Matthew did it for her. "You don't believe me."

"I didn't say that."

"You didn't have to. You're staring at me like I'm Timothy Leary." He stood up. "I'm sorry about Derek, Mom, and I'm sorry you had a shitty day. You think I'm a druggie. I know I'm not. Seems like that's all there is to say. Unless you've got some bamboo shoots to shove under my nails, I'm going to my room."

The remark stung, but Samantha let it pass. What choice did she have? She heard Matthew's door slam shut, then music blared from behind the thin plywood door—screaming guitars, thumping drums, gravelly voices. She knew Matthew was baiting her, hoping she would stomp into his room to complain about the noise so he could get in a shot or two about his right to privacy. She gritted her teeth to the onslaught of rebel yells and mangled riffs and only hoped that Beatrice wouldn't phone to find out what was going on.

Eventually Matthew grew tired of the game and the apartment was miraculously quiet. The telephone beside her beckoned. She began to dial Chris's number. Midway through, she hung up, determined not to use Chris for a sounding board yet another time. Her troubles, for now, would remain her own. And anyway, it wasn't sympathy or empathy she needed. She needed answers.

She went to the kitchen, dropped the pills into a Ziploc bag, and put the bag into a seldom-used soup tureen. From the rear window, she could see yellow lights illuminating rectangles of glass throughout the neighborhood. In so many homes, life was going on as planned. Supper dishes would be cleared away, families would be reading newspapers, children doing homework or arguing over the evening's TV viewing.

But not here. And not at the Townsends'. Tonight, while others laughed, ate popcorn, read bedtime stories, the Townsends would be planning a funeral, phoning relatives, asking themselves why.

Again she felt her throat constrict, her eyes well up. Quickly, she opened the cupboard under the sink, snapped on rubber gloves, grabbed the scouring cleanser and attacked. The sink glistened, the stove shone, the refrigerator was relieved of food beyond its best-before date. The floor was next, and after that she moved to the bathroom. While scrubbing the countertop, Samantha caught sight of herself in the vanity mirror and was taken aback. Her forehead was deeply lined and slick with sweat, her puffy eyes ringed with gray. Her lower lip was blood-red from biting on it.

She made it to the front closet in eight strides and lugged the vacuum cleaner from its resting place. Repeatedly, she dragged the vacuum over the small rag rug until a sleepy-eyed Matthew poked his head into the room.

"Enough already. What'd that rug ever do to you?" Before she could apologize, he slammed his bedroom door.

She ran toward his room, longing to wrap her arms around him, tell him they would work things out together. Her hand stroked Matthew's bedroom door, fingers reached for the knob. Then she stopped herself. She had told Derek Townsend they would work things out together too.

The phone rang and Samantha flew at it, not wanting to risk another snarl from her son. It was Tom, checking on her. She cut the conversation short, sick of talking, sick of everything.

She hauled the vacuum cleaner back into the closet and got ready for bed.

But sleep wouldn't come. In the darkness, she thought of Matthew in the next room, probably wrestling with the covers as he often did, with Gisele Bündchen letting him struggle alone. Samantha felt a sudden longing for the Barney the Dinosaur days; she would have even settled for the Michael Jordan days, when things were less complicated, less charged with emotion. A simple request, she thought, to turn back the clock. To have Matthew's clarinet case hold nothing more than a clarinet, to put that stupid water pistol in Derek's hand instead of . . .

The sound of the gunshot reverberated in her mind. She sat up, clicked on the lamp, and squinted until her eyes adjusted to the light.

The espionage novel she tried to concentrate on left her bewildered. Too many characters, too much jet-hopping to exotic locations, too many unpronounceable names and spy acronyms. She couldn't tell the good guys from the bad guys. The letters on the page blurred into a smeared, graying mess.

She realized she was crying.

18

HE HAD THEIR ROUTINE DOWN pretty good. At 7:45, she usually came out of the house and headed for her car. By the time she got the motor running, the kid would beetle out from behind the house and jump in the Toyota, too. He would watch them drive off, then he'd have to put his foot to the mat to get to Lou's on time.

This morning, though, things were different. He'd slept in, barely had time to do the three S's and make it to her place. She was unlocking the '92 Corolla when Frank turned onto the street. He parked well back. The trees had lost most of their leaves, giving him no cover, and he wasn't about to get another lecture from his parole officer. Not just for watching.

She looked great, even though her hair was pulled back again, not long and loose the way he liked it. The kid was coming out now, and she was saying something to him. Right away, Frank knew there was trouble. The kid didn't answer her. He hardly even looked at her, and he didn't get into the car either. He just stood on the walkway and faced the other direction as she drove off. There was no wave, no smile, no honking of the car horn. Frank put his key in the ignition, pulled his car up closer to the house and let it idle at the curb. The kid was some pissed off, all right.

The front door opened and the skinny old lady stuck her head outside. The sight of her seemed to cheer the kid up, and he flashed the old girl a big smile.

That was when Frank almost crapped his drawers.

The light was good. Though it was a bugger of a cold morning, the sun was coming out, and he got a good look. The kid's smile. He knew it like his own. It *was* his own.

It was like looking in a goddamn mirror.

He heard the eight-o'clock news come on the radio. Shit. If he was late, Lou would report it to his probation officer. But something smelled important here, real important. He'd have to check it out.

During his lunch hour, he marched right into the school's front office like he had every right to be there. The reception area was full of computers and a bunch of other machines he didn't even recognize. Machines aside, the school was a big, old-fashioned place just like the one he'd gone to until he dropped out.

He smiled at the first face to look up. A woman in a thick sweater, wearing even thicker glasses, got up from her desk and came over. Her legs were thick, too.

"May I help you?"

"Yeah." He cleared his throat. "I mean *yes.*" What the hell. It was worth a shot. "I understand the Quinlan boy goes to this school."

"Matthew?"

"He must be getting pretty big. 'Sbeen a long time since I've seen him. Matthew." The name sounded strange coming from his mouth.

"He's in the ninth grade." Quickly, she put her hand to her mouth.

Frank picked up on the signal. "You must wonder why I'm asking. I'm a friend of his mother's and I'd like to buy the boy a birthday present. Thought he was born around this time of year."

"Why don't you ask his mother? She's on staff here." The woman stepped over to an ancient metal box covered with levers, knobs, and dials. Her skirt was shorter in the back than in front, and from where Frank stood, the view was godawful. "I can have her paged."

"No!" he snapped.

The woman flinched. Another gal sitting at her desk looked up.

More softly he added, "I wanted it to be a surprise. For both of them."

"I'd like to help, Mr.—" The secretary paused. Frank kept quiet. "But we're not allowed to give out personal information."

"Sure. I understand. Guess I'll just mail a card."

Frank left the office, glad to be away from that damn homely woman and her stupid rules. He was about to leave the building when he caught sight of the kid, about six car lengths away, making love-eyes at a small blond with braided hair. He was all set to move in for a closer look when a buzzer sounded. In seconds he was in the midst of a stampede. Kids were all over the place. Ahead, dozens of lockers in varying shades of industrial green were slamming shut. He couldn't see the kid now, just a swarm of faces all whizzing past like he was invisible.

Frank got shoved against a locker. Automatically, his hands became fists. He whirled around, but in the crowd, he couldn't tell who had pushed him. Quickly, he shouldered and elbowed his way through the mess of people until he found himself outside. He took half a dozen greedy gulps of air and counted to twenty, slowly, until he felt his heartbeat return to normal.

Schools. Shit. It all came back to him, and so did his reasons for quitting. Too many rules. Too many assholes giving out stupid orders, finding fault with something you wrote, something you said, something you did. He had more freedom in jail.

He looked at his watch. Double shit. He'd have to miss eating again to get back to work on time.

No matter, he told himself. He still had a beer left in the car.

19

FOR THE REST OF THE WEEK, the weather was dreary, the school and home front drearier. The school flag flew at half-staff, and after Wednesday's private funeral, Samantha's office flooded with grief-racked teenagers.

The teachers were subdued. Some canceled classes, others conducted impromptu discussions or quiet reading periods. The only one who could muster any energy was Hank Ehrhart, who worked his athletes even harder than usual. For once, Samantha was grateful for Ehrhart's stamina—it kept him in the gym most of the time and out of her hair.

Between ministering to the kids and dealing with her own grief, Samantha struggled to come to grips with all that had happened since the appearance of ten little black pills. She couldn't afford to be naïve about her son. He was exceptionally bright, which didn't make him immune to the pressures of adolescence; if anything, his giftedness contributed to his problems. He faced the same social ostracism of many of his peers. He and his small circle of friends had taken a lot of ribbing, some of it normal, some of it even deserved, but much of it cruel. Around school, those in the gifted English class were known as the Menstrual Society, a vicious Mensa pun. Samantha could understand Matthew, like any other kid, wanting to fit in, no matter the cost.

Matthew took a pounding in other areas, too. He wasn't mechanically inclined. Nor was he athletic. In the two short months since he had enrolled in high school, his artsy tendencies earned him the whispered label "fag," which cut deeply.

Still, something wasn't right. Matthew wasn't demonstrating any of the general symptoms of drug use. He wasn't withdrawn, his grades hadn't dropped, his eyes weren't red or glazed over. But she needed more information.

Over the phone, she described the pills to Chris. "Sound like amphetamines," he told her. "Speed. We used to call them black beauties at Tufts. Guys took them all the time, cramming for exams, yours truly the exception, of course. The medical name is Benzedrine. Where's all this coming from?"

"I'm concerned about a student at school," she replied. Not exactly a lie. "Amphetamines? You're sure?"

"I ought to be. Paxton Pharmaceuticals makes them. Anyway, if this student you're worried about is abusing speed, you'd know it." Chris rhymed off a list of symptoms: insomnia, irritability, short temper, confusion, euphoria. None of these described Matthew. Nor had he been vomiting. There were no complaints of nausea or diarrhea, and there certainly wasn't anything wrong with his appetite. Though they'd eaten breakfast in near-silence that morning, Matthew still managed to polish off a bowl of oatmeal, two pieces of toast with peanut butter, a banana, and a tumbler of orange juice. Heading out the door, he'd grabbed a box of raisins.

Samantha thanked Chris and hung up. Had Matthew been telling the truth? She hoped so, wishing their relationship could return to normal. Even though it had been only two days, she already found herself missing her son, his sense of humor, their

Scrabble games when there was nothing decent on television. For a moment, she felt relieved, nearly positive that Matthew was drug-free, but just as quickly a horrible thought took hold: if the pills didn't belong to Matthew, then how did they get into his locker?

The idea that someone else could have placed them there seemed a far more sinister prospect. Had another teacher conducted the locker search, the news of Matthew Quinlan's drug use would have been all over the school within minutes. Samantha scribbled random thoughts on her notepad, her efforts to sort through the quandary only increasing her confusion. Either Matthew was taking drugs or he had an enemy, one who played dirty.

20

ON A TIRED BLOCK OF more tired business establishments, Frank could see there wasn't much business going on. The window of Rhonda's Beauty Emporium displayed faded pictures of women wearing hairdos that no one would ask for. Next door, in Nonna's Alterations, you could get your pants hemmed for six bucks, discounts for seniors. He wondered what the kid was doing walking down a street that everyone else had forgotten about. Then Frank spotted it: an arcade on the corner, most of the marquee's round lightbulbs burned out.

The kid was late getting out of school. It was already past six o'clock, and instead of going home for a hot meal, he was ducking into a pinball joint. Frank got out of the car and crossed the street.

The kid was at the back of the place, already yanking like crazy on a lever. Frank sauntered along. The clanking, whistling, and buzzing that surrounded him fueled his need for a drink. There was barely room for him between the rows of machines. Every shape and size of ass jutted into the aisle. Finally, he stood over the kid's shoulder. On the screen, a yellow happy face gobbled up a bunch of dots and cherries. Then the screen changed to bright blue and the action sped up, the pathways became more complicated, the escape routes fewer. The cherries turned to peaches. Within seconds the screen went blank.

"Hey, you're pretty good at that."

The kid looked around behind him. "Nah. I can never get past that second screen."

"Better'n I could do. I've never seen a game like that before."

"Pac-Man? Are you serious? It's the oldest game in the place. Where have you been, on Mars?"

Frank smiled. "Want me to spot you a quarter?"

It was like an alarm went off in the kid's head. He glanced toward the exit. "No, thanks. I was just leaving." He started to pick up a little black case from the floor.

Frank spoke in a rush. "How come you play this game if it's so old? Why not one of those other ones? Seems like they've got more action." He looked at the pinball machine next to Pac-Man. Two busty blondes, wearing strategically unbuttoned combat shirts, smiled from the lighted plastic panel of a game called Commando.

"Too violent. I don't like shooting at things. In fact, I'm not much of a pinball junkie."

"So what are you hanging around here for?"

The kid took a long look at him as though trying to decide whether he should say anything. Then he set the case back down on the floor, straightened up, and said, "Letting off a little steam, I guess."

"Tough at your age, huh?"

"Sometimes." He paused. "Ever get blamed for something you didn't do?"

Frank laughed. "Story of my life." Now it was his turn to hesitate. "Yeah," he said after a time, "I remember what it was like at your age. What are you, 'bout fourteen? No, wait, I bet you're closer to fifteen." He searched the stale air, then snapped his fingers. "Birthday sometime in December, am I right?"

"Hey! Yeah, the tenth! How'd you do that?"

Frank laughed again, a full belly laugh. "Everybody's good at somethin'."

The kid smiled then, and Frank felt something funny in his stomach. One thing was for sure—she'd done a good job raising the kid. *Matthew.* He'd have to get used to calling him that. He seemed decent, polite, except maybe he needed a few pointers on getting some street smarts. It was a rotten world, and if Matt didn't toughen up a little, he could get chewed up.

"I've really got to go now," Matthew said again, picking up the case.

"How come?"

"I've got to practice my clarinet, finish writing a poem for homework. I'm making an anthology for English. See you."

Poetry? Clarinet? Shit. It looked like Frank had gotten here just in time.

So the kid was born in December, and Frank knew that Sam and the jock hadn't made it together before their wedding. It didn't take a genius to count to nine months. But birthday or no birthday, it was the smile, and that was proof enough.

It just might put a whole new spin on things.

21

From the moment I wake
You are there with your smile
To walk alongside me
Through life's uncertain miles.

At times my boyish stories
I, at length, do share
You listen so patiently
And show that you care.

So seldom it seems
Can words clearly express
The tender emotions:
Love, peace, happiness.

But all these you bring me
Day in and day out
For these are the things, Mom,
That you're all about.

Samantha choked back the knot of emotion in her throat and returned the poem to the folder. Knowing he had band practice, she had gone into her son's room on a snooping expedition, not quite certain what she was searching for, only discovering that if Matthew was involved in any way with drugs, there was no evidence here, not even in the lyrics of his favorite musicians' songs.

She wondered when Matthew had written the poem and if, during the past few days, he had ever been tempted to tear it up. When she heard her son's footsteps on the stairs outside, she hurried to the living room, sat on the couch with an opened magazine, and tried not to appear guilty. Matthew was in the kitchen now, lifting the lid on a stainless steel pot.

How different things were. Usually, Matthew hollered, "I'm home!" to which she would respond, "I thought you looked familiar," or some other nonsensical phrase that was guaranteed to get his eyeballs rolling. If she arrived home later, she would proclaim, "It's me, your favorite mother." Matthew's typical reply was something like, "But you're nothing like the one I ordered from the catalogue." Now, because he hadn't greeted her, she looked up from her magazine and announced, "Spaghetti. Specialty of the house. Ready in ten minutes."

"Smells good, Mom."

Three words, Samantha thought. A definite improvement. Not quite a flood, but better than a drought. She really missed her son, and the effects of their strained relationship were beginning to show. Even Tom noticed the change and asked her frequently if she was all right. She avoided any references to Matthew, telling him instead she was still upset about Derek. Again, not exactly a lie.

"How was band practice?"

"Mr. L.'s a sadist. We're learning Wagner's *Lohengrin*. Triple tonguing. I thought my face would fall off."

Matthew came into the living room and scouted for the remote.

"Leave it off a minute, could you?" she said. "Come. Sit."

"Uh, if it's all the same to you, Mom, I'll just stand. Last time you told me to sit beside you, I didn't like the way it turned out."

"Maybe I'll surprise you this time." He settled down beside her, his proximity bringing out her nervousness. The words tumbled out. "Look, Matthew, this motherhood business is a tough gig. If I took a thousand courses and read a million how-to books, I'd still mess up once in a while. I've never promised that you'll like every decision I make or every sentence I say, but I'm doing the best I can."

"Because you care," he said softly. "And you want what's best for me."

"You know I do. This stuff with the pills, it's all new territory—"

"Are you saying you believe me now?"

Samantha pursed her lips. She couldn't lie, not to her son. What credibility would she have if she couched the truth? "I wish I could say I did, Matthew, but the best I can give you right now is that I'm leaning more your way."

"Geez, Mom—"

"I'm sorry if it's not what you wanted to hear. Drugs are everywhere, you're a growing guy with all the pressures that go along with it . . ."

Samantha studied his face. Since last Monday, Matthew had worn an uncharacteristic scowl, one that Bert Halloran might envy. Now that expression was replaced by a look of utter defeat, as though some invisible vacuum had sucked away all his anger, leaving him with a bottomless sorrow and eyes that were damp with tears. In a lifeless voice, Matthew asked her, "What's making you think I *might* be telling the truth?"

"It's the drugs. They're speed. Amphetamines. Chris told me."

"Oh, no," he wailed. "Chris knows?"

"No. But I've been thinking that you're not acting like any

hopped-up kid. So unless you're dealing the pills or unless it's your first time using them, there might be some other explanation. I'm open to ideas from the floor."

"Better get out your notepad," Matthew told her. "You always think better when you write things down."

Over their spaghetti dinner Samantha scribbled furiously in her notebook, conceding several points to Matthew. Why, if he knew drugs were in his locker, would he have risked her going through his things to bring him a book? What would he want with ten uppers anyway? He had plenty of energy. If he wanted to sell drugs, he wouldn't pick amphetamines—they weren't the drug of choice among the high-school crowd. He'd stand a better chance of making money by getting steroids for the wrestling team. Samantha was momentarily taken aback at her son's savvy about illegal substances, but the more they spoke and the longer she wrote, the more puzzled she became. Something wasn't adding up.

"Let's come at it from the other direction," she said, her fork twirling a cyclone through her pasta. "The drugs aren't yours. You've got nothing to do with them. How do you suppose they got into your locker? And more importantly, why?"

"*How's* the easy part. I've already told you those lockers are useless. May as well leave all my stuff out in the hallway. But why? To make trouble for me, I guess."

"What if you found the drugs instead of me, though? There'd be no trouble at all then. You'd just flush them down the toilet, right?"

"Probably. So, someone knew there was going to be a locker search. Was maybe even hoping another teacher would find the pills, raise a stink." Once again, Samantha saw a pained expression cross her son's face. "Who hates me that much?"

With some difficulty and even more reluctance to squeal on any potential culprit, Matthew eventually furnished her with a small list of suspects, two sophomores who originated the Menstrual Society label and a few classmates who'd given him grief recently. "I guess any of them could have stolen the pills from a parent's medicine cabinet. It just seems like the wrong kind of drug to plant, that's all."

Samantha agreed. After an hour they were no further ahead. They cleared the table in silence, Matthew offering to wash the dishes while Samantha dried.

It wasn't until he was scouring the pot that held the spaghetti that Matthew spoke again. "I guess we're back to me being a druggie, then."

"Wait a minute," she said at once, a dreadful idea taking hold. "What if this whole thing has nothing to do with you at all?"

"Huh? You've lost me, Mom."

"What if it's *me,* Matthew. What if someone wanted to destroy my reputation? Or our relationship?"

"Then I guess we're rephrasing the question: who hates *you* that much?"

22

SAMANTHA WAS KEENLY AWARE that over the span of her ten-year tenure at Somerville Central, she had ruffled a good number of feathers. During the panic-fueled chaos in the moments after Derek's death, any one of the staff or students could have seized the opportunity to stash a handful of pills in locker 156, a deed that must have already been in the planning stages. She forced herself to eat lunch in the staff room for an entire week, keeping her friends close, her enemies closer. Tom appeared puzzled by the turnabout, her previous reclusive nature now abandoned in favor of a more glib, extroverted Samantha. "Time to get on with the business of living," she had told him on their Wednesday-night outing with Matthew.

If it was strange behavior she was after, then the genie in charge of dysfunctional folks granted her wish. Her notepad was quickly filling up with hasty jots of unusual sightings, sentences with dual meanings, occurrences that were not quite right. At work, she kept the notepad in her oversized shoulder bag at all times, removed from the prying eyes of those who might think her paranoid, or worse.

Tony Puglia, who, as it turned out, thought Samantha was a real babe, made regular pilgrimages to her office, inventing a host of inane problems and gripes as excuses to spend time with her. In the halls, he shadowed her constantly so that she found herself ducking into washrooms, latching on to other teachers, faking conversations on her office phone, anything to avoid that forlorn basset hound stare. Tom had given her a heads-up on Tony—his father, if gossip amounted to anything, was a middle-rung racketeer. "Don't make the kid mad," Tom warned her. "You could find yourself wearing a piano-wire necklace and admiring the marine life from the bottom of the Inner Harbor."

Bert Halloran was feeling the agonizing pinch of thumbscrews —his phone rang constantly, with none of the callers praising his administrative capabilities, so the gossip went. He was, in turn, deflecting his pain onto Samantha. During another pants-tugging, pouting session in his office, the principal complained about Meredith Paxton, how her visit had left him with the overpowering urge to deck the woman. She had big ideas for the school's major fundraiser, each of them better than anything Halloran or his committee could come up with, in Meredith's opinion. If he would only step aside and let her run the show, she would prove it. Halloran thumped his head with the heel of his hand. Did Samantha know what she was getting into by marrying into that family?

Then the principal informed her that Derek Townsend's father had been by asking a lot of questions about how his son had died. There were rumors, it seemed, about a male teacher who had tried to intervene but was prevented from doing so, and what did Halloran know about it? He explained the situation to John Townsend as best he could, the implication being that Samantha now owed him her right arm. Bert Halloran didn't like parents who asked questions, which he made quite clear to Samantha, his usual scowl having metamorphosed into a snarl.

She couldn't forget about Halloran's loyalty to Jim Petrella either, particularly now that the noon-hour grapevine was circulating the news that Petrella's wife had left him. While a few staffers muttered that it was about time, there were more who banded together in support of the industrial arts teacher. Petrella was a straight-up guy. Petrella was a good teacher. Petrella was framed.

But was Petrella in the building the day of the shooting?

On the Friday of the second week in November, as Samantha was preparing to leave for the weekend, Hank Ehrhart burst into her office. "You've really done it this time, Quinlan." The coach's energy could have run a major kitchen appliance. "I thought you always took the kids' side. What have you got against Grantham?"

Star of the volleyball team, six-foot-two Bryan Grantham had a killer spike that could knock over the opposing teammates like so many bowling pins. Unfortunately the athlete also drank as though tomorrow was his last day on the planet. "I have nothing against Bryan. What's eating you?" She wanted to add "this time."

"He went to his parents for help. About his drinking. Advice courtesy of one Nosey-Parker school counselor. Now Grantham and his folks are going to some weekend retreat run by their church to sort out their problems."

"So?"

"*Next weekend.*"

"So?"

"You live under a goddamn rock, Quinlan? The championship tournament is next weekend and Grantham will be off communing with nature or the Alcoholics Anonymous god. The point is, he won't be playing net on my volleyball court."

The lines were all there in her head. Had Ehrhart trained his athletes to play as a team, they wouldn't be so stuck without superstar Grantham. Didn't Ehrhart want Grantham to stop drinking?

Wasn't the boy's health more important than some game? And how could she have known about a retreat scheduled for the same weekend as the tournament? He couldn't blame that on her.

The arguments went unspoken, for in the seconds it took her to form her words, Ehrhart was already scuttling for the door. He spun around to face her. "You'll get yours, Counselor. One of these days, your cookie-cutter perfect world will cave in and you'll get yours."

The enemy was well armed, and he was everywhere. The encounter with Ehrhart left her shaken. After donning her coat and heading to the staff parking lot, she scouted for signs of the beady-eyed coach and his reconditioned BMW, wondering what little motivation he might need to run her over.

Enough sleuthing, she decided. She was scaring herself, thinking every shadow hid a villain and that malevolent, glowing eyes watched her every move.

"Have a nice weekend, Samantha!" Delia Petros called out from her parking space.

The shrill voice startled her, but Samantha recovered quickly and waved back. "You too!"

The secretary had already started her Christmas baking and the pounds were clearly visible under the wraparound coat that couldn't. "Say, did your friend ever catch up with you?"

"What friend?"

"Guy came in, last week sometime. Said something about a present for Matthew's birthday."

"Who was it? What did he look like?"

Delia's description, right down to the mole at the corner of the mouth, would have delighted a police sketch artist.

Samantha's blood went sub-zero.

"I didn't catch his name."

"When was he here?"

"'Bout a week ago, maybe more. I can't remember exactly."

"Was it the day of the shooting?"

Delia paused for a moment. "Could have been. I'm not sure. That day's all a blur."

In her Toyota, Samantha cranked the heat on high. *Who hates you that much, Mom?* She had her answer.

23

THE HUNTINGDON CLUB IN Brookline was a haven for the who's who of the area's physicians, lawyers, politicians, and executives. They mingled in lounges furnished with sumptuous damasks and velvets. Polished Italian shoes moved from Aubusson to Aubusson while dour faces stared down from gilt-framed portraits. This was Meredith Paxton's stomping grounds. Chris's mother, looking chic in an ivory wool suit, blended in well with the pastel-and-pearl crowd. A frothy designer scarf poufed from her neckline, framing her pale skin. Once they were ushered to their table in the dining room, she removed tan gloves, an exact match to her tan shoes and handbag. Samantha, in awe of the place with its quiet elegance and its quietly elegant clientele, slid her unpolished black pumps farther beneath the floor-length tablecloth.

Chris, in surgery all day, would be joining them later but first intended to unwind by playing racquetball with the anesthesiologist. Samantha hoped he wouldn't be too long—she had been alone with his mother only once before, and in spite of her years of dealing with all sorts of people, she found herself tongue-tied around Meredith. There had already been an awkward moment at the coat check; she didn't know if she should hug Chris's mother, kiss her cheek, or just grasp both hands. And should she call her Meredith or Mrs. Paxton? *Mom,* she knew, was out of the question. After a clumsy shuffling and a dumbstruck stammer, Samantha was rescued from her dilemma by Meredith herself who said, "Allow Gustav to help you with your coat, Samantha."

Now she caught the woman's appraising stare from across the round table. Samantha was clad in one of her favorite outfits—solid black slacks and a double-breasted plaid jacket—yet she felt as though the words *country mouse* blazed neon from her forehead. For a brief moment, she wondered what Georgina MacPherson would have worn to dinner at the private club, then dismissed the thought. *Chris is marrying me,* she told herself firmly. *The sooner Meredith realizes that, the better off we'll all be.*

A tuxedoed sommelier uncorked a bottle of Montrachet at their table. The pale gold burgundy went down a little too smoothly, and Samantha forced herself to sip slowly. Getting pie-eyed would not improve her standing with Chris's mother.

"How are things at school, Samantha? That dreadful ordeal with that poor boy . . ."

The mere mention of Derek brought another flood of emotion to her cheeks. "It's been difficult. For everyone. Police have been in and out, questioning the kids. They've sent in a team of psychologists, too. And Derek's father is hanging around, badgering the principal, wanting to see the cafeteria where his son died. He's always been what we call a problem parent, constantly badmouthing teachers, causing a commotion at sports events. I don't know what this tragedy will do to him."

"Desperate people can be driven to desperate acts, Samantha."

"That's what I'm afraid of. But please, enough of this for now. Thank you again for having my clothes cleaned. It was one less thing for me to worry about."

Meredith waved away the gratitude. "Not at all. And Matthew? He's doing well?"

"Yes. His marks are good. He's enjoying high school." She avoided Meredith's gaze, fearful that her face would betray her obvious concealment of the larger issues plaguing her.

"How nice. It seems that everything I read lately describes how rebellious teenagers can be, especially boys. I was lucky with Christopher, of course. Never a moment's worry. But these days, with all one hears about gangs and the trouble they get into, the stealing, the drugs, it's almost a miracle to raise a well-adjusted child with decent values."

"It's a challenge, yes, but so far, so good," Samantha replied.

"Especially given your situation, raising a son alone. Does Matthew's father help out? Financially, I mean?"

Samantha reached for her wine. "Matthew's father is dead, Meredith." She took a long drink, then reluctantly set the glass down. "I assumed Chris had told you."

"Oh, dear! I'm so terribly sorry!" Meredith toyed with her serviette and straightened the cutlery. In spite of her fluster, her cheeks remained pale as porcelain. "No, I don't believe he mentioned it. How long ago?"

Samantha gave Meredith an encapsulated version of her relationship with Scott and the years of struggle afterward. Chris's mother listened with rapt attention, offering all the correct platitudes, condolences, and woeful sighs. Through it all, Samantha sensed that Meredith did indeed know Samantha was widowed and not divorced. Why, then, did she pretend otherwise?

Meredith said, "We must turn this conversation to more pleasant matters. I'm assuming you and Christopher will want a long engagement. Your wedding will take quite a bit of careful planning, and these things must be done properly."

"Actually, I think Chris prefers a small, simple affair. Around fifty or so guests, and we had talked about marrying during spring break."

"*This* spring? Oh, my!" The exclamations were huffed on rapid bursts of breath. It was some moments before Meredith was composed enough to add, "We must get busy, then. But do think about the guest list. We know so many people, and we don't want to disappoint anyone."

Samantha knew Chris would be adamant about the wedding, and both were keen on marrying not in Boston but on a beach in Virgin Gorda. Still, now didn't seem to be the time to make an issue of it, especially with Chris not there.

As if hearing his cue, Chris strode into the dining room, the maitre d' motioning him toward their table.

"Christopher, my darling!" Meredith's arms were outstretched, her cheek upturned.

Chris gathered Samantha into his arms for a warm hug before kissing his mother on the proffered cheek. To Samantha, the disapproval on Meredith's face was obvious. "How are the two best-looking women in the room?" Chris asked, taking his seat.

"We're just fine, Christopher, dear," Meredith said hurriedly. "But you—you look so tired. That job of yours will be the death of you. I'm so afraid you'll catch some terrible germ from one of those people you operate on. Just look at him, Samantha. Is this the man you want to see at the end of the day? When he does come home, that is. You must already know the hours he puts in."

One look at Chris's haggard face told Samantha he was in no mood for one of his mother's crusades to get him to leave his practice.

"How did the surgery go, Chris?" Her interruption of Meredith's latest campaign elicited another look of disapproval that the woman quickly hid behind a sip of wine.

"The tumor was malignant. I think we got it all. My patient's jaw is clamped shut now. She'll be wearing the dental equivalent of a football helmet for a while. There's no jawbone to splint. Only thirty years old, too. She—" Chris took hold of Samantha's hand. "Enough shop talk. Looks like it's been a rough couple of weeks for a lot of us. How are you holding up?"

"Better," she said. "Especially now that you're here."

"Let's order dinner, shall we?" Meredith said.

Chris's mother sent back her breast of duck, proclaiming it too dry. Her second choice, a Dover sole à la meunière, wasn't fresh. She made do with a generous garden salad and profuse apologies from the chef.

Samantha expected more wedding talk from Meredith, and predicted the woman would apply firm, steady pressure until Chris caved in to her idea of the perfect society wedding, but the subject never arose. Instead, Meredith focused again on Matthew, peer pressure, and a newspaper article she had just read on the problems facing youths being raised by one parent.

"Matthew's a super kid, Mom," Chris said. "Samantha's done a great job."

Meredith turned her attention to the dessert menu.

Samantha was partway through her chocolate mousse when Chris again took hold of her hand. "Samantha, honey . . ." Samantha and Meredith looked up at the same time as a gray shadow marred the white linen tablecloth.

Frank Ventresca, reeking of too many beers and the foul mingling of motor oil and sweat, loomed over Samantha, the doorman in charge of security rushing up behind him. "Sammy, we gotta talk." His voice oozed in Samantha's ear.

Her mouth went Sahara dry. "Go away," she said feebly.

"Sir, you must come with me," the doorman said in a hushed, firm voice. "This is a private club."

Instead Frank stepped closer. "Come outside a minute, Sam. It's real important."

"She's not going anywhere with you," Chris said.

Frank ignored him. "Look, I don't want no trouble, Sammy."

"Then leave."

Meredith snapped her fingers at the doorman. "Robert, call the police." The maitre d' turned toward the table. The other diners were staring.

"The kid," Frank said, hurrying to get all the words out. "Matthew. Born in December. He's mine, isn't he."

"No," Samantha said, but the weakness of her answer betrayed her.

"Never mind. I don't need to hear it from you. It was his smile. I knew it right away."

The maitre d' approached the table, but the doorman motioned him toward the telephone in the entry. "911," he said.

"Please, Robert," Meredith said, "do escort this man out. He doesn't belong here and he's quite obviously been drinking."

"My apologies," the doorman said. His starched collar appeared to wilt with his shame. "The gentleman rushed by me, said he had the lady's keys and important information about her car."

The doorman cupped Frank's elbow, but Frank jerked away. "I know where the door is," he sneered. "Keep your pants on." He looked at Samantha again. "Kids get into a lot of trouble nowadays. A boy needs a father. His *real* father." It was then that Frank faced Chris, directing a look so filled with contempt, Samantha felt a shudder reverberate through her.

Chris glared back. Then Frank was gone. In half sentences, Samantha searched for appropriate words, an explanation, an apology, but found none. Chris withdrew his hand. His expression was unreadable, but Meredith seemed to know what he was thinking. She cast a sympathetic glance at her son, allowed a little sigh to escape, then gently took his hand.

Samantha's hands remained in her lap.

24

HE DIDN'T MEAN TO BLAB it all out, especially not in front of the wimp, the rich dame, and that room full of people all staring at him like he was a steaming pile of dogshit. But when she wouldn't even talk to him, when she told him to go away, now that wasn't right. The whole thing about the kid just flew out.

The news hit like a stink bomb, and it had shut everybody up, too. Maybe that wasn't such a bad thing after all. The fancy folks might already be thinking twice about *associating* with Sam, and without the wimp dentist and all that money in her corner, she might just realize she wasn't so high and mighty. Then things could be like they used to be.

He figured he'd have almost an hour by the time the tab was paid and they dropped off the old gal wherever she lived, so in Somerville, he parked his car, slouched behind the wheel, and watched the house. The kid and the stick lady were downstairs. He could see the TV screen flickering blue and white. He dug at the grime under his fingernails, used a spit-soaked thumb to rub away the dirt that settled in the creases on his palms. He was getting antsy. A long swallow of whiskey took the edge off, but not much.

A bright red pizza delivery car pulled up in front of the stick lady's chain-link fence. It parked illegally, its headlights shining on Frank's car. He screwed the top back on the thermos and beelined toward the delivery boy.

"Here, buddy, I'll save you the trouble," he said, fumbling in his jeans for his wallet. "How much do I owe you?"

The kid, a real chub cub with a blizzard of forehead zits, looked confused. He hung on to the grease-soaked box. "Say, how do I know you're not gonna run off with this? I saw you get out of that car over there." He nodded in the direction of the Trans Am. "I don't know this is your place."

"You're pretty sharp, kid," Frank said. "I hope my son Matthew's as careful as you are."

The kid looked at the name on the delivery slip. "Matthew?"

"Quinlan. May as well treat my family to a pizza since I'm so late getting home."

The boy relaxed and smiled. "That'll be seventeen dollars." He held out his hand.

Seventeen dollars. Shit. He hoped he had that much. Things had sure gone up in price. Where was this pizza from, France?

He pulled a twenty out of his wallet. His last bill. Lucky tomorrow was payday. He waited for his change, but the kid kept shooting him funny looks, taking forever to fish around before reluctantly coughing up the three bucks.

Jerk. Frank grabbed the pizza, pushed open the gate, walked up the narrow concrete sidewalk, and knocked on the door.

When the door opened, Matthew stared for a moment, then Frank saw his expression change.

"Hey, it's the man from Mars!" he cried out. "You're the guy from the arcade."

From another room, Frank could hear the old lady holler, "What did you say, Matthew?"

"Is this what you do for a living?" the kid asked, ignoring the old lady's question.

"Part time," Frank answered.

Matthew took the pizza and set it on a nearby table.

"How are things going, kid? You were pretty down in the dumps last time I saw you."

"Okay, I guess. Better."

The old lady hollered again. "Matthew, I thought you were starving! What's taking you so long?" There was a clatter of cutlery, then a kitchen drawer slammed shut. Frank wanted to wring her skinny neck.

"Coming, Mrs. Bea!" Matthew hollered back.

"Play much pinball lately?" Frank asked, but the kid was more interested in pizza than talking. He read the amount on the delivery slip and held out the money, plus an extra dollar. "Thanks. 'Night."

The door shut in Frank's face.

He must have stared at the faded green paint for a full minute before gathering his wits enough to move his feet. He'd been fluffed off again, and he was getting damn sick of it. He took a quick peek in the living-room window, and seeing the kid and the old lady hunched over the coffee table eating pizza and watching TV, he ducked under the window and made his way to the back of the house.

25

STING WAS SINGING the acoustic version of "Roxanne," and Matthew was doing a reasonable accompaniment in his bedroom. When Samantha knocked and peeked in, her son was drumming on the desktop with a pair of rulers. Impulsively, she rushed over and hugged him.

"Too much wine with supper, huh, Mom?"

"Not nearly enough, I'm afraid. Chris's mother is something else." She went to his bed, sat down on the striped comforter, and patted the space beside her. Matthew turned off his music and trampolined onto the mattress.

She told him briefly about the evening, highlighting superficial details—the luxurious interior of the club, the delicious food—but omitting the crucial episode with Frank storming the tuxedoed barricade, intent on his search-and-destroy mission.

"Matthew, would you agree that we're quite a team?"

Her son paused briefly, then said, "Not too good in the sleuthing department. Any leads on the black pill caper, Samantha Spade?"

"None. But in the mother-and-son department, how do you think we rate?"

"That's a funny question." He examined his bulletin board, where Heidi Klum was now keeping Gisele Bündchen company. Getting no answer from either model, he said, "Well, no offense, Mom, but you don't throw a baseball very well, and neither of us can fix a leaky pipe or a loose railing like Mr. L., but I guess we're stuck with each other."

"I'm serious, Matthew. In spite of the rough patches, are we okay?"

"I'd say we're a pretty good partnership. Hey, this isn't about Chris, is it? You're not having second thoughts, are you? 'Cause I really like him."

No, I'm not having second thoughts, but Chris might be. After tonight, she would be lucky if Chris ever spoke to her again. All along, he had believed Scott was Matthew's father. Now they had this monstrous deception between them, not the strongest foundation on which to build a marriage. Chris had been prepared to take on Matthew, but why should she suppose for one miserable moment that he would take on Frank? How much of her baggage was he expected to carry?

"Mom, you and Chris—did you have a fight?"

"Not really. More of a misunderstanding. Let's just let things take their course." After the look she had seen on Meredith Paxton's face, Samantha knew exactly where the woman would steer Chris. Georgina MacPherson never looked so good.

"Well, at least we've got each other, right?" Matthew said a little wistfully. "Some people seem so lonely. Like the man from Mars."

"Who?"

"The guy who delivered the pizza earlier tonight. He really needs somebody to talk to."

Samantha was aware Matthew had inherited her empathy for the underdog. Still, she didn't want him reaching out to total strangers, even though he reminded her almost daily that he was nearly fifteen and could take care of himself. If anyone could write a book on how projecting an air of sympathy could make a person vulnerable to predators, Samantha could. She tried to keep the rising concern out of her voice. "How would a pizza guy strike you as lonely? He hands you food, you give him money. Where in that brief transaction is there an opportunity for you to size somebody up like that?"

"Relax, Mom," Matthew said. "I've seen the guy before. He talked to me once at the arcade. Must have a tough life. He's holding down two jobs."

"How do you know that? Did he tell you?"

"Nah. But there he was, delivering pizza and wearing a jacket from Lou's Service Center."

A cold finger of fear traced the back of her neck. Frank had been wearing a red jacket with a yellow insignia when he crashed their dinner. She fought for calm, though she already felt the flush in her cheeks. "What did this man from Mars look like?"

"Why?"

She recovered quickly. "Matt Hammer, what kind of sleuth are you if you can't give a decent description? Detectives are supposed to be observant."

He seemed convinced. "Dark, straight hair, mole at one side of his mouth." He stopped and thought. "I don't remember which side. Red nylon jacket, yellow lettering. Stood about five eight. Wearing jeans, black sneakers. Oh yeah, I almost forgot—he drove a black Trans Am. Older model, but still a nice enough car for someone down on his luck, now that I think of it. Well? How did I do?"

A black Trans Am. Of course. Frank, caught in a fifteen-year time warp, would have stored his prize possession. "You pass the official detective test with flying colors." She tried her best to sound carefree, but she heard her voice quake. Quickly she rose to her feet and ruffled her son's hair. "What do you think? Time for all gumshoes to turn in?" At the door, Samantha turned around. "Matthew, I don't think you should talk to this man anymore. You just never know. There are all kinds of crazies out there. And plenty of them prowl the arcades, schools, any place where they know kids hang out."

"This guy didn't seem like a pervert, Mom. More like a pathetic loser. Not dangerous."

If you only knew, she thought. "Showing up twice in your life? What are the odds?"

"I guess you're right. I'll be careful. But, Mom, stop worrying about me, would ya?"

"I know, I know. You're almost fifteen. Night."

She gave her son a rubbery smile and closed the door softly behind her. As she went for the phone, her legs trembled and she had to sit down. She shivered at the thought of that man near her son and was determined it wouldn't happen again. The partnership of Quinlan and Son would continue its business without any interference from Frank Ventresca, and Matthew's face would not be seen on the side of a milk carton or on an episode of *Missing Treasures*. She dialed the phone.

It wasn't until she was preparing for bed that she got the jolt that would keep her awake for much of the night. In the drawer of the end table Samantha rooted for a pen and her notepad to add to the growing list of catastrophes that had befallen her of late. Tucked into the corner of the drawer, where she always kept it, was the brass heart-shaped frame that held a picture of her and Scott. For years, the photo had rested on top of the television where she couldn't miss staring at it. Then it moved to the end table, where it stood beneath the lamp, the two of them encircled by a halo of light. Eventually, Samantha felt ready to shed the grieving-widow routine, and the picture went into the drawer.

It was a silly picture, one a friend had taken of the two of them in front of a grand Georgian home in Beacon Hill, as though one day they might own it. Samantha hadn't felt the need to look at it for some time, but now she turned over the frame and held the picture up to the light. A ripple of fear skimmed her spine.

In the photo, she was smiling, her hair blown away from her face as she said "cheese" on cue for the friend whose name she could no longer remember. And Scott was smiling, too, having just promised her the home behind them, or one like it. At least, he should have been smiling. Someone had removed Scott from the picture.

26

Frank snapped the tab on his last can of beer and paced the tiles from the kitchen to the pull-out couch. He didn't know why he'd done it, going up to the door like that; he only knew that waiting around was making him crazy. He was an action guy and he wanted to make things happen. He couldn't blame the kid for not talking to him, not really, especially when he didn't know who Frank was.

The kid was almost fifteen. He deserved to know the truth. Once it came out, once the shock of it was over, Matthew just might cozy up to the idea. And with a little more experience, Frank would get better at this fatherhood thing. He could take the kid places, show him things, maybe teach him how to take apart an engine. They could have good times together, not like when he was growing up.

Frank plunked down on a folding chair and fought the memory, but it came anyway.

"Daddy, it's almost time for my soccer game. Come on."

"Not tonight, Franco. I'm too tired. Get me a beer on your

way out." His father was reading the newspaper, the pound puppy whimpering at his feet.

"You promised, Daddy. You haven't been to one game all summer."

"Franco, when I say I'm tired, I mean I'm tired. I don't need you nagging me like your mother. Now get me that beer."

Beer in hand, he tried one more time. "Maybe after you finish your beer, you could walk down to the park then?"

The puppy whimpered again.

"Franco, did you feed that damn dog?"

He gulped. "No, Daddy. I'll do it now."

He heard the newspaper crackle shut. The beer bottle thunked onto the coffee table. His father rose to his feet.

"When are you gonna learn some responsibility? I work hard for a living, trying to make ends meet. All I ask is for you to do one little thing. You begged me for a dog. I got you a dog. Is it too much to expect you to take care of it?" His father moved toward him. Frank backed away. "I guess I'm gonna have to teach you a lesson."

He backed up as far as he could, until he was cornered in the nook under the stairs where he always cowered, waiting for the first blow.

Instead, his father held out his hand. "Come on."

Cautiously, the boy took his hand and emerged from his hiding place. His father grabbed the keys to his Pontiac, then picked up the puppy. Frank smiled. His father was taking him to the game after all and bringing Happy along, too.

When they passed the park, Frank saw his teammates doing their warm-up drills on the field. His father kept driving. "Where are we going, Daddy?"

His father didn't answer, not even when they were way out of town, but he knew they weren't lost. If they were, his father would have been swearing by now. Instead he was calm, even though his mouth made a straight line across his face. Frank sat quietly in the passenger seat, petting Happy, who had curled up in his lap.

Eventually, the car slowed down. Happy sat up, front paws on the dash, and wagged his tail. They were on some kind of forest reserve. Frank had sounded out the word "reservation" on the sign when they'd turned in. The trees were huge, mostly maples and oaks, he decided, remembering his second-grade leaf project. Happy barked.

"Give me the dog, Franco. It's gotta pee." Frank handed the dog to his father. He watched his father carry Happy over to the trunk of a gigantic tree. The puppy lifted its leg.

Frank was confused. He couldn't figure out why his father hadn't hit him yet. He seemed mad enough. Why was he taking him for a ride?

His father was playing with the puppy now, throwing twigs around for Happy to chase. He picked up a really big stick, held it up in the air over the puppy's head, then brought it down near Happy's nose. The puppy sniffed. His father raised the stick again, and again he brought it down. Happy was going crazy now, jumping up and down, enjoying the teasing game. The third time the stick went up, his father hurled it deep into the forest. Happy took off after the stick.

He watched his father run toward the car. He slammed the door shut. The Pontiac surged forward.

"Daddy! You forgot Happy! Look!" He clutched his father's shirtsleeve, then pointed at the puppy. Happy was bounding out of the trees into the roadway, the huge stick in his mouth.

His father stared straight ahead. "You thought the dog could go without being fed. Let's see if he can. And don't you dare cry, Franco."

Frank turned around in his seat. Happy had dropped the stick and was running after the car. Frank crawled into the back seat, closer to his puppy. He rolled down the rear window and cried out, "Happy!" His father pressed on the accelerator. The rear wheels kicked out dirt and gravel, leaving the puppy in a cloud of brown dust.

He held his head back to keep his tears from falling onto his face. His eyes stung, but he knew his father hated crying. His nose threatened to drip, too, but he didn't dare sniffle.

For weeks, he hurried home from school, thinking Happy might have found his way out of the reservation like Lassie did in the movie and would be waiting on the front steps, wagging his tail.

But there was no Happy, then or since.

Frank drained his beer, got up, and set the bottle on the kitchen counter with the rest of the dirty dishes. He looked around the apartment, the place he was so proud of. It was all he had. Until Matthew.

He hadn't thought about Happy in a long time, but he remembered too well what it was like to lose something. He thought about the prison guard who had made the mistake of trying to take something away from him. Sam, too, had lopped fifteen years off his life, like he was worth nothing. All that time, spent pining away for someone who didn't have a clue what real love was.

In four giant steps, he made it across the room. He took her picture from his wallet and shredded it into dozens of pieces until he couldn't recognize her. He threw the bits onto the worn-out rug and walked all over them, grinding his work boots into the carpet.

"How does it feel to be down in the dirt with the rest of us?" His voice echoed in the apartment.

A long chapter of his life was over, but somehow, he wasn't sad. He would have Matthew. No one was going to take his kid away.

No matter how rich the competition. He thought of the wimp dentist and felt his blood boil. That guy was going to be out of Frank's family picture.

27

TWO DAYS HAD PASSED since the fiasco at the club and Chris hadn't heard from Samantha. Though he missed her terribly and hoped she was okay, he stubbornly refused to pick up the phone and call her.

She owed him an explanation, dammit. That guy in the restaurant—was he really Matthew's father? If so, why hadn't she confided in him?

It was insulting, and he was hurt, so he dug his heels in yet again and stayed away from the telephone. He needed a break. To clear his head. To assess their relationship. And what kind of relationship was it if Samantha couldn't tell him the truth? Yet when his phone rang, he dove at it. Instead of Samantha's voice at the other end, he heard his mother's. A friend had suddenly canceled, and could Christopher accompany her to the ballet this evening? It was *Swan Lake,* one of his favorites, and the principal dancer, a brilliant fifteen-year-old prodigy from Croatia, was making her debut.

"Sorry, Mother, but I'm just not up to it."

"Do you the world of good, dear. A little diversion. You simply can't sit at home brooding over that girl and her problems."

At length Chris relented. Perhaps the distraction would do him some good at that. If nothing else, he could lose himself in his mother's gossip about who was doing what to whom in Boston.

"Your ticket will be waiting at the box office. And Christopher, dear, do wear your dark suit with that striped tie. You look so handsome in it."

The Wang Center for the Performing Arts, on Tremont, served as the hub of Boston's ballet season, and hordes of people were cramming themselves in for the evening performance. Inside the front entry, mink and satin mixed with denim and cotton. Chris scouted the densely packed space for some glimpse of his mother, who would certainly raise a critical eyebrow at the eclectically dressed crowd. Seeing no sign of her and assuming she was already seated, he stepped up to the ticket window, gave his name to the attendant, and moments later found himself ushered to Row F in the orchestra section. To please his mother, he'd worn his dark suit; the '40s-inspired tie, he wore to please himself.

Wafts of heady perfume, liberally applied, assailed his nostrils as he sidled in front of four bejeweled women to his place. After ensuring he had stepped on no one's feet, he looked up to discover that his mother did not occupy the adjacent seat.

"Georgie, what are you doing here?"

Georgina smiled up at him, a perfect, expensive smile. "Hello, Chris." She tilted a cheek toward him. His tight lips landed coolly on her smooth skin. "I hope you don't mind. Your mother called me about an hour ago, said she had a splitting headache and wondered if I might be able to use her ticket."

Chris sat down and stared at Georgie, impeccably coiffed and gowned in soft pink silk. Her makeup was flawless, her manicure perfect. His mother had not called an hour ago. Georgie had been getting ready all day.

A little diversion. Engineer Paxton had done it again.

Chris, with all his accursed manners, resisted the urge to run pell-mell from the theater. Instead he sat straitjacket still, inclined stiffly toward the perfumed woman on his right, and made small talk about his job, city traffic, and the Boston Bruins until the curtain went up.

Rich Tchaikovsky music filled the hall. As the house lights dimmed, Georgina leaned toward Chris, who was now feeling suffocated on both flanks. Once more he forced himself to remain seated and tried to endure a nagging cramp in his side, trapped in an impossible situation with a woman who shot Novocain through his veins. He knew then that as soon as the dancers took their final bows, he would bolt out of this place and head straight to Samantha.

He had been a fool, a heartless, unfeeling bastard. Samantha was terrified of that character in the restaurant. She hadn't confided in Chris because she was afraid he would judge her, which, of course, he had. He had provided her no comfortable environment in which she could express her feelings and open up about what was tormenting her. He had further slammed the door on any potential communication by acting like a miffed schoolboy. He hoped some of his mother's pomposity wasn't beginning to rub off on him.

With each crescendo, his desire to be with Samantha intensified. He ached with missing her and found himself blotting out the dancers onstage, their lithe, graceful forms replaced by a full-blown image of Samantha, her long, wavy hair, that endearing dusting of freckles, her emerald eyes.

Georgie slipped her hand into his, jarring his reverie. On stage the prince, torn between honoring his word and his love for Odette, was leaping into the lake. Georgie allowed a well-timed sob to escape. "It's just so moving. So sad." She continued to whimper as the swans embraced their beloved Odette, distraught at the tragic fate of her true love.

The temptation to hustle Georgina into a cab after the performance was overwhelming, but Chris knew that once again, good manners would prevail. As they exited the building, Georgie draped a diaphanous pink stole over her bare shoulders. When they hit the street the evening air was fresh and crisp. Georgie seized the moment, her body suddenly clinging to Chris's like plastic wrap.

From somewhere in the crush of people, a camera flashed.

28

Samantha lay in her bathtub, her body surrounded by hillocks of raspberry-scented bubbles. She had lit nearly a dozen fat candles and poured herself a glass of chilled Riesling, but though this formula for surefire relaxation might work for soap opera divas and stars of bubble bath commercials, it was having little effect on her. A nagging band of tension still pulled between her shoulder blades, and the steady throb of a dull headache pulsed behind her eyes.

At school during the week, she had found herself looking for Derek Townsend, so many times expecting his hesitant knock on her office door, to see his crooked grin and the hunched-over way he walked when entering a room. At times, during scarce quiet moments, she heard his deep, slurred "Hi, Mrs. Q.," and she would look up, only to face a vacant doorway and to feel her heart sink still lower.

Hank Ehrhart hadn't yet put his grudge to rest about volleyball star Bryan Grantham. He continued to save his best snarls and grimaces for whenever he crossed Samantha's path, which she tried to ensure didn't happen too often. It didn't help that Jim Petrella had been kicked out of his house and was staying at the Hallorans' until he could get himself together enough to look for a place. There were some who said they'd seen the shop teacher around the school once or twice, trying to stay out of sight while some of the boys from the auto mechanics class winterized his old Alfa Romeo.

Samantha still didn't know what to make of the black pills. Matthew was behaving normally, eating well, studying hard, but two things about her son bothered her. He hadn't yet told her anything about his interest in Kelly Frid. Even more disturbing was the photo with Scott virtually beheaded. Matthew denied knowing anything about it, but he had to have torn it. Who else could have done it? The more she tried to encourage him to talk out his feelings—was he upset about her engagement to Chris? Or that he'd never known his father?—the more vehemently he claimed ignorance about the photograph.

At least there had been no further contact with Frank. Matthew hadn't reported seeing him—could she count on her son to be honest about that?—and now that Samantha had followed Chris's advice and gotten an unlisted number, there had been no phone calls either.

And none from Chris. In her mind's eye, Samantha could still envision Chris's expressionless stare, Meredith's disdain, Frank's sneer. So many pieces of her life were eroding like friable asbestos, leaving her exposed, unprotected.

She picked up a loofah and tried to scrub away her stress, succeeding only in chafing her already dry skin. She finished her wine, drained the water from the tub, and stepped onto the fuzzy yellow duck-shaped bathmat, a Christmas gift from a much younger Matthew that she still couldn't bring herself to get rid of. As soon as she toweled dry, she would pour herself some more wine, scan the TV channels for a goofy late-night comedy, and hope she fell asleep before she realized how truly miserable she was.

She wrapped herself in a worn Viyella robe, cleared the condensation from the mirror with her palm, and untangled her hair with a wide-toothed comb. As the last of the bath water gurgled down the drain, she heard a faint thump. Matthew, in his restless sleep, must have knocked something onto the floor.

Moments later, the noise came again, and as she moved into the living room, she realized someone was knocking on her back door. She looked at her alarm clock on the end table. It was nearly midnight. She froze, half-expecting Frank with another bouquet of hideous purple flowers. Or worse. She glanced at Matthew's door and saw it was firmly shut. She yanked her bathrobe securely around her and peeked into the kitchen.

Through the slightly parted curtain on the back door's window, she saw Chris, his hands cupped around his eyes, peering in at her. Her heart returned to its normal place. For a mad second she fluffed her hair and smoothed her robe, then, deciding the whole thing was hopeless, she went to the door and opened it.

In a rush he came toward her, arms outstretched. "I've been such a shit," he murmured against her damp hair.

She folded against him. "I should have told you. No more secrets. I promise."

Kisses and apologies were traded back and forth until Samantha and Chris drifted to the sofa and sat close together. Her words spilled out calmly, easily. "Frank raped me. Fifteen years ago. I pressed charges, put him in jail. Now he's out, and he's made contact with Matthew—"

Chris's face went ashen. "Rape? Samantha, my God."

For the first time, she told the story on her own, without being probed for details, without someone seated across from her putting pen to paper. Without feeling she was on trial. Chris sat quietly, nodding imperceptibly from time to time, his expression traveling a range of emotions—confusion, humiliation, fear—the same emotions she'd felt on that night and so many times since. Chris was reliving the attack with her, feeling her pain.

He waited until she had finished, and again Samantha saw his expression change. His jaw tightened, his mouth turned downward at the corners, his eyes glinted with anger. "That bastard," he said.

She loved him for that. She had wanted to see this kind of rage from Scott, had wanted to have someone hate Frank as much as she did, but the reaction never came. Scott had bandaged everything, thinking a honeymoon and a new life would be the tonic to erase what had happened. And when their first few nights together hadn't measured up to his fantasies, he took to the skies, looking for his thrills far away from her. Odd how she'd forgotten Scott's eagerness to brush Frank, her needs, and the rape under the carpet. For the first time, she wondered if their marriage would have survived the ghost of Frank.

"I didn't want the rape to make a difference, to have it affect how you treat me. And I was afraid of losing you. It's not uncommon."

"I'm not going anywhere," he said, his tone earnest.

"I won't hold you to that. Frank will never leave, you know. He can move away, go back to jail, but a rapist is always with you."

"Ventresca's been in jail all this time?" Chris asked.

"Yes. He beat me, too. He smashed my face black and blue. That's how I got this." She pointed to the bump on her nose. "He broke it."

"Jesus."

In spite of everything, she smiled. "I guess now you see why my thaw took so long."

"Trusting takes time, especially after abuse like that."

"But not fifteen years, right? Frank is an old story, but some others along the way haven't exactly played nice either. I was pretty soured about men and sex until one particularly attractive oral surgeon showed up." She drew her knees to her chest and wriggled her bare toes under his warm thighs.

Chris wrapped his arms around her knees and rested his head on top of them. "And that son of a bitch is Matthew's father?"

Samantha shrugged. "I've always thought of Scott as Matthew's father. Mom, Dad, and I knew when my baby was born early that it was possible that Frank was his father, but we never spoke about it. Ever. Scott's name is on Matthew's birth certificate and that's good enough for me." Chris's frown ripped through her. She fingered the engagement ring, twisted it nervously on her finger. "I should have told you, Chris. I'm sorry. If this is all too much for you, I'll understand—"

He put a finger to her lips. "It's heady news, yes. But not for the reasons you're thinking. For what's happened to you, Samantha, I could kill the bastard with my own hands. And for leaving you alone these past few days, with all you've gone through, I'll be a while forgiving myself. But if you think any of this changes how I feel about you, well, you're just nuts, that's all." He tapped her nose with his finger and then he smiled, a wonderful smile, and Samantha felt some of the burden she'd been carrying wash away. Things would be all right. They were made of good stuff, she, Chris, and Matthew. Whatever cards were dealt to them, they could handle.

"Just let that Ventresca try and come between us," Chris continued, taking her hands in his. "I'll pull all his teeth out. One at a time. No anesthetic."

"Now I know why I love you so much."

"My sadistic nature?"

"Something like that."

Their kiss was long, tender, and Samantha felt a swell of warmth. With the briefest addition of pressure, another moan of pleasure, their tenderness could have easily become passion, but neither yielded to physical abandonment. They were content to feel comfortable, sensual, happy. When Samantha drew away, she said, "Chris, where were you coming from, all dressed up, so late at night?"

"Brace yourself for this one," he murmured close to her mouth. "Besides Frank Ventresca, there's someone else who won't be interfering in our lives anymore."

29

BY MONDAY MORNING, the raw edges of grief had scabbed over, and the school was beginning to thrum with the steady pulse of normal activity. From her office, Samantha could hear lockers slamming and girls laughing loudly to capture the attention of nearby males. The males belched to impress each other.

She had witnessed similar adolescent behavior in the staff lounge moments earlier, when Ehrhart had come into the room with one of the substitute teachers, bellowing the punch line to a particularly lewd joke she'd heard him tell half a dozen times. New face, new audience. These days, Ehrhart was never without a quart bottle of distilled water, and he frequently made grand deliberate gestures of hiking up his trackpants and retying the drawstring.

"Losing weight, Hank?" Rupert Stanfield asked.

"Ten pounds," he announced proudly, thus beginning a monologue on the hazards of too much coffee consumption and the benefits of five small meals a day.

Samantha, in line for coffee, rolled her eyes. On any given week, at least one person at school was on some diet or another, and now Ehrhart was the latest enlightened fanatic to espouse his healthy regimen. Three or four months hence, Samantha knew, Ehrhart would be back shopping in the portly section of his favorite men's store, disillusioned and packing on more pounds than he'd started with.

The everyday banter, both in the staff room and in the halls, was a sure sign that people were moving forward, putting the tragedy of Derek's death behind them. Samantha knew this was positive and healthy, but it depressed her too. She wondered how often others thought about Derek, whether they stopped, as she did, in the middle of some mundane activity because a memory suddenly surfaced. At times she was able to conjure up a vivid image of Derek, but then bits of him—his brown eyes, his unruly hair—would disappear into shadow. She wished she had a decent picture of him, not just the yearbook photo, with Derek's face partially eclipsed by the frizzy hairdo of the girl standing beside him.

Yvonne Colford jarred her from her thoughts. "Sorry to hear about what happened, Samantha. Let me know if there's anything I can do."

Before Samantha had a chance to ask the English teacher what she was talking about, Yvonne had disappeared down the hallway.

Samantha had a good session with Pete Sinclair. With her help, the boy had found a part-time job, enabling him to be out of the house and away from his father two evenings a week. The other nights were spent studying and completing homework at a friend's house, where the peaceful atmosphere allowed him to concentrate. Pete's grades were improving, but in spite of the sunny outlook, Samantha kept Pete in her office for an additional fifteen minutes to make sure the picture was as rosy as she saw it. There would be no more Derek Townsends.

When Tom came by to check on their lunch plans, his face was somber. "How are you managing?" he asked.

"Fine. Why?"

"Just must be tough, that's all. Say the word if there's anything I can do."

"I give up. What are you talking about?"

"Hey, it's me, remember? You don't have to pretend you're not hurting."

"Tom, for God's sake, fill me in, would you? I've been getting strange looks all morning."

"Oh, no. Don't tell me you haven't seen— Ah, me and my big mouth. Well, now what am I supposed to do?"

"Tell me what the devil is going on."

Tom closed the door. With some reluctance, he set a *Boston Globe* on Samantha's desk. "Page ten."

It was a picture of Chris, and on his arm was an ethereal blonde, the epitome of the expression "you can't be too rich or too thin." The caption below the photo read: "Heir to Paxton Fortune Squires Georgina MacPherson." The brief article mentioned a few of Boston's elite who had also attended Saturday's performance of *Swan Lake* at the Wang Center, with a paragraph devoted to Chris and Georgie's longtime friendship.

Samantha refolded the paper and handed it back to Tom. "Is that all?"

"What?"

"Oh, Tom, you're so sweet to worry about me, but that picture means nothing. Turns out Chris's mother engineered one of her little fix-ups. In fact, it wouldn't surprise me if she had something to do with getting that photograph in the paper. But there's nothing to it, and after Chris gets through with blasting his mother— Well, let's just say I wouldn't want to be Meredith Paxton this morning."

"So the engagement's still on? Everything's okay?"

"It better be. Chris is taking me to the Cape this weekend. We really need to get away."

Tom plopped down into a chair. "Whew," he said. "You've been through so much lately, I wasn't sure you could handle your relationship with Chris going sour. Well, I'm glad everything's okay. You want Matthew to stay at my place?"

"You're off the hook—he's going to Jeff's. But thanks anyway. You'll be able to work your way through your blue book again."

"Good. I've just finished with the M section." He shot her a boyish grin.

"So it's Nancy or Noreen's lucky weekend?"

"Nicki, actually. Dots her *i*'s with hearts, but she's still a great girl. Say, maybe I could stop by your place during the day and fix that leak under your kitchen sink. Save Beatrice a few bucks, and you and that brat kid of yours won't be in my hair."

"Tom, you do so much for us already—"

"You know I love to putter."

"If you don't mind, then who am I to stop you from exploring your inner handyman? I'll let Beatrice know you'll be by and she'll give you a key."

"I know the drill."

"You really are quite a guy, Lundstrom." Samantha smiled and reached across the desk to pat his hand.

There was a knock on her office door and Bert Halloran burst in. His gaze fell immediately on Samantha's hand resting atop Tom's. The principal cleared his throat, scowled, then seemed to have forgotten what it was that he needed to see her about. With another gargle of phlegm and a few muttered stammers, Halloran made a hasty exit.

"What the hell was that?" Samantha asked.

"That jackass. Saw me come in here. Probably waited outside for a few minutes then came in here hoping to catch us humping like mad up against your filing cabinet."

That elicited a spasm of laughter from Samantha. Tom grew

serious once more. "This mother of Chris's, she really is a dragon lady, isn't she. Why would she set Chris up with that skinny blonde when she knows he's engaged to you?"

"Wishful thinking, I guess. Trust me, it won't happen again."

"Watch out for her, Samantha," Tom warned, his frown deepening. "That's a pretty cold, calculating thing to do. That type could be dangerous."

30

BY THE TIME THURSDAY rolled around, Samantha was willing to walk, crawl, or pogo-stick her way to Cape Cod, whatever it took. She couldn't remember ever needing a weekend away more. After four days of nearly nonstop rain, her spirits were becoming waterlogged as well. The meteorologists predicted sunnier skies ahead, and Samantha hoped better weather would lift her dark mood.

At school, Jenny was milking her connection to Derek Townsend for all it was worth. *She* had broken his heart so he concluded life wasn't worth living. *She* was very nearly killed. *She* was the one who would have to live with the memory, the anguish, the trauma. After not being cast by Tom in the musical, Jenny had still managed to find herself a starring role, and she was playing it like a true prima donna. Her overacting, however, was wearing thin after only two weeks, so to gather more sympathy from her friends, Jenny had upped the ante—she intended to join a convent, she announced one day. She would devote her energy to helping others and serving God.

Jenny's father, eyewitness to his daughter's shattered psyche and uncharacteristic ascent into goodness, decided that litigation might just be the answer, but as of noon Wednesday, Karl Rideout still hadn't determined who would be the recipient of the lawsuit—the school, Derek's parents, or Samantha herself.

This latest scrutiny proved too much for Bert Halloran, who couldn't muster the energy for even the slightest scowl. As Samantha had seen him do countless times before, Halloran was booking off sick for the remainder of the week. One of his cluster headaches, he had told his secretary.

Samantha had already slipped on her coat, so that when Thursday's final buzzer went, she bolted out the door in order to beat the bottleneck of traffic leaving the parking lot. A quick stop at the drugstore for a few essentials, then she could go home, pack for the weekend, put her feet up, and try to forget about work for a few blessed hours. On tired feet that refused to be seen in sensible teaching shoes, she headed to her car, sidestepping puddles and dead worms.

At the drug mart, she grabbed a red plastic basket and moved from aisle to aisle, stocking up on toothpaste, deodorant, razor blades, and travel-sized containers of shampoo and hand lotion. She passed by the tampons with a relieved sigh and made her way to the pharmacy at the back of the store to pick up her prescription of birth control pills. The pharmacist, a dour-looking East Indian, was slipping the small pink compact into a paper bag as she approached the counter. After paying for her purchase and exchanging complaints about the weather, Samantha turned around and slammed into a wall of a man.

"Oh, excuse me, I—"

Jim Petrella's sneer left her cold. "In a hurry, Quinlan?"

He looked like hell. It had been a few days since he'd shaved, and the stubbly beard gave him a dark, street-smart edginess that Samantha found unnerving. He hadn't showered either, and his hair looked like it had been slicked back with Valvoline.

"Well, actually, Jim, I am on my way—"

"What's wrong? No kind words for a guy down on his luck? Usually you have *plenty* to say." He shifted his weight onto one hip, assumed a cocky stance, hands on his hips to block her way.

"These are tough times for everybody, Jim. I suppose you heard about Derek Townsend . . ."

A smug huff of air issued from his nostrils. "Yeah. The Townsends have lost their kid, I've lost my job, my wife. You, though, seem to be doing all right." His deliberate stare moved to the package in her hand. "Tell me, what's it like, Quinlan, watching everyone's lives fall apart. Don't you feel just a little . . . responsible?"

She swallowed hard, tried to meet his stare but found his steely gaze too penetrating. His face was rigid with anger, locked in an expression of malevolence she'd seen once before, in his classroom, when he'd clutched the hammer in his hands. Her own nervousness caused her eyes to flicker to the dinosaur-shaped vitamins over Petrella's left shoulder, the display of condoms on his right, and back again. "None of what happened is my fault, Jim."

"Somehow, I don't see it quite that way. Your goddamn interference has cost some people plenty. How'd you like it if someone went poking around in your business?"

"Is that man bothering you, Miss?"

Samantha turned to face the pharmacist. "Yes," she answered, "actually, he is. But," she whirled back to Petrella, "I think he's finished now. Aren't you, Jim."

This time, just before she brushed by him, she fixed Petrella with an icy stare of her own.

"Yeah, Quinlan," Petrella replied. "I'm finished. For now."

She knocked over some boxes of condoms as she hurried around the corner, but she kept on going. Only when she reached the parking lot did she turn around, half expecting to see Petrella chasing after her, relieved to see that he wasn't.

As she inserted her key in the lock of her Toyota, she was gripped by a disturbing thought: Petrella lived in Boston's North End. If rumors were true and he was staying with Bert Halloran, then his temporary home was in Woburn. What, then, was he doing in a strip mall in Somerville? Had he been hanging around the school? Or had his accidental "meeting" with her been no accident?

She knew she was thinking like a crazy woman, but Petrella's presence had unnerved her. She checked the back seat, then groped in her purse for her cell phone. Reassured, and not knowing what other precautions to take, she got into her car, slammed the door, and locked it.

She yanked at her seat belt but it wouldn't budge. Lately, the thing had a habit of twisting itself inside its molded plastic housing, and no amount of biceps strength could coax it to cooperate. She had complained to the second-year auto mechanics students about it as well as the squeaky fan belt and a slow leak in one of the tires, which they promised to get to but hadn't. Samantha tugged again but the seat belt still wouldn't come free. She gave up, knowing she risked getting a ticket.

Key in the ignition, Samantha scanned for an easy-listening radio station and took a few deep breaths behind the wheel. She needed to calm down before driving home, though the distance was short and she was eager to put as much distance between herself and Petrella as possible.

A looming shadow at her car window made her jump. Reflexively, her hand hit the horn and the startled man beside her dropped a bag of groceries. He reeled, hurling a barrage of curses at her. She mumbled an apology, hoping he could read lips as well as she, then she threw the Toyota into reverse.

Matthew was ravenous as usual, polishing off not only his own dinner but also half of Samantha's. After a few attempts, Matthew stopped trying to coax her to talk about what was bothering her. He retreated to his bedroom to practice his clarinet, and Samantha hoped to lose herself in anticipation of her weekend with Chris. She descended the rear stairs and continued on to Beatrice's basement, where she kept some of her possessions in storage. The cellar, like the rest of the woman's house, was tidy and clean. Samantha tried to extend the same courtesy by keeping all of her belongings in a well-organized corner. Behind a barely used exercise bicycle and her three garment bags of summer clothes, Samantha found her gray overnight bag.

Trudging up the stairs once more, Samantha was struck by the words uttered by the officer from the Department of Correction just a few weeks ago. *Make sure you have a deadbolt lock on your door.* Which she hadn't. Too much had gone on, and at the end of each day, it was all she could do to steer herself home, decide what to make for supper, then crawl dog-tired into bed. A detour to the local hardware store was too onerous a task. Perhaps, if he didn't mind, Tom could put a new lock on the door this weekend. She would ask him tomorrow.

Samantha slid the chain across its slot and began assembling her outfits for the weekend, then the toiletries, and, finally, she thought with a tingle of pleasure, her new lingerie. She remembered the last time she had worn the black lace camisole and panties, when Chris had taken her to dinner in Cambridge. The lingerie was extravagant, she knew, but she didn't treat herself often, and besides, she rationalized, it was a treat for Chris, too. She went to the large antique pine chest that doubled as her dresser and opened the bottom drawer. The ivory faux-filigreed box from the lingerie store was where she'd put it—nestled toward the back of the drawer under some sweatsocks and cotton T-shirts.

But the box was empty.

31

Twenty more hours until the weekend. Some time between now and six o'clock tomorrow, Samantha would have to talk to Matthew, find some way to reveal the secret she had kept from him for nearly fifteen years. She continued to stall, sitting on the sofa and looking from the packed overnight bag near the television to the notepad on her lap.

Now her written meanderings had a title—Enemies I Have Known—and she had filled four pages with unfocused jottings of the strange events that had punctuated her life these past weeks. Following the discovery of the black pills, Samantha had added:

—Frank barges in at club, drunk
—Scott's picture torn; Matthew?
—Ehrhart still mad about Grantham and Petrella
—Meredith sets up date with Georgie
—Jenny Rideout's father: lawsuit?
—Jim Petrella: following me?

And finally,

—underwear missing

On paper, it all looked so silly, especially the underwear bit, but she'd looked everywhere—in all her drawers, in Beatrice's washing machine and dryer—but the lingerie had indeed disappeared. Though her landlady hadn't seen anyone skulking around, Samantha knew someone had been in her apartment. She knew who, but she didn't yet know why.

Words Frank had spoken at the country club suddenly took on a sinister meaning. *Kids get into a lot of trouble nowadays. A boy needs a father. His* real *father.* Was Frank Ventresca delusional? Or was he dangerous? And how far was he willing to go to prove how much a boy needed a father? Enough to frighten her, turn her world upside down, then rush in to save the day?

The answer didn't matter. She had to warn Matthew, to prepare him for what might lie ahead, and for that, Matthew needed the truth.

She heard Corelle plates clunking in a sink full of sudsy water. Matthew was lifting the last of his supper dishes into the drainer, his feet still shuffling to whatever tune throbbed through his headset. He'd grown so tall, all at once, it seemed. Not a boy anymore. What would this do to him?

Water gurgled down the drain, the last of it slurping into the leaky pipe below the sink where large, pendulous drops would plop into a margarine container until Tom's plumbing skills would remedy the problem. He would install a deadbolt for them, too, though now, somehow, that seemed small consolation. If Frank couldn't enter via the kitchen door, a window would do.

Matthew draped the blue J Cloth over the stainless faucet and when he turned around, she motioned to him. He set his Discman on the counter and came into the living room, where he sat cross-legged on the small rug in front of Samantha.

"Matthew, how'd you like to join Chris and me on the Cape?"

Samantha had been ready to cancel her weekend plans. She needed to tell Matthew the truth, and she needed to know he would be all right. It was Chris who had found the most reasonable solution, suggesting that Matthew join them. The getaway would do them all some good.

He laughed. "That's a good one, Mom."

"I'm serious. There's plenty to do, the—"

"Mom, what gives? Jeff and I have our weekend planned. His folks are expecting me."

"What exactly are your plans?"

"You know, stuff. Hang around, maybe catch a bus downtown, see a movie."

"Is Kelly Frid part of those plans?"

He tried for a surprised look but couldn't quite pull it off. "Uh, yeah, she might be. Don't worry, Mom. I won't make you a grandmother. You're too young."

"And so are you. Matt—"

"Geez, Mom, no offense or anything, but sometimes you take this motherhood thing one step too far."

The comment chafed, but Samantha couldn't be angry with him for challenging her. They had always talked things over, always negotiated for rules, amended whatever needed amending. She admired her son's independence, yet now she was fawning over him like a protective animal with injured, helpless young. Matthew needed an explanation.

"Let me be straight with you, Matthew. I know I've been acting just like the kind of parent I swore I'd never become—"

"This is still about the pills, isn't it."

"No. It's about the pizza man."

"Who?"

"The pizza man. The man from Mars. I think he wants more from you than you realize."

"Think he's a pervert? Or maybe a drug dealer?"

"No, Matthew, I don't."

"'Cause I saw him again today. At the doughnut shop. After school. Just kind of hanging around. He looked like he wanted to talk to me, but I was with a bunch of the kids—actually, I was with Kelly. He sat there, staring at me with a sort of sad look."

"He's dangerous, Matthew. Stay away from him. Promise me."

Matthew sat for a long time, picking at the rag rug, trying to shove loose threads back where they belonged. Eventually he said, "You know the man from Mars, don't you."

She didn't bother choosing her words carefully, she simply let them gush forth until, by midnight, Matthew knew the truth about Frank Ventresca. Samantha ached to hold her son, yet she knew it would be the wrong thing to do. When she looked at his face, she saw the same expressions she had seen a few weeks earlier, in the high-school auditorium, when she spoke about Derek's suicide. He was puzzled, shocked, searching for answers to questions that were too difficult.

"That guy raped you?" His voice squeaked. "Broke your nose? Now you're saying that someone like that could be my father?" His fingers knotted together. "But you said Dad—Scott—was the first. Those times we talked about sex."

"And he was. Scott was the first man I ever made love with. And unfashionable as it sounds, we waited until we were married. But Frank—the rape, it was about power. Violence. What took place with Fr—"

"What took place with Frank may have produced a child. Me."

"*May* have, Matthew. Biologically, it's possible. But neither you nor I are great fans of science, and I don't care what any blood test reveals, you are Scott Quinlan's son. You have his name, and you are the son of two people who loved each other."

For a moment, Matthew seemed satisfied. But a worried look came over him. "If that Frank guy tries to prove I'm his son, goes for custody, tries to become buddies, well, I don't think I can—I can't deal with it." He crumbled then, and Samantha went to him. They huddled together on the small rag rug, arms around each other.

After a while, Matthew broke away. "I wish you'd told me sooner. You always said I was a man in kindergarten."

"That's why I'd like you to come with Chris and me. Frank is a ticking bomb, and I don't know what he'll do when he gets it through his thick head that neither of us want anything to do with him. I know what he's capable of, and there's something else. I think he's been in this apartment. Some—things of mine are missing."

"The picture? Did he do that?"

"Yes. So come with us, Matthew. It'll be fun."

Matthew's response was quick. "I'm not going to the Cape, Mom. Period."

"Let's not forget who's in charge here. Haven't you heard a word I've said? Frank is dangerous."

"And you holding my hand won't make him less dangerous. I want to go to Jeff's, Mom. I need to be with people my own age. Besides, I've got a lot to think about."

At length, Samantha agreed, not just because Jeff was a nice boy and Matthew did need his space. Both Jeff's parents were police officers.

The next night, as her son was going out the door, she reminded him that Tom would be calling to see how he was doing, and that he would be around for a while on Saturday if Matthew needed anything. "Have a great weekend," she called after him, "and say hi to Kelly. She's a nice girl, Matthew. Good picking."

Yet as much as she knew she had to let him go off on his own, she hated the thought of it, knowing the team of Quinlan and Son would be separated for the weekend, with crazy Frank out there, just waiting to pounce.

32

FRANK GOT OUT OF THE shower and shook his wet hair. He thought the pulsating water would loosen him up and make him feel better, but the tightness in the back of his neck just wouldn't let go. In fact, it was getting worse.

Not enough sleep. That was the problem. When he did manage a few hours of shut-eye, his dreams were filled with the way things used to be, with the old Sam, the one who was so easy to talk to, the one who always knew just the right thing to say in that low voice of hers. Then he would snap awake, realize that she wasn't saying those things to him anymore. On those nights, he would lie awake, trapped in some purgatory between anger and frustration, unable to return to sleep because of rampaging emotions and sodden sheets that stank of stale sweat and grease. She was a stranger, a woman who looked down on him just like everybody else. It was the photograph of that stranger that he'd ripped to ratshit.

All he'd wanted to do was buy her a coffee, talk about old times, maybe make a date for the movies. Get to know her all over again. Sure, maybe she'd changed some, but so had he. Given a little time, he was sure he could win her back from the uppity boyfriend. Now he could see that maybe she'd changed too much; his patient approach wouldn't work. Besides, hadn't he waited long enough? What she really needed was to be cut down a peg.

He dried himself off with a scratchy striped towel and wrapped it around his waist. He ate a cold can of SpaghettiOs over the sink, then filled the empty can with water. From the cupboard overhead, he grabbed a bottle of aspirin and shook three into his palm. The last one lodged in his throat, its bitterness making him gag.

He looked at the clock. Nearly six. Better get a move on if he was going to keep tabs on her this weekend. Probably had a date tonight. There was a half a bottle of warm beer still on the counter, left there since two that morning, when he'd thought it might help him sleep. No sense letting it go to waste. He threw his head back, opened his throat, and downed it all at once.

Maybe this new Sam wasn't so bad after all. With that high and mighty attitude, it could be fun trying to tame her, to reel her in. Then what? Dump her? Give her a taste of her own cod liver oil? He didn't know much of anything anymore, except that old habits died hard, and he just couldn't shake free of this one. She was a part of his life, for better or worse, as they say, and to suddenly stop following her, checking up on her, well, it didn't seem right. It didn't seem *normal.*

From far away Frank heard a faint tinkling. It reminded him of wind chimes, and wind chimes reminded him of that night they spent together. Under the tree. Her fingernails raking at him, her tear-stained face whipping back and forth. He felt himself go hard. He pressed his groin against the cupboard. For a moment, there was a strange warmth, then a stabbing pain.

He looked down at his hand. The beer bottle had shattered, a spiky shard wedged into his palm. The sink was red with blood.

33

THEY DROVE PAST COUNTLESS MOTELS, mini-putts, and not-so-quaint seafood diners before jockeying for position in the traffic circle at Buzzard's Bay.

"Not the prettiest stretch of road, is it," Chris said once they were safely out of the rotary and crossing the Sagamore Bridge. "Samantha?"

"Pardon? I'm sorry, Chris."

He reached across the console for her hand. "Take it easy. Matthew's perfectly safe with the Filions."

"You're right. I know."

"And we need this weekend, agreed?"

"Right again."

Chris changed the music selection, abandoning the '70s rock station for a mellow jazz CD. As they made their way east on Route 28, Samantha forced her body to relax. She pressed her shoulders down, tilted her head from side to side, and took a few deep breaths, but though the tense muscles in her neck may have eased, her mind raced at dizzying speed, surpassing the velocity of the northeasterly wind that the weather station had accurately predicted. It shrieked around the car, roiled the water in the bay.

She was burning out, the list of occurrences in her spiral-bound notebook occupying too many of her waking hours, so much so that she had little left for Chris. Samantha had made another call to the Department of Correction; they were aware of her concerns about Frank and the possibility of his rooting around in her apartment. They encouraged her to proceed with securing a restraining order. Beyond that, there was little she could do at this point. For this weekend, the Petrellas, Ehrharts, and Ventrescas of the world could take a flying leap.

She reclined the seat a little and settled back, fully intent on conjuring up a juicy fantasy about Chris and the promise of two blissful nights together when another annoying thought intruded. She wondered if Chris's mother knew about their weekend plans and if her attitude had changed now that Chris had warned her about her interference. She wasn't sure how to broach the subject with Chris, and was surprised when he brought it up.

"You'll be relieved to know that Mother was quite contrite about her shenanigans with the ballet. She's offered to atone by throwing us an engagement party. Her place. I warned her, though. Nothing fancy. Just a few friends. Maybe the week before Christmas. How does that sound?"

"It sounds fine. I hope the scene wasn't too ugly."

"Not to worry. She'll recover. Mother's very resilient that way. One thing you have to learn—with her, you can't be subtle. Hit her with a brick, she'll get the message."

Samantha hoped she wouldn't have to resort to any brick-slinging and that Meredith Paxton would come to accept her for who she was. And for who she wasn't.

"Does she know about this weekend?"

"Uh-huh."

"And her reaction was . . . ?"

"Not too thrilled, to be honest."

Samantha sighed. "She'll never accept me, will she."

Chris shrugged, gave Samantha's hand a squeeze, and focused on the road.

Last-minute bargain-hunters were leaving the factory outlet malls, slowing traffic to a near standstill. Chris allowed a fair share of vehicles to squeeze ahead of him, but lost his patience when a beat-up van roared out of a side street, cutting off his Saab.

"Shit!" He slammed on the brakes. "You son of a bitch!"

Instinctively, Samantha reached out for the dashboard, then quickly whirled around in case they were going to be rear-ended. Behind them was a low, black sports car. She gripped Chris's thigh.

"Sorry," he said. "I didn't mean to scare you. Bastard should have his license revoked. Are you all right?"

She looked over her shoulder once again. "Chris, back there. The black car behind us. Is it a Trans Am?"

Chris glanced in his rearview mirror. "Could be," he replied. "But it's hard to tell. Damn high beams are shining right in my mirror. Why?"

"Matthew said Frank delivered the pizza in a black Trans Am. What if that's him? What if he's following us?"

"Lots of people drive black sports cars, Samantha."

"I know, but the restraining order . . . What if Frank somehow found out that I picked up an application for one and it made him furious? What if he's trying to prove that a little piece of paper can't scare him off?"

"That's a lot of what-ifs." He stroked her hand. "You're not really going to let Ventresca spoil your weekend, are you? I think you're too smart to give him that much power."

"You're right. I'm panicking for nothing. And that's just an ordinary black car back there with an ordinary person behind the wheel."

"That's the spirit. Now could you loosen your grip on my thigh? You're cutting off the circulation to some vital parts of my anatomy."

She released her fingers. They drove for a while saying nothing, a Chuck Mangione CD playing. She knew Chris thought she was being paranoid, though he had the good grace not to say so. She looked over at him tapping absentmindedly on the steering wheel. Periodically, she lowered her vanity mirror, pretending to check her lipstick. Each time, she saw the black car, close behind.

Chris wasn't fooled. "Relax, *please,*" he urged her. "You're safe with me."

His words did little to soothe her. Her mind frantically sorted out bits and pieces of what she knew about Frank. He'd gone crazy before, when she'd told him she was marrying Scott. Had he somehow learned of her engagement to Chris? As she stared transfixed at the digital readout on the dashboard clock, Samantha wondered what time had done to Frank. She could almost hear the inexorable ticking of minutes, the tread of prison-issued shoes across a stone-cold floor, as Frank counted down the days, weeks, years until he could emerge to claim what he thought was his. Fifteen years of biding his time, building up steam. When the explosion came, Samantha did not want it unleashed on Matthew. Or Chris. She had worked hard to make a life for herself. She deserved happiness, and those around her deserved safety. And she would see that they got it.

They drove through quaint Cape towns—West Yarmouth, West Dennis, Bass River—though their New England charm was lost on her. The dark vehicle still tailgated. By the time they reached Harwichport, Samantha had endured enough. Chris stopped for a red light, and Samantha unbuckled her seat belt and bolted from the car. With purposeful strides she marched up to the black car and pounded on the tinted windows. She could hear

Chris calling her, his car door slamming, the whir of the vehicle's dark windows being lowered.

The cloying stench of marijuana wafted from inside the car. A flustered teenage girl sitting in the passenger seat slammed the ashtray shut. Her companion, a boy with dyed blond hair, gawked at Samantha, wide-eyed.

Samantha, speechless, stared back.

Chris was at her elbow. "Sorry, you two," he said quickly, grabbing Samantha's arm. "We thought you were someone else."

Back in the car, the air was thick with tension. Chris shut off the CD player, preferring, it seemed, the music of the howling wind. Samantha chewed away her lipstick, bit the inside of her cheek, picked at the nail polish on her baby finger.

"Say something," she demanded, finally.

"Dammit, Samantha, that was a crazy thing to do. Darkness and traffic aside, what did you intend to do if it had been Frank behind the wheel? Give him a stern lecture?"

The words tumbled out on a rush of breath. "I didn't want him spoiling our weekend, hounding us like some slimy private detective chasing adulterers. I had to take some kind of action. Don't you see? Frank has loomed over my life for so long. I won't be a victim anymore." When she was finished, she realized she hadn't answered Chris's question. Had she come face to face with Frank, she didn't know what she would have done. A moot point now, since the ominous black Trans Am had turned out to be a Camaro.

"No one's asking you to be a victim, Samantha. Look, you can take on Ehrhart at school, kick Petrella's ass, tell Bert Halloran to go to hell, and I'll cheer you on every time. But with Ventresca you're way out of your league. And remember, he won't spoil anything for us unless you let him."

The meaning of Chris's last sentence came through stiletto-sharp. Frank wasn't spoiling this weekend—she was. A sob threatened to erupt. She swallowed past it. Chris deserved better than this, better than her. Could she turn it around, bring more into this relationship besides a history of baggage and a series of battles she always seemed on the verge of fighting?

"I won't mention Frank again," she said in a tired voice. "And I'll handle him. You don't have to worry."

"You still don't get it, do you? If Frank is upsetting you, then he's upsetting me. And of course you can talk about him. This is a partnership, Samantha. No secrets. But answer me this: why was Ventresca in jail all these years?"

"You know why. For what he did to me."

Chris shook his head. "A first offense. Jails are overcrowded. Ventresca would have been released years ago."

"I'd always assumed he was out, and that he'd moved away."

"But now we know from the Victim Services Unit that he was behind bars. Like I said before, Ventresca couldn't have played nice in prison. They kept him locked up, meaning it wasn't safe to have him walking around with the rest of us. That should be reason enough for you to understand you can't just *handle* someone like him."

Samantha poked the CD button, and Chuck Mangione's flugelhorn played through for the second time, the selection upbeat and danceable. Chris stared at the road ahead, his eyes focused on the taillights of a Dodge Neon. Samantha picked at the polish on her thumbnail.

When they reached downtown Chatham, she let out a little laugh. "Guess we just had our first big fight."

Chris didn't laugh at all.

34

FRANK TAILED THE WHITE CAR all along Route 28, keeping several vehicles between them. A few times, he broke a sweat thinking that even in the inchworm traffic he might lose them, but he glued his car to the bumper of a Saturn and hugged the center line, the rich bastard's Saab always in view.

He was stumped when, at an intersection in one of the rinky-dink towns, he saw Sam get out of the car and make her way to the driver of the car behind. Frank almost ducked lower behind the steering wheel before he realized he didn't have to. He was three cars back, and she was so focused on whatever was happening ahead, she wouldn't have spotted him unless he was stark naked and sitting on the hood. The commotion was over fast, and he saw Sam being hustled away from the car.

So he kept cruising along, driving with his one good hand, the other mummified beneath layers of gauze, the cut stinging like a bugger. He wondered why they weren't pulling in to one of the motels that flanked the road. They were all decent enough—heated pools, cable TV, a few with waterbeds or free breakfast. Lots of vacancies this time of year, too. He passed one place advertising Jacuzzi tubs and special honeymoon rates, that familiar throb pulsing in his groin.

It wasn't until he saw the sign for Chatham that he figured the bastard wasn't taking Sam to a motel. They were going to one of those snooty inns where a guy needed to wear a jacket and tie just to get a meal. Frank cursed out loud. He stood a better chance of seeing what was what if they'd gone to a motel; in most, once you paid your money and got your key, nobody much gave a shit what you did.

The Saab continued slowly through town. The Saturn was long gone but Frank let an older-model BMW take its place. There was hardly anyone on the streets. The wind howled like an ornery bitch, and the few morons who were out on this rotten night scuttled like roaches for the nearest restaurant.

At the end of Main Street, the road came to a T, and the car turned left onto Shore Road. Frank followed, aware of the crashing Atlantic just yards beyond.

Funny place for a hotel, out in the middle of nowhere. The Chatham Bars Inn, the sign said. Set back from the road but close enough for Frank to see chandeliers hanging in the dining room and white-jacketed waiters jumping for tips. Sam and loverboy didn't turn in, just kept on going, and Frank wondered how long they'd keep driving. On not much sleep and no supper, he was already headachy and feeling like he wanted to ram the white car into a tree trunk.

On this stretch of road, the houses were on large lots, and when Frank rolled his window down for fresh air, he could almost smell money. A few had little red stickers shaped like stop signs on their fences, some almost every twenty feet, warning "Stop! These premises protected by Devlin Security Systems." In case you were too stupid to get the message from just one sticker. The Saab's right signal blinked and the car turned onto a long gravel drive and rolled through a pair of white wooden gates supported by stone columns.

Shit. He knew the guy had bucks, but this place had to be worth some serious change. Frank caught a glimpse of the house as he passed by, a huge gray thing with too many windows, which is what his mother would complain about if she saw it. *Who'd want to clean all that?* she would say every time she opened a decorating magazine in the doctor's office. Like she ever had to worry, living in the shitbox he'd grown up in.

He edged his car farther down the road, pulled over onto a wide patch of lawn outside the weathered cedar fence, and killed the engine. Off in the distance, he heard a dog bark.

Well, now what? All this way, with a boomer of a headache, and no plan. In ten minutes, Sam and the dentist would be in the sack, and what was he gonna do about it? Shinny up a drainpipe and watch?

The dog barked again, and Frank unscrewed the top on a mickey of Captain Morgan. Happy used to hate storms, too. Frank remembered how the dog would burrow under Frank's blanket, its warm body shaking against his thigh.

He heard ocean waves crashing off to his right, the wind beating against the car windows. In his head, his father's voice. *Come up with a plan, genius. You think you're so smart.*

"Shut up!" He pounded on the steering wheel.

Smack! *Goddamn kids think they know everything.*

He pounded the wheel again. Once more. Another.

Soon he became conscious of another noise, one that blotted out the ocean waves, the fierce wind, the terrified dog, his father's voice. It was his own scream—one continuous keen, a discordant siren wail that erupted, swelled, and heightened until at last there was nothing more than a cracker-dry rasp. He was drenched in sweat, gulping for breath, and when he looked down, he saw the gash on his hand had split wide open, the once-white gauze now saturated with blood.

35

AT THE END OF THE DRIVEWAY, Samantha caught her breath. Before her stood an enormous Dutch colonial, its porch lanterns gleaming. The front rooms were aglow, as was a tiny crescent-shaped window tucked under the gambrel roof. Though the house was large, it appeared homey and welcoming, especially on a cold night with the wind howling.

The ground was littered with fallen twigs. Samantha trod carefully toward the front door, shouldering against the wind as Chris lifted her overnight bag from the trunk.

Inside, the living room alone could have housed Samantha's entire apartment. Oversized sofas formed a U before a fieldstone fireplace. The dining area consisted of a pine refectory table and ten ladderback chairs positioned near a triple set of French doors facing a floodlit beach. Braided rugs warmed the wide plank floors.

"Oh, Chris, it's just beautiful," Samantha said. "Did you spend your summers here growing up?"

"Yes. Lots of sand castles, cookouts on the beach. There were some great times."

Samantha wondered how many of those great times included the MacPhersons and their blond daughter Georgina.

Chris set the luggage at the bottom of the stairs. "Coming here always reminds me of Dad. He loved this place."

Charles Marlborough Paxton, from what Chris had told Samantha, was a tireless worker, often putting in sixteen-hour days. But he always came home for dinner with his son, and he ensured that weekends were sacred, for family only. His death, when Chris was sixteen, was a crushing blow, and perhaps, to Samantha's way of thinking, all the more reason for Meredith to cling ferociously to her son.

At the back of the house, the kitchen was a chef's dream. Old cast-iron pots and utensils hung from the beamed ceiling. Clamped onto the end of the long butcher-block counter was a big antique coffee grinder. Every modern convenience was here, too—a six-burner cooktop, double wall ovens, an espresso maker.

"Your mother's domain?"

"Hardly. Dad was the cook. He used to whip up some great stuff in here." Chris pointed to a shelf full of cookbooks. "Now, come on. Let's get settled in, then I'll build us a fire and see what we can do about some drinks."

She followed Chris up the rear staircase to a blue and yellow room above the kitchen. The bed was a cherry four-poster with a crocheted canopy and mountains of Battenburg lace pillows. She shivered in anticipation of the two of them, naked, with the flicker of candle flame and embers in the hearth casting a warm glow over their bodies. This, she vowed, would be a weekend to remember. She would devote herself fully to Chris, savor each touch, each word. Nothing would interfere with their pleasure. Already, the memory of a black car with tinted windows seemed as distant as the moon.

"Closet," Chris said, pointing, "bathroom, drawers for your

stuff. Why don't you get yourself organized then come back down and give your order to the bartender?"

She rose on tiptoe and kissed him. "I'm so glad we're here."

He pulled her closer. "In a few hours, you'll be ecstatic." He winked and kissed her forehead.

Samantha unpacked quickly, throwing sweaters and jeans into a cherry highboy. She stashed her empty suitcase in the closet and deposited her cosmetics bag on the bathroom counter. In the bedroom, as in the rooms downstairs, a wall of windows faced the beach. She could see a large flagstone terrace below, and beyond that, a stretch of scrubby foliage, then yards and yards of ripply sand. No wonder Chris's father loved the place. It was quiet, the sounds coming not from traffic and machinery but from nature. Out here, problems were left behind and there was peace, contentment.

Or did the isolation leave her vulnerable? *No.* She had to stop. Negative thoughts and paranoia had no place here. She was with Chris. She was safe.

She dug out her cell phone and punched in the Filions' number, and she was relieved to hear from Matthew that no black sporty cars had been spotted there either. Matthew and Jeff were making an adventure of it all, taking turns doing sentry duty at the window, logging observations of suspicious characters and conducting hourly sweeps of the back yard, communicating to Jeff's parents on walkie-talkies. Once again, she was learning from her son. *Lighten up.*

From below, she heard the crunch of coffee beans being ground and as she descended the stairs, the aroma of freshly brewed coffee filled the kitchen. She took a deep, appreciative breath. Chris had his shirtsleeves rolled up and was assembling the last of their supper on glass plates.

"Chris, while we were driving along the Shore Road, I noticed a lot of the homes had security systems. Do you have one here?"

He returned mustard, lettuce, and smoked turkey to the fridge. "Dad used to think that security systems were a great way to advertise that you had something worth stealing, so he never had a system installed. In fact, he used to keep a hundred-dollar bill on the hall table just inside the front door. That way, if a burglar came in, he might just take the money and get the hell out." He poured coffee and a shot of Frangelico into each of two large stoneware mugs. He handed her a plate and mug, his mouth tightly pinched into a frown. "Ventresca won't come here, Samantha. He didn't follow us, and he's not gonna pull a frogman stunt and rise up out of the water. Current's too dangerous. Okay?"

"I'm done now," she said, holding up her plate. "I swear on this turkey sandwich. No more foolishness about you-know-who. Now let's eat, drink, and—well, see what other ideas we can come up with."

They went into the living room and settled onto the braided rug in front of the hearth. While Chris stacked kindling, Samantha struck a match and lit half a dozen fat pillar candles that decorated the antique sleigh that functioned as a coffee table. In minutes Chris had a fire blazing. He dimmed the lights, and they sat down to snack on sandwiches, carrot sticks, and store-bought brownies. The liqueur-laced coffee went down warm and smooth, and when Samantha asked for a refill, Chris obliged.

"Drink it slowly," he cautioned, his voice low. "I want you fully conscious."

"And I don't want to miss anything."

He kissed her deeply, easing her back onto the rug. She gave herself over to the sensations, the delicious feel of Chris's mouth on hers, his firm thighs pressing against her, teasing fingers tracing feathery lines beneath her sweater. She breathed in the woodsy scent of his cologne, burrowed into the hollow of his throat, and felt the throb of his pulsing heart. She reached behind her, grabbing the hard cool metal of the sleigh runner, Chris's touch more insistent, probing, urging. She stretched her body long, longer, extending each inch of skin to receive more of his caress. Samantha knew then that having him close wasn't enough. The fantasy of the blue and yellow bedroom would wait. She wanted him here.

"Chris—," she whispered between kisses. She broke away, held his hands still. "What was that?"

"What's wrong? Did I do—?"

"That snapping noise. Didn't you hear it?"

"Must have been thinking about something else," he murmured, his tongue doing a carefree dance along her neck toward her ear.

She moaned, eager for more, when another sharp crack split the night. Samantha wriggled out of Chris's arms and raised herself up on her elbows. "I know you heard that. It came from over there." She pointed at the curtainless black glass facing the beach.

"Of course I heard it," he told her, smoothing hair away from her face. "It's okay. A branch snapping. Some of those trees are over a hundred years old. This wind will wreak its share of havoc tonight. Remember all the twigs on the ground?"

She reached for her coffee and took a long drink. A louder snap, this time from the front of the house, made her jump. "My God, we're surrounded," she said, trying to make light of it all.

Chris wasn't fooled. "I didn't know you were scared of storms."

It's not storms I'm afraid of, she wanted to say. And the sound she heard didn't sound like decayed branches giving themselves up to the wind. She was certain she heard footsteps, although now, with the wind bellowing, she didn't know how she could have heard anything above it.

"We're safe here, Samantha."

"You're sure?"

"Yes, but there's only one way to make *you* sure. Be right back." He kissed the tip of her nose, then rose to his feet and went to the front stairs, where his suede jacket still hung from the newel post.

Samantha rushed over to him. "Please, Chris. This isn't necessary." She grabbed his arm.

"Relax, would you?" he said. "Once I make a tour of the outside and assure you there's no bogeyman in the bushes, we can continue where we left off. I think I was somewhere around here." He softly planted a kiss on the side of her neck. "Now, I'm off to inspect the premises, as they say. Wish I had a plaid cap or something."

She protested again, but he would not be dissuaded. He flipped open the front of a drop-leaf desk and pulled a brass letter opener from its pigeonhole. Chris executed a dramatic slash, followed by several thrusts and parries.

"How's my technique?"

"As a kisser, terrific." She wrapped her arms around him. "As a fencer, I'm less confident. You don't have to do this for me, you know."

"For you? You think I'm doing this for you?" He tightened his hold on her. "This is completely selfish, I promise you. When your conquering hero returns, he's going to be expecting his just reward. I'll head out the back and come in the front door. Meanwhile, you get over by that fire, sit down, and figure out exactly what pleasures of the flesh I deserve for my bravery."

She followed Chris into the dining room, and he opened one of the French doors and held up a victory fist.

"Samantha," he said, "if I really thought there was someone out there, do you think I'd arm myself with this piddly thing?" Then he disappeared.

Samantha returned to the hearth, drew back the mesh screen, and picked up an iron poker. An ashen log crumbled on the grate, the fire reduced to a few orange embers. She tossed on two more logs and prodded with the poker until the flame rekindled. On the mantel above her, a Seth Thomas clock ticked away the minutes.

I don't think Ventresca played nice in prison.

Where was Chris? She should have checked the time before he went out the door. How long had he been gone? They had been seconds away from making love when she'd let her fears and her imagination intrude. Now Chris was out in the storm instead of here with her.

Perhaps he was already in trouble, grappling with whoever had made the noise she was now convinced she heard. Again she looked at the clock. Five more minutes. She decided she would wait no longer than that before she ventured outside herself. To find Chris. To bring him inside. Or to call the police.

Still gripping the poker, she stood and went to the French doors, pressing her face against the cool glass. Squinting through the darkness, she could see the beach, deserted, and far off to the left, a boathouse. Perhaps Chris was inside, checking to make sure it was empty. Which he wouldn't have to be doing if she had just left well enough alone.

She stared at the boathouse, waiting for Chris to emerge, but the doors remained closed. The poker felt rock-solid, reassuring in her hand. She would take it with her outside when she—

"Ah, Jesus! No! Oh, God!"

"Chris!" She bolted for the front door.

From the other side came Chris's voice again. "Samantha, stay there! Don't come—"

She opened the door. And screamed.

36

SAMANTHA SAT WRAPPED IN an afghan at the end of a sofa, her knees drawn to her chest. The stiff postures and stern expressions of the officers seated opposite told her the Chatham police took their work and the concerns of the townspeople seriously.

Police Constable Ferenc didn't make himself too comfortable. He'd barely settled into the chesterfield when he was up again, excusing himself to have a look around outside, leaving his partner to hold up the public relations end. Samantha watched Ferenc go out the front door, lifting his short legs over the grisly obstacle in his path.

Notepad poised in her lap, Constable Barnes asked, "Did you hear anything outside?"

"I thought I heard twigs snapping," Samantha said, her voice still quivering as she struggled to banish frightful images from her mind. "Maybe footsteps. It was hard to be sure with the wind blowing."

"And you?" Constable Barnes looked up at Chris, who was angrily pacing across the braided rug.

He shook his head. "Nothing. But when Samantha said she'd heard something, I went outside to check. Went out that door there." He waved toward the French door. "Looked up and down the beach, by the boathouse, but I didn't see anyone, or anything, not until I found that—" Chris cast a disgusted glance toward the front door. "It just made me si—"

From the kitchen, the kettle shrieked. Samantha shrugged out of the afghan but Chris held up his hand. "Stay where you are. I'll get it."

Once Chris left the room, Constable Barnes pressed for more details. Where exactly had the sounds come from? Around what time had Samantha heard them? Could she describe what she heard more specifically? And oddly, how long had she and Chris been dating?

"Nearly a year. Why?"

The constable scratched the information across the page. "Anyone else live on the property?"

"The house belongs to Chris's mother, Meredith. It's used mainly as a summer place and weekend retreat, I think."

"No housekeeper? Gardener?"

"Not sure. Chris can tell you better."

"Both," Chris answered, coming into the room carrying a tray with all the paraphernalia for tea. "Mr. and Mrs. Stayner. They live here in Chatham and they take care of the place for us. But maybe you should be chasing down an older-model black Trans Am."

This got the officer's interest. She looked up from her page and motioned for Chris to sit down. "Why do you say that? Do you have someone you suspect?"

Samantha opened her mouth to reply but Chris beat her to it. "Yes," he said. "Frank Ventresca. V-e-n-t-r-e-s-c-a. He's an ex-con and he's been terrorizing Samantha."

Constable Barnes's pen was up and moving again as Chris

explained about the flowers, the phone calls, Frank's contact with Matthew. "He's the only person we know who could do such a thing. Everybody around here loved Buster."

Buster was the seven-year-old Irish setter belonging to the Paxtons' neighbors to the east, the Renquists. According to Chris, the setter was the friendliest dog on the Cape and a local hero, too, having dragged a drowning toddler from the treacherous undertow five summers ago. Now Buster lay on the Paxtons' Welcome mat, his life cut short by one lethal puncture wound made with what may have been a screwdriver.

Again Samantha had to revisit the scene of the rape as Constable Barnes sought to fill in the links between Samantha and Frank. By the time the officers were ready to leave, Samantha was exhausted. She caught parts of sentences—"check out this Ventresca . . . drive around town, see what's what . . . talk to the neighbors . . ."

Constable Ferenc, who reported seeing nothing out of the ordinary on the Paxtons' property, had already wrapped the dead pet in a plastic sheet. To Barnes he said, "Well, I guess we'd better get next door and tell the Renquists that Buster won't be coming home."

Still in the same clothing they'd worn in the car, Samantha and Chris curled up on opposite ends of the sofa, the afghan draped across their feet. Thoughts of passion and desire for intimacy were as dead as the poor creature the officers had taken away. In the hearth, the dwindling fire licked the last remains of a silvery birch log, then the final orange embers died too.

During the night, while Chris slept, Samantha rose from the sofa and groped her way toward the fireplace. As soundlessly as possible, she tugged at the chain of a floor lamp, and the room was bathed in soft, blessed light. She could not bear the darkness. In the darkness came visions of that still, cold creature, killed because of her, and a grinning face that repeated, "You are mine. Forever."

There was another vision, too, of the note that had been tucked inside the slain pet's collar: *Have a Nice Weekend.*

37

THERE WAS DRIED BLOOD on the steering wheel. He was freezing, but the jumbo-sized thermos of rum-spiked coffee was empty. Frank slid the heater switch over to maximum and eventually his shivering stopped, but he passed a good number of motels and souvenir shops before he could unclench his teeth. From somewhere through the starless night, his father's voice growled at him. *If you want something, Franco, you go after it with all your guns firing.* He'd taken that advice once, and it had landed him a suite in the Iron Bars Bed and Breakfast. Stood to reason if it was lousy advice then, it was probably still bullshit.

He stretched his mouth into an exaggerated grin, then dropped his jaw wide, but the tension in his face persisted. He tried to focus on the road but he'd had too much to drink. The center line blurred into one long, fuzzy caterpillar that disappeared from time to time under his tires. His mouth and tongue were coated with wool. A chain of knots tightened across his shoulder blades, and a few times, he tasted the booze-laced coffee coming back up. He had to lay off the liquor. It made him do stupid things, and earlier tonight he even thought he'd had a hallucination. He'd blinked a few times but the vision was gone.

Then all hell broke loose. There was noise from the house—a scream, he thought, then the sound of a police siren, something that made him sit up in a hurry, start his car, and get the hell out.

They left the Cape early the next morning, neither Chris nor Samantha commenting on the shambles made of their romantic weekend. Along Route 6A, the scenery was a shambles, too, the aftereffects of the night's windstorm blotting the landscape. Groves of shallow-rooted locusts in Eastham were decimated. Oaks, pines, and maples had been pruned by the fierce, salt-drenched winds.

"No shortage of firewood this winter, that's for sure," Chris stated. Beyond that, he said little.

Samantha understood his anger, and she shared it. Once again, Frank had come between them, and though both had tried, neither could banish the image of the Renquists' dog lying on the front porch. Chris, who abhorred violence, swore that if the police didn't bring Ventresca in, he would hunt him down himself.

Samantha promised to apply for the restraining order as soon as she got home, though inwardly she pondered the futility of such an exercise. Her years as a counselor had taught her that many restraining orders weren't worth the paper they were written on. She'd seen her share of battered wives and teenagers who'd been forced to hire bodyguards to ensure their safety from abusers who priced human life cheaply and were undeterred by legal scraps of paper. Again she pictured the body of the Irish setter, trying to imagine the anger such an act would have required. What would a restraining order do to Frank's anger?

The drive to Somerville seemed endless. The silence between Chris and Samantha came not from the comfortable ease of two lovers who didn't need to fill quiet time with inane chatter but rather from people who had no words left. Their emotions were so raw and mangled and confused that conversation, on any level, would be stilted.

Chris finally pulled up alongside the curb in front of Beatrice's. He got out and reached in to retrieve Samantha's suitcase from the back seat, but she had swiveled out before him and had already hefted the overnight bag up by the shoulder strap. It felt as if it was weighed down with bowling balls. If Meredith Paxton were nearby witnessing this scene, Samantha was certain she would be grinning triumphantly.

Chris said, "Let's just get you safely inside."

"It's okay, Chris," she said, her hand firmly on his chest to stop him. "I'm as safe here as anywhere. I'll be fine. Really."

He gave her a long look to be sure, then planted a tender kiss on her cheek. "We'll try again another time."

She felt an apology forming in her mind. What came out instead was, "I'm disappointed too."

Chris nodded, asked her again if she was all right, then circled to the driver's side of the Saab. "The restraining order," he said. "Right away, okay?"

Then he was driving off, and Samantha couldn't bear to watch. Bone-deep sorrow welled up within her, threatening to erupt in a burst of tears. Her relationship with Chris was crumbling; perhaps it was already over. She needed to get inside. After a good cry, maybe she would be able to find a way to set things right, make it all up to Chris somehow. If it was still possible.

Beatrice was on the front stoop gathering colorful bundles of junk mail that had been rolled up and stuffed into the curlicues of her wrought-iron porch railing. "Why, Samantha," she said, tugging her patterned cardigan around her, "I didn't expect you until later tomorrow."

"Long story," Samantha replied, swallowing hard.

"Your friend is here. Putting a new lock on the door."

"Tom?"

"That's him. Reattached my mailbox, too. No more wobbling." She reached up to where her pitted brass mailbox used to dangle from one rusty screw. It was now firmly anchored to the aluminum siding. "Such a nice man."

"He is that," Samantha said. "Now get inside. You'll catch cold."

"A real cutie, too," the landlady added, then disappeared behind the faded door.

When Samantha lugged her totebag up the rear stairs, she saw Tom, clad in stone-washed jeans, work boots, a plaid shirt, and fleece vest, closing the lid on a red metal toolbox.

"What the hell?" he said, turning when he heard her footsteps, "you're not supposed to be back until tomorrow. What gives?"

"Got an hour? Come on in. I'll make coffee."

With a pot of hazelnut decaf and a plate of double chocolate chip cookies on the kitchen table, Samantha told Tom about the weekend that never was.

"Sweet mother of God," he said when she was done. "Ventresca killed a dog? Left it there for you to find? That guy is really sick. Seeing you and Chris must have tipped him over the edge." He poured coffee for the two of them, emptied a packet of sweetener into Samantha's, then added milk. "At least the cops will get on his case. Tell you one thing for sure. Frank Ventresca won't bother you here. I installed the Rolls-Royce of deadbolts on your door."

"He can still break the window. Crawl in . . ." Samantha looked at the single pane of glass on her kitchen door.

"And make so much noise, by then you've already dialed 911. Short of installing a moat full of crocodiles, this deadbolt is the best we can do. There's three keys on your counter," Tom said, nodding toward the sink. "One for you, one for Matthew, and one for Beatrice."

"Who's quite fond of you, I might add. 'A real cutie,' I believe were her exact words."

Tom smiled broadly. "Maybe I oughta ditch my little blue book and just hook up with the Queen Bea. Who knows? Underneath those prim dresses and hand-knit cardigans might lurk the body of a temptress."

That made Samantha smile. But only for a moment. "Tom, what'll I do if Chris decides he's had enough? Maybe this last thing with Frank was all he could take." She remembered the look on Chris's face as they turned onto her street. A mixture of disappointment, anger, and what else—accusation? Did he somehow blame her for all that had happened?

"Don't be ridiculous."

"I mean it. Maybe Meredith Paxton is right. Georgina MacPherson has known Chris for years. They come from the same background, and she's baggage-free."

"Samantha, give the good doctor more credit. If a guy really loves someone, then he's in for the long haul, baggage or no baggage. You just wait and see what kind of stuff Chris is made of. I bet he comes through this even crazier about you."

"You think?"

"I do. Plus, Ventresca won't be able to keep this game up much longer. Sooner or later, he'll either get tired of it or he'll do something stupid that lands him right back in jail."

"It's that second one I'm worried about."

"Nah." Tom waved away her concern. "Could be Ventresca's just a big delusional palooka with a perfect-family fantasy. When he sees you don't share his dreams, he'll move on. Besides, he's already made his first real mistake. That thing with the dog? Even if the cops can't prove he did it, they'll be watching him. If he so much as wears mismatched socks, they'll be ready with the handcuffs."

"Oh, Tom, I know what you're trying to do, and thanks." She patted his hand. "But big delusional palookas have been known to take butcher knives to their loved ones."

Tom pursed his lips together. "Hey, work with me on this one. If you're not going to meet me halfway, how can I make you forget your troubles? Listen, Samantha, you're either surrounded by people at work or you're with Matthew, Beatrice, or Chris. And yours truly is only a speed-dial away. What's Ventresca going to do with all those people around you?"

"I was with Chris in Chatham, and Frank managed to do plenty."

"Kid stuff. You weren't in any real danger, were you?"

"I suppose not."

"There you go. You'll rally from this, and you'll be able to tackle that bitchy future mother-in-law of yours, too."

"Let's hope so. Right now, I don't seem to be handling anything particularly well. Except these cookies," she said, staring at the last one on the plate. "How many have I eaten?"

"Been a rough time," Tom said. "Don't bother counting."

Unlike herself, Tom wasn't a chocoholic. She offered to fix him a salami sandwich but he declined. "Salami is *verboten* on the Lundstrom diet," he told her. "Chocolate, too. Reacts with my medication. Anyway, I'd better be off." He rose and headed for the door.

She thanked Tom for replacing the lock and reached for her wallet but he refused to take her money. "Consider it an early Christmas present," he said.

Once Tom had gone, Samantha phoned Matthew at the Filions. The boys were in the rec room playing nine-ball with Jeff's father.

"Mom, what—?"

"If you say I'm not supposed to be home until tomorrow, I'll cuff you upside the head."

Once again, Samantha found herself relating the story of what had transpired in Chatham. She fought to keep emotion out of her voice, but Matthew wasn't fooled. "Mom, that's sick," he said, echoing Tom's sentiments. "We've seen enough biographies on TV to know what's happening here. Frank's rage. It's *escalating.* This guy's gotta be stopped."

She assured him that the Chatham police would coordinate their efforts with the Somerville force to ensure their safety. "Are you staying at Jeff's tonight? Because I'll need to know when you're coming home. Tom's put a new lock on our door and you won't be able to get in if I'm not here."

Matthew told her he would probably stay the night at the Filions'. "Jeff's mom made lemon meringue pie and I think we're having roast beef for supper."

"Can't compete with that," Samantha said. "Have fun."

Samantha unpacked her suitcase, returning unworn sweaters to their drawer, reminded again of her missing lingerie. She thought too about the spoiled weekend, the time that should have belonged to her and Chris. Was Tom right? Would this somehow draw the two of them closer together?

How could it?

Tom was just being his usual optimistic self, trying to buoy her spirits. He wanted her to focus on something other than Frank, even going so far as to distract her with thoughts of Chris's mother. But minimizing the threat Frank posed was no good. Samantha knew firsthand how dangerous he was, and now Chris and the Chatham police knew it too.

Frank's rage. It's escalating.

If that were true, then why kill a dog? If Frank was so dangerous, why didn't he come after her directly? Or Chris? He had been bold enough to venture onto the Paxtons' property, march onto the front porch. What prevented him from coming inside and acting out his rage all over the place? What was gained by killing a poor animal?

Samantha settled on the sofa and tried to sort things out, recording the events of the previous night in her spiral-bound book. On paper, everything seemed straightforward. Frank, tired of waiting, was playing a cruel game, terrorizing her and trying to come between her and Chris in the most vicious, senseless way. Yet from somewhere, another thought niggled and teased at her, but she couldn't urge it forward.

As she boiled water for tea, she doodled on a blank sheet of paper, hoping the exercise would rid her of the uncanny sensation that she was missing something. It was no use. Eventually, cup of tea on the table beside her, Samantha curled up on the sofa and let the tears come.

38

MATTHEW CHECKED HIS WATCH, then double-checked his transit map, making sure he knew exactly where to transfer to the Orange Line. If he didn't hurry up, not only would he miss out on Mrs. Filion's lemon meringue pie but he'd catch hell for worrying Jeff's parents, too.

He left Jeff at the doughnut shop, telling his friend he had a few things to do and would catch up with him later. Jeff, occupied with trying to get the attention of a cute girl on the junior basketball team, didn't seem to mind. He'd already packed away three crullers and two mugs of hot chocolate so the owner wouldn't kick him out.

Matthew's feet were soaked. New Nikes were on his birthday wish list, but that was still a few weeks away, so slushy water flooded through the dime-sized hole in his sneakers and squished between shriveled toes. On the streetcar, he thought about Mr. Stanfield's introductory lesson on genetics and the structure of DNA. The textbook illustration showed the double-helix formation and the chapter described how, using an enzyme, the chain could be cut, the fragments put on a gel so they lined up. Matthew had been fascinated with the process and wished he could carry out the procedure on his own twisted thoughts—separate them into nice neat, straight bundles so he could analyze them one at a time. Instead, everything in his head was distorted, mangled, twisted into knots.

Bad enough what Frank Ventresca had done to his mom, but now, the possibility that the creep might actually be his father—well, genetics or no, Matthew wasn't having any part of it. Worse than a creep, Frank was a stupid creep—that much Matthew could tell from the few times he'd spoken with him. His mother used to caution him not to be smug about his intellect, but there it was—he didn't want a dummy for a father. It was embarrassing. Neither did he want anyone in his life that would break a woman's nose, rape her, and kill a dog. More serious than embarrassment was anger, and Matthew had reached his limit.

Once all his thoughts had sifted down, he knew he would have to do something. His English teacher was a huge believer in quotes, spouting them off by the score in class. A favorite was Heroditus: "The worst pain we can have is to know much and be impotent to act." She often recited this one when someone had an incomplete assignment, but now, for Matthew, the quote had a different significance. He did know much. And he was not powerless. Matthew intended to act. Frank would have to answer for all he had done. Face to face. Man to man.

Lou's Service Center was in the streetcar suburb of Roxbury, an area stacked with tenement housing, three- and six-family triple-decker apartment buildings. Matthew stepped down from the trolley, landed squarely in a puddle of slush, and walked away from the transit stop with a confidence he didn't feel. The neighborhood was bleak, gray, cold, and not the kind of place he wanted to find himself in when it got dark. Suddenly Somerville, with its simple homes, neat yards, and safe familiarity seemed too far away.

The gas station was three short blocks away from the transit stop. Matthew spotted Frank adding a quart of oil to a Chevy Citation, the man's gloveless hands the color of raw hamburger.

"Hey, kid! Long way from home, aren't you?"

"We've got to talk."

"Go on inside." Frank jerked his head toward the empty service station. "This weather's a bitch."

Matthew heard the Citation's hood slam shut and he watched from inside as Frank completed the transaction with the customer. A few minutes later, Frank was heading toward him, hands jammed under his armpits. When the outer door closed behind him, he stomped slush off his boots, then blew on his hands.

"Jesus H., it's getting cold. How'd you know where to find me?"

Matthew pointed at the yellow insignia on Frank's jacket. "I can read."

Frank glanced down and laughed. "How 'bout that. So, what brings you by?" He hoisted himself up on the counter. His coveralls were grease stained, his fingernails filthy. He was outlined against a wall of clipboards dangling from hooks, a shelf of motor oil, and a poster advertising Peretti tires.

Matthew was struck by the absurdity of the situation. It looked as though Frank actually thought this was some kind of father-son reunion. His face wore an eager, hopeful expression. "I've got a few things to say to you."

"You do? Well then, pull up a chair and let's get to it."

The only chair was a brown vinyl and chrome standard-issue, but a good three dozen dog-eared car magazines were piled on top of it. "I'll stand, thanks. This won't take long."

"Suit yourself."

"I know about you and my mom."

Frank's smile was close to sheepish. "Yeah, well, I figured you'd find out sooner or later. I've always had a thing for her. Always will."

"Even if she doesn't want to have anything to do with you?"

The smile turned cocky, a corner of Frank's mouth upturned. "People can always change their minds."

"Especially if you try to change it for them, right?"

"Huh?"

"Like you did fifteen years ago. When my mom said she was going to marry Scott. You tried to change her mind that night, didn't you. Under the lilac tree in Grandma and Grandpa's yard."

"Now wait a minute—"

"No, you wait. You hurt my mom. And she had you put away for it. She doesn't care about you. What is it with you anyway? Jail's supposed to teach you something, but you're just as dumb as you were when you went in."

Frank's mouth formed a flat line. A tic pulsed below one cheekbone. "Hey, who you callin'—?"

"You heard me. What would you call a guy who can't take no for an answer? And here you are, after all this time, popping up all over the place and trying to break up my mom and Chris."

A low growl was coming from Frank. At first Matthew thought the man might leap from the counter and attack, but then he realized Frank was counting, the rhythm of each syllable becoming louder. He sensed it wouldn't be long before the explosion. He had to hurry. "The phone calls, the flowers, they were just plain stupid, but that thing with the dog? You're sick, you hear that? You're sick, and we don't want you anywhere near us."

The man's brow furrowed, and he jumped down from the counter and gripped Matthew's arm. "Now listen here, kid. What goes on between grown-ups is their business, and what's this—?"

"Let go of my arm," Matthew said, trying to jerk free. "I know how this looks, an older man grabbing a teenage boy. If anyone drives by and sees this, you'll be back in jail before midnight, and that's a promise."

Frank let go.

Matthew whirled away and raced out of the service station, not slowing down until he reached the streetcar stop. His heart still thudded loudly even as he hurried up the Filions' front steps close to forty minutes later. Inside, Jeff was setting the table, his mom was in the kitchen, and his dad was on the phone.

"Never mind, he's just come in the door, Mrs. Quinlan. Yes, he's fine."

He was given dry socks, a cup of tea, and the space he needed to calm down. After a second helping of pie, Matthew told the Filions everything. He thought he should feel satisfied, that at least he wasn't sitting back allowing Frank Ventresca to control their lives. But there was no satisfaction, nor any peace. Instead, Matthew felt sick to his stomach and twice during the conversation thought he might need to bolt for the bathroom. He remembered Frank grabbing his arm, and how by some miracle he'd persuaded him to let go, and a lucky thing, too, because during the entire time Matthew had been in the service station, not one car had pulled up to the pumps. He was right about that part of Roxbury—it wasn't a place where anyone could count on being rescued.

He envisioned bizarre scenarios—Frank hitting him over the head with a tire iron and driving the getaway Trans Am to Nome, Alaska, or some other outpost where a body could lie frozen for years before being discovered. He'd taken a big chance with his safety, and he didn't feel the least bit heroic. Frank wasn't going to be stopped by a few harsh words from a fifteen-year-old. In fact, the only thing Matthew thought he might have accomplished was to make Frank angrier. For such a smart kid, his meeting with Frank was probably the stupidest thing he'd ever done.

39

ON THE FIRST MONDAY in December, Boston received its first snowfall of the year and the city was transformed into a Hallmark card. Bare branches glistened white. Shrubs were mounds of puffy cotton. Samantha loved winter and welcomed the snow the same way she had done as a child, by sticking out her tongue and letting a few flakes melt there. She made a mental note to bring her wreath and box of ornaments up from the basement. Some pre-Christmas cheer was certainly called for.

She drove to school hoping the new coverlet of fresh snow would provide a needed boost to staff morale, but her hopes were in vain. When she arrived, the building was more chaotic than usual. Rather than braving slippery commutes from distant suburbs, eight staff members had called in sick, and there was a frantic scramble to get classes covered. In the aftermath of Derek Townsend's death and the publicity it received, substitute teachers were turning down jobs at Somerville Central. In the teachers' lounge, several grumbled about giving up spare periods. Bert Halloran grabbed a quick cup of coffee, avoided eye contact with everyone, and retreated to his office to avoid the fallout.

Hank Ehrhart complained the loudest, and to no one in particular. "Damn it all. I just played poker with Halloran on the weekend. You'd think friendship would stand for something." Ehrhart had to fill in for an absent geography teacher. "Reading period, that's what the kids'll get. I'm not doing any geography lesson."

"Could be worse, Hank," Samantha told him. "I'll trade you for one of Tom's music classes."

The coach turned on her. "Why don't you go play Norman Vincent Peale someplace else? If I'd wanted your power of positive thinking, I'd have asked."

What had she done now? Ehrhart's irritability was becoming legendary. Phys. ed. students griped about him every day, including some of Ehrhart's star athletes. "We're all going to get through this day, Hank," she said. "Try to keep a sense of humor."

Ehrhart pressed his fingers together in prayer and gave a mock bow. "Thank you, Our Blessed Lady of Perpetual Advice."

Nearby, someone muttered "bastard," but Samantha couldn't tell who it was.

"Oh, by the way, an admirer of yours sends his regards."

She didn't ask, she merely raised an eyebrow and waited.

"Petrella." Ehrhart sneered. "Remember him? Used to work here?"

That did it. A few more teachers had stopped talking and were staring in their direction. Samantha had a choice—fight or flight. She opted for a little of both. Rising to her feet, she said, "Have fun in your geography class, Hank. Maybe one of the students can direct you to the exact spot where you left your brain." As she left, she heard brief applause from a brave few and more grumbling from Ehrhart.

On the stage in the auditorium, the first-year music class was already tuning up, the huge room filled with squeaks, crashes, and trombone farts. The discordant noise made Samantha want to escape to the relative quiet of her office, but taking one music class was the least she could do for Tom, who was home with a sore throat and low-grade fever. She'd lost count of the number of favors she owed her friend.

Thanks to four years of piano lessons while growing up, Samantha could read music. One of the students had located Tom's collection of scores, so for the next sixty minutes, she had "The Theme from the Pink Panther," "Colonel Bogey's March," and "Hello, Dolly!" to look forward to. The clarinets and flutes formed a semicircular front row. Matthew should have occupied one of the chairs, but he was home today too, with chills and sneezes, Samantha blaming his sodden feet from Saturday night.

Matthew's tale of his confrontation with Frank had knocked her sideways. "What could you have been thinking?" she lit into him. "Frank's an ex-con," she said, thinking it wasn't so long ago that Chris reminded her of the same thing. "And you gave him hell? Oh, Matthew!"

At first he tried to lie his way out of it, telling Samantha he had left Jeff to meet Kelly, but for that, he caught it worse. Samantha had already spoken to Mrs. Filion, who told her about Matthew's adventure in Roxbury.

The session with her son had lasted nearly an hour, with Samantha's voice decibels louder than usual. Matthew agreed he owed Jeff's parents an apology for causing them worry, and Jeff too. By suppertime, he had taken over a bouquet of carnations and a thank-you note. He apologized to Samantha for lying but not for going to see Frank.

"He can't scare us, Mom," Matthew explained, his chin jutting forward. "He has to know nobody messes with Quinlan and Quinlan."

Matthew admitted he didn't know the effect his words had on Frank; indeed, he hadn't given Frank much chance to get a word in edgewise. He admitted, too, that he'd been scared, not just of Roxbury's menacing atmosphere but that Frank might actually slug him, or worse.

"What were you thinking?" she said again. Yet, all harsh consequences meted out, Samantha was proud of her son and told him so. His actions demonstrated courage beyond his years, and his determination to confront the bad guy while placing his own safety at risk clearly showed how much he loved her. A rare breed, that boy of hers.

Samantha heard a throat clear, then a whispered, "Mrs. Q.?" It was Kelly Frid.

Samantha flipped open one of Tom's scores and tapped the white baton on the metal lectern in front of her. " 'Pink Panther,' guys," she said when they'd quieted down. "Let's make Henry Mancini proud."

By the end of the period, Samantha held Tom Lundstrom in even higher regard. The percussionist, no Ringo Starr or Phil Collins, had given her a throbbing headache, and the floor near the brass section was dotted with saliva. While many of the budding musicians showed promise, as a group they butchered not only Mancini's composition but the rest of the songs as well.

At noon, Halloran proclaimed himself another victim of the flu bug and flew the coop, the noisy muffler on his Audi giving away his premature exit. Samantha knew Halloran was no more sick than she was. The going was getting rough so he was getting out.

By the time the dismissal bell rang, a wind had come up from the east and was blowing snow everywhere. The radio was warning of whiteout conditions, so everyone rushed to their cars, eager to get home. The parking lot was slick as Samantha made her way toward her Toyota. Hank Ehrhart was already skidding out onto the street, his BMW unable to stop at the corner. There was a loud blare of a horn, then another as Hank tooted back at the angry driver. Even on the road, the coach wasn't making any friends.

Concentrating on her footing and squinting to see through the whirling snow, Samantha was nearly face to face with the stranger waiting at her car before she saw him.

Her heart constricted. Then she realized it wasn't Frank, and she relaxed a little.

Standing beside her Toyota was a tall man, well over six feet, his broad torso exaggerated by a heavily padded parka. Though Samantha was sure she had never met the man, there was something familiar about him. "Can I help you?" she asked.

"You're the one, aren't you," he said, his voice slow and deep, the syllables eliding into one long, mushy word.

"I beg your pardon?"

"You're the one who let my son die."

Derek's father. And he was drunk.

"Mr. Townsend, I know this must be a terrible time for you and your wife. It's a terrible time for all of us. Derek was very special."

"Yeah, so special you didn't stop him from putting a gun to his head."

Samantha quickly scanned the parking lot. Others were intent on scraping windshields, getting into their cars. No one glanced in her direction. "Mr. Townsend, I feel awful about what happened to Derek—"

"What happened to him? He *died,* that's what happened to him. Can't you even say it?" He reeled slightly to the left, then steadied himself.

"Mr. Townsend," she said, not sure what approach to explore next, "I think we should talk. Why don't you come by the school tomorrow afternoon?"

"I got nothing to say to you," he said, a globule of spittle dotting his lower lip. "I just wanted to see what kind of person would let something like that happen."

Samantha's heart ached for the man. His guilt must be tremendous. The gun Derek had brought to school exactly one month ago had belonged to Mrs. Townsend, bought for her by her husband after she'd been attacked a year ago in her own driveway. Two thugs had knocked her down and grabbed her purse. Samantha knew Mr. Townsend's intentions had been good, but he had to be thinking that if the gun hadn't been in the house, Derek might still be alive.

What could she say? There had to be something. She'd missed her opportunity with Derek. She couldn't let his father go without trying to help. Somehow.

Derek's father turned and walked away. "Mr. Townsend! Please!" she called after him, but he continued walking. Relieved that at least he wasn't getting into a car in his condition, she watched as the man headed across the parking lot and down the street with his shoulders stooped and head bent low. He had the classic shuffling gait attributed to one who is severely depressed. She debated going after him, but knew Derek's father wasn't ready to accept help, and he certainly didn't want it from her.

Samantha scraped pebbles of ice from her windshield and brushed snow away from the headlights and off the hood. She slid into the seat, started the engine, and turned on her rear defroster. Once more, her seat belt got stuck and she sighed in exasperation. While she waited for the car to warm up, she dialed Tom on her cell phone. "I can pick up soup from the Chinese restaurant," she offered. "Or a burger, if you need a grease fix."

Tom declined. "Just get home safe, you. It's storming like a bugger."

"I'm on my way," she assured him. She was tempted to tell him about her encounter with Derek's father, but then decided against it. Tom's voice still sounded raw, and he was staying home tomorrow, too. He didn't need to listen to yet another of her problems.

Like Ehrhart's car minutes ago, the Toyota skidded into the middle of the intersection. Samantha took her foot off the gas and coasted down the road.

The car ahead of her fishtailed along the street. One taillight was smashed, and the driver was signaling a left turn with a snow-covered arm. Samantha was glad the tech boys had serviced her car and winterized it not long ago, and she relaxed a little behind the wheel.

40

THE TOYOTA HAD A MIND of its own, sliding all the way down Massachusetts Avenue, across the Harvard Bridge, and into Boston. Another dusting of snow had fallen during the supper hour, the fresh white blanket a perfect mask for the treacherous black ice beneath.

Samantha knew it was foolish to be out when the roads were so slippery—in fact, Matthew told her she was nuts—but Chris's mother had made special arrangements to have an exclusive Newbury Street boutique stay open after hours. She gently reminded Samantha of that detail when Samantha had phoned to suggest rescheduling. Samantha sensed now was as good a time as any to put the Georgina-at-the-Ballet fiasco behind them and work at building some kind of relationship. That Meredith Paxton was helping Samantha find a dress for the engagement party was an encouraging sign. Perhaps Chris's talk with his mother had done some good after all, and Meredith was finally accepting her. Chris was highly skeptical and hoped Samantha wasn't setting herself up for a huge disappointment. Samantha hoped so, too.

The boutique resembled an aristocratic drawing room, the

walls painted a complexion-flattering soft pink, the vast floor space broken up by an assortment of thick area rugs in muted pastel tones. Meredith Paxton was seated on one of four striped bergère chairs that surrounded a glass cocktail table. She wore a pale lavender knit ensemble and sipped champagne from a delicate crystal flute.

"Sorry I'm a bit late," Samantha huffed, checking her watch. "The weather's terrible and I had trouble getting parked."

The proprietor, a tall, lithe strawberry blonde, introduced herself as Candace and took Samantha's coat. Samantha slipped off her boots and saw her stocking feet were now damp and stained blue from the lining of her overshoes. As she passed a trio of full-length mirrors, she caught a nasty glimpse of the rest of her. Her damp hair was quickly becoming a frizzy mess and her clothes bore telltale wrinkles from the cinched belt of her overcoat. Still, she adopted a confident air.

"Samantha is a guidance counselor, Candace," Meredith explained to the blonde. "And anyone knows what dedication it takes to be a teacher these days, especially with all the gangs and drugs and weapons. Why, not that long ago, there was a shooting at Samantha's school. You must have read about it in the paper. Samantha was right in front of the boy. She could have been killed!"

While Samantha was presented with dresses from the boutique's extensive collection, Meredith regaled Candace with several anecdotes about Samantha's achievements at Somerville Central, information that she could have gotten only from Chris. Suddenly Samantha was the darling of the hour, and while she was pleased at Meredith's turnaround, she found herself embarrassed by the frequent gushes of praise.

The dresses kept on coming, changing into a white parade of silk, satin, and taffeta as Chris's mother asked to see some of the bridal gowns. Many were lovely, but they were all too expensive.

Samantha tried on a few of the simpler styles, then one lavish gown with a long seed pearl train that Meredith admired, but as Candace fastened the last in a series of ornate buttons, Samantha decided she wasn't interested in any of the lacy, frilly hoopla. She wanted Chris, a beach, a bespectacled minister, and she didn't much care what anyone wore to their wedding, herself included.

She emerged from the fitting room and Meredith gasped. "Oh, Samantha, it was made for you! And with your hair up—"

She felt ridiculous. The full skirt billowed around her, rustling like an unfurled sail in the wind. There was enough fabric to make tents for a small African village. The row of buttons down the back ended in a huge bow. Yes, the dress could be stunning, provided the bride was twenty years old and had $10,000 to spend. Samantha pasted on a rubbery smile and allowed Meredith a few more moments of swooning. She had braved the blustery weather so she could bond with Chris's mother, and bond she would. There was plenty of time to burst the bubble later.

"We don't have to make a decision tonight," Samantha said, eager to remove the frothy contraption. "In fact, looking outside, perhaps we should all get home. There's quite a blizzard brewing out there."

There was an exchange of thank-yous, we'll-get-together-soons, and cool cheek kisses, then the trio disbanded. Meredith stepped gingerly into a waiting black Mercedes, the door already opened for her by a driver now faceless behind darkened windows. Samantha trudged along the snow-covered sidewalk until she reached her car. Once again she scraped her windshield and hoped her trip downtown had been worth it.

Exhausted and craving a cup of tea and warm pajamas, Samantha poured herself into her Toyota, wrestled with her mangled seat belt and lost. Nice and easy, she cautioned herself as she pulled out into the street.

The snow was falling steadily now, Cream of Wheat granules doing a maniacal dance outside her car. The wipers thwacked against the windshield, the motion and sound so hypnotic Samantha turned on her radio to help her stay awake. Her eyes stung and she struggled to keep them open.

There were few cars on the icy street, and Samantha knew Matthew had been right—she was nuts. Future mother-in-law be damned, there were some sacrifices that just shouldn't be made and ignoring personal safety to score points with the likes of Meredith Paxton was one of those. Her favorite radio station was playing hits from the '70s. The Doobie Brothers belted out "China Grove," and Samantha cranked up the volume, but not even the hard-driving guitar could prevent her from feeling woozy. It had been such a long day, and seeing Derek's father certainly hadn't helped. Her body ached for rest. Another few minutes and she would be home.

She shouted along with the Doobies but the song was over too soon and now James Taylor was lulling her into a near trance. Snapping awake, she rolled down the window an inch, but pelting snow blew into the car and the wind whipped her hair across her face. She cranked the window shut, glad at least that she'd refused Candace's offer of champagne, opting instead for mineral water. Now she wished she'd chosen coffee.

The car's heater switch was slid over to High and the fan was blowing full blast, but the windows were fogging up. With a bare hand, Samantha wiped the condensation away and turned up the collar on her coat. She was freezing. She cupped her hand over the vent. Cold air rushed through her fingers.

Five more minutes, she told herself. She trembled with cold, heard the wipers skid noisily across the icy windshield.

It wasn't until she passed the Boston Common and was driving down Charles Street that she realized something else was wrong. She checked her speedometer. Thirty-five miles per hour.

Gently, she applied a steady, controlled pressure to the brakes.

Nothing happened. The speedometer still registered thirty-five.

Samantha pumped the brake again, once, twice, a third time. Her foot hit the mat.

Ahead, an elderly couple was crossing the street, pulled by their German shepherd. At the sight of her approaching car, both froze. The dog broke free of its leash and barreled across the street.

Samantha leaned on her horn. She thought of her emergency brake and pulled. She shut off the ignition. The Toyota slid toward the couple. The German shepherd barked.

At the last moment, the couple began to run like crippled marionettes. Decibel for decibel the squeal of tires matched Samantha's scream. She cranked the steering wheel to the right and sent the Toyota crashing headlong into the front window of an antiques store.

41

IT WAS THE EERIE HUSH, the absolute nothingness that roused her from a dead sleep. Samantha listened for the hard edge of a Bon Jovi song, even the yabba-dabba-doo of an after-school *Flintstones* rerun, but rock stars and cartoon characters had vanished.

With her eyes adjusting to groggy consciousness, she stared at the varicose-veined ceiling, its net of capillaries and other swollen signs of water damage reminding her of where she was. Bouquets of flowers sat on the window ledge—yellow daisies, white roses, an extravagant spray of Stargazer lilies. Matthew, Chris, and Meredith, she guessed, relieved that there were no purple arrangements anywhere. A teddy bear nestled between the flowers. Beatrice?

Samantha's right leg was in traction. She raised her hand to touch a bandanna of gauze that encircled her head. It hurt to breathe. In the distant corners of her mind she heard a piercing squeal, the shatter of glass. Her skin prickled with the sensation of millions of pins. She jolted fully awake.

"You gave us quite a scare there, Mrs. Quinlan."

The voice startled her. At the foot of the bed, a white-coated doctor with a scrub pad of gray hair peered over her chart.

"But you're out of the woods now, as they say." He came around the bed and stood near her shoulder. "Of course, you won't be doing any ballroom dancing for a while. How are you feeling?"

"Like I've been in a garburetor." Even talking was painful. "What are the damages?"

"For starters, you've got a compound fracture of your right tibia and fibula. Happens when all your weight comes to bear on the leg that's locked on to the brake pedal. Your tongue's in rough shape—you bit down on it pretty hard. And to cap it off, six broken ribs and a collapsed lung. No air bag in your car?"

She shook her head.

"You'll be with us awhile."

The doctor explained what had been done during surgery. Her tibia was now the proud owner of a titanium nail and five screws. She sighed.

"There was an elderly couple. Crossing the street. Are they—?"

"Safe and sound. No worries there."

While the doctor returned his attention to her chart, Samantha looked over his shoulder. On the wall behind him, a brass-framed print depicted a clipper ship sailing the high seas. She supposed the picture was meant to lend a jaunty maritime air to the room, but instead it made her seasick. The room was cheerless, funereal, the walls painted an industrialized grayed-out turquoise that clashed with the royal blue in the picture. The pinch-pleated curtains were fashioned from a drab beige-and-turquoise check, the synthetic fabric sagging in places from too-frequent laundering. Indeed, the whole room seemed to sag.

"Are you sure I need to be here so long?" she asked as the doctor tightened a blood pressure cuff around her arm. "Hospitals are terrible places to get well."

The doctor smiled. "I didn't figure you for trying that dissatisfied-patient routine. Shame on you. We're keeping you for a couple of weeks, no matter how cranky you get. That leg's got to stay elevated, and we're still monitoring your internal injuries. Don't want your spleen dropping onto your kitchen floor, now, do you?" His smile broadened. "So get used to us." He released the tension on the cuff, the steady hiss of deflation echoing how she felt.

"Here. Maybe these'll cheer you up." Dr. Buchanan gathered greeting cards from her nightstand and handed them to her. "From your legion of fans."

While the doctor continued prodding and poking, Samantha opened the first card, its generic get-well-soon message in silver calligraphy above a dewy basket of tulips. It was signed simply: "The Staff." Tom had sent a Far Side card—two cows dancing on a coffee table while another pair watched in disgust from the sofa. The caption read: "I told you not to invite the Holsteins for drinks!" Tom had written in his cramped backhand, "Hurry up and get well. The herd is driving me crazy." In spite of her misery, Samantha smiled and could easily imagine Tom in the card shop, deliberating over the store's selection until he found the perfect card.

By the time Dr. Buchanan finished his examination, Samantha again felt her eyelids drooping. The black type on the physician's nametag began to blur. Her eyes closed, and as she succumbed to fatigue, she felt the doctor slip her get-well cards from her grasp and heard the curtains slide shut.

On the edge of sleep, she was haunted by hazy images, shadows of memories flitting in and out, irritating as houseflies. There was a flash of the accident, her foot pumping a useless brake, the sickening crunch of metal. She'd had the car serviced, hadn't she? Perhaps she'd only thought so, just like she'd thought she'd gone to the dentist for her checkup, until a toothache reminded her it had been two years. Then another flash, of her Toyota on that snowy night, parked on a Back Bay street, unguarded while she had tried on dresses she would never own. Plenty of time for someone to tamper with her brakes. Was that what happened?

Frank. It had to be. He knew how to fix cars. He would know how to unfix one. And if he found out she was still alive, what would he do?

In her mind a tug-of-war raged. She fought against bandages, pain, and the harness that trapped her leg. During brief moments closer to wakefulness, Samantha knew she wasn't moving at all. She was bound to her bed, not only by her injuries and the mechanics of technology but by a body that betrayed her.

42

He was in deep shit. He paced the shag carpet of room 104 and pressed a towel full of ice cubes against his jaw. It would be black and blue by morning, but he didn't think it was broken. For a wimp, the hotshot dentist threw a hell of a punch. Quick as a striking rattler, too. No way could he have seen it coming, especially not from him.

First it was the kid mouthing off about some dog, then the society boyfriend ragging on something fierce about her car. Frank had never been too interested in school, but he could still add two and two, and much as he tried, the only answer he kept getting that made any sense was, Run. Run and hide.

He'd stuffed his clothes into a sports bag and taken a last look around his apartment. For a split second he felt sad. He'd planned to spiff up the place, especially with Christmas coming. He would have bought a fake tree, strung some colored lights around his window, but now all that had turned to shit, too. He looked at his used TV, bought with his first paycheck, then turned his back and walked away. Abandoning his Trans Am—now that really hurt, but he couldn't risk being followed, so he left the keys in the cash drawer at the service station with a note: *Thanks, Lou. You been good to me.*

The sign outside the Seawinds Motel said: Bring Your Best Gal. There were three pickup trucks in the parking lot, and one black foreign job. Frank decided the motel was as good a place as any to hole up for a day or two. When he opened the door to the end unit, he thought that anyone who brought his best gal here had no intention of turning the lights on. Not exactly top security either, but it would have to do.

It was quiet outside, not many comings and goings, so for a while at least, Frank felt safe. Once more he scanned the angled parking spaces outside his window. Same three trucks, same black car. He closed the orange striped curtains, propped both pillows against the veneer headboard, stretched out on the bed, and clicked off the bedside lamp. In the blackness of the room, he shuddered, trying to make sense of everything, but it was no good. Since that night he'd driven to the Cape, he'd been feeling like someone had put a garter snake down the back of his shirt. Much as he tried to fight it, the creepy-crawlies were with him all the time now. The quiet, the darkness—neither were much help. He still couldn't think.

Frank flicked on the television.

Three stations came in clearly, and the rest were gray fuzz. His choices were a panel of women discussing menopause, a rerun of *The Brady Bunch,* and a movie. He picked the movie.

The television screen was black, except for a pair of mean-looking eyes glaring out of the darkness. Frank looked for the write-up in the TV listings. *The Spiral Staircase,* the blurb said. "Handicapped women find themselves the victims of a deranged killer in this classic suspense film. Starring George Brent and Dorothy McGuire." When Brent's hand clamped over the woman's mouth, Frank shut off the television. Why were the networks running this kind of crap so close to the holidays?

His sandpaper throat was dying for a beer, but he didn't dare go out. The ice inside the towel was melting, water dripping between his fingers, so he tossed the whole mess into the bathroom sink. He flopped down on the bed again. Then he laughed. He couldn't help himself. This was worse than jail, this room with the ugly brown corduroy bedspread and curtains the color of a rusty tailpipe. And he had run here because he didn't want to go to jail. It was damn funny.

Who was he kidding? He'd end up back in prison anyway, sooner or later. He had tried to make it on the outside, but he was like the oil slicks on the garage floor and the rest of the world was water. Like his old man, he didn't know how to do much except screw up. He rolled over on the bed and picked up the phone.

Moments later, he hung up, the knots in his stomach twice their size. *She's still in the hospital, thanks to you.*

His next call put him no further ahead. Like so many times lately, she wouldn't listen. Well, that was bad. *Unacceptable.*

The only thing he could do now was to make sure she got the message. The whole message. He had to make her listen.

43

"*Watch your back, Sam.*"

She cringed. The voice on the phone slithered across her skin.

"Ya gotta listen." Just like that night so long ago. He said it again. "Listen t'me."

"No," she said as forcefully as she could, the haze of painkillers stripping her voice of its power.

As she lowered the receiver she thought she heard "member-happy."

It didn't matter what Frank said. The police would catch him, throw him back in jail, and she and Matthew would be safe. Once again, she could turn her back on the past and look to a wonderful future. With Chris. About time.

She must have drifted off. The next voice she heard whispered, "I get her Jell-O." Followed by, "It's green. You can have it."

Matthew was beside her bed, peeking under the lid of her lunch tray. His boyish features seemed to have faded, the light dusting of freckles, the long eyelashes overshadowed by a determined jaw and serious green eyes.

Chris was holding her hand. "Sleeping Beauty awakens."

"More like Sleeping Ugly, I bet," she replied. "Do I look as bad as I feel?"

"Your hair could use a shampoo, Mom."

"Is that what you look like without makeup?"

"Thanks a lot, you two."

Chris laughed and brushed a light kiss on her lips, his mouth landing fuzzily, barely penetrating the numbing fog surrounding her.

She reached for the small hand mirror on her bedside table, looked at her image, and moaned.

"You look fine, Samantha."

"I look like Cochise," she said, fingering the layers of gauze that wrapped around her forehead. "It's no use." She handed the mirror to Matthew with a disgusted wave. "Break it to me gently, Chris. Is Georgina MacPherson starting to appeal to you more these days?"

He looked up at the ceiling and thoughtfully scratched his head. She swatted his arm. "Traitor. And you," she said, pointing at Matthew, "looming over my green Jell-O like a starving vulture. Shame."

"Sorry, Mom." He held out a pink wicker basket. "Mrs. Bea sent these."

"What's in it?"

"Girl stuff," Matthew and Chris said together.

There was an assortment of bath products—body lotion, shampoo, conditioner, bubble bath—and Beatrice had even knit a pair of pink slippers. Samantha smiled, knowing the woman's feet were always cold. Chris set the basket on top of a two-drawer cabinet opposite the bed.

"She would have come with us, Mom, but her phlebitis is acting up again."

"Well, be sure to thank her for me, and for the cute teddy bear, too."

"That one? Mrs. Bea didn't send that. It's from Mr. L."

She should have known. When they were teenagers, she and Scott frequently double-dated with Tom and his girlfriend of the week; a favorite outing was a Saturday afternoon at an amusement park in Agawam, where, try as they might, the guys could never snag the large stuffed animals the girls coveted.

"Mr. L.'s still sick—strep throat, I think—so he says he'll visit when he's not contagious. And Mom? Frank phoned. And I did a dumb thing. I told him you were here. Well, not here exactly. But in the hospital."

"He phoned here too, Matthew." She saw the alarm on her son's face, Chris's too. "Kept saying I had to listen to him. Which I didn't, of course. I can't believe the police haven't picked him up yet. What are they waiting for?"

Chris glanced at Matthew. "They can't find him."

"What?"

"He's ditched his car, quit his job, cleared the clothes out of his apartment. He's gone."

"The phone call!" She struggled to sit upright, but excruciating pain across her abdomen made her cry out. "We've got to tell the police," she said between gasps. "They can get phone records, find out where he was calling from—"

"They've got that information, Samantha," Chris said, gently easing her back onto the bed. "Everyone's been alerted. The hospital's posting a security guy to watch your room. And the doctors have done their damnedest to keep the police out of here so you could recuperate, and I intend to see that continues. You don't need to worry about Frank. They'll catch him, Samantha. Remember, you told me he's not that smart."

And you told me we don't know what he's learned in jail.

Chris reached for her hands with both of his, and it was then that she noticed the knuckles on his right hand, blackened and swollen.

"What in God's name?"

"Chris had a collision too, Mom. With Frank's face."

She sighed. "You didn't."

"'Fraid so."

"My two shining knights," she said. "You're both out of your minds. You know that?"

They turned the conversation to school trivia—Tom's difficulty in casting the lead for the spring musical, Jenny's new love conquest, the latest Ehrhart tantrum. Eventually sensing her fatigue, Matthew and Chris decided to leave.

"Mother said she might stop by after dinner," Chris said. "I'll have the doctor on standby with a sedative."

"All I do is sleep," she complained.

"You should eat something, Mom."

Samantha smiled at the role reversal. "I know. My girlish figure is turning into a boyish figure."

Amid kisses and good-byes, Samantha promised to eat, and while Chris and Matthew were at the movies and having pizza, she'd have plenty to distract her—crossword puzzles, a deck of cards, three paperback mysteries. Worries about Frank wouldn't enter her mind, she assured them.

She was on her fifth round of solitaire when a "Hi, Mrs. Q." interrupted her game. She looked up to find Tony Puglia at the foot of her bed.

"This is a surprise, Tony," she said, staring down her white cast at the boy who followed her everywhere. Now here he was again, wearing that same hangdog look, and with her broken leg and other injuries, there was no getting away.

"Nurse says I can only stay five minutes. You need your rest."

She owed the nurse a box of chocolates. "It's nice of you to drop by. How're things?" Instantly she regretted the question, knowing Tony would probably tell her.

"Pretty okay, I guess. Mr. Lundstrom gave me a part in the play. I'm gonna be a mad scientist, you know, like in *Young Frankenstein*. I get to wear a curly wig, lab coat, these big glasses. Should be cool."

Just like that, Tony stopped talking. Samantha waited but there was only dead air. "Tony, is something wrong?"

"Your car, Mrs. Q.," he wailed, gesturing frantically. "I don't get it. Everyone's saying someone messed with it. But I worked on it myself. Remember?"

"*You* worked on it?"

"Checked all the fluid levels, flushed your antifreeze, put new stuff in. Your brakes, the pads, all that was fine. There's no way that car should have been unsafe. I told the police that, too."

Samantha forced herself to breathe slowly. "Tony." She paused, the boy clearly upset. "Did anyone else work on my car besides you?"

"No. Just me. It was kind of like a test, you know, to see if we knew our stuff. Mr. Petrella checked the work himself."

44

THOUGH SHE STILL HAD little appetite, Samantha welcomed the sound of squeaky casters rolling down the hallway. Food, if not delicious, was at least a diversion in this place where one day was exactly like the one before it. For at least a moment, she could pretend that her assembly-line meal had been flown in from Paris on the Concorde by a five-star Michelin chef.

A plump Filipina wearing a pastel smock set Samantha's tray on her swivel table. She raised the bed to a sitting position. "Feeling better after your nap, Mrs. Quinlan?"

"Nap? How long was I out?"

"Two hours anyway."

She must have fallen asleep after Tony's visit, or maybe even during it. She had napped this morning, too. "Why am I so tired?" To her own ears she sounded mush-mouthed, like someone doing a bad Bogart impersonation.

"You were in a serious accident, Mrs. Quinlan. Your body's trying to tell you something. Listen to it."

Samantha nodded. "I like your pin."

Affixed to the girl's collar was the head of a plastic Santa.

When she tugged on a short string, Santa's nose and cheeks lit up. "It's a big hit down in Pediatrics."

"I wonder if I'll get home in time for my son's birthday."

"When is it?"

"The tenth."

"What does your doctor say?"

"I believe his exact words were 'no way in hell.' "

"Maybe if you get a little stronger," the girl said, trying to sound hopeful. "You'll feel better after you've eaten something."

Samantha hoped so. The sluggish, dazed feeling alarmed her. Had the accident done more damage than the doctor was telling her? Perhaps Chris and Matthew were hiding the truth from her, too. She had suffered a recussion, the doctor had said. Upon impact, her brain had sloshed forward then sharply back against her skull. There was permanent damage, she decided, and no one wanted to tell her.

Great. Stupor, and now paranoia. She could be an entire chapter in a medical textbook. Samantha knew the nurse was right. She needed to eat.

The chicken was anemic, the vegetables soggy and lukewarm. The potatoes had the consistency of slurried wallpaper paste, but she dug in anyway, chasing down bland mouthfuls with gulps of tepid apple juice.

"Michelin star, my behind," she grumbled. "More like Michelin tires."

She set her cutlery on the tray and glanced self-consciously into the hallway. "Yes, I'm afraid so, Doctor. In addition to being whacked-out and paranoid, the patient in 602 is talking to herself."

"Did you say something, Samantha?"

Meredith Paxton, in one of her signature pale outfits, this one a winter white wool dress with matching coat, entered the room.

Oh fine, Samantha thought. Now Chris's mother has heard me

talking to myself and is probably reserving me a spot on the goony-bird branch of the Paxton family tree.

"Hi—" The word hung awkwardly in the stale air, Samantha still not sure how she should address the woman. "Chris mentioned you might be stopping by."

Meredith removed her coat and, seeing no place to hang it, draped it across the blankets at Samantha's feet. She pulled a lurid orange plastic chair alongside the bed and sat down. Samantha raised herself on her elbows and tried to get comfortable, but no matter what she did, some part of her ached or stabbed or itched. She was bone-tired too, and hoped Meredith wouldn't stay long. Judging from the woman's stiff posture and the tentative way she perched on the edge of the chair, Samantha guessed the visit would be brief.

"I hope you're eating," Meredith said, glancing over at the supper tray.

"Doing my best, given the quality of the cuisine. I hoped that eating would help me get my strength back, but so far, it's not working. I feel wobbly and lethargic most of the time, but my doctor says there aren't any pills for feeling just plain rotten."

Meredith stared at Samantha but she didn't reply. While the woman appeared to be listening, Samantha had long ago learned to recognize the look of someone whose mind was elsewhere.

"And how are things with you?" she asked, not knowing what else to say.

Meredith's smile was pinched, and quickly disappeared.

Pins and needles ran the length of Samantha's arm and she struggled to prop pillows behind her. Meredith made no move to help.

"Candace certainly had some beautiful dresses in her store," Samantha said in a rush of garbled *s* sounds. "Though it's hard for me to believe people can spend so much money on a dress they'll only wear once. I guess I—" She stopped herself, embarrassed at her babbling and unable to remove her gaze from Meredith's quizzical stare. Again it came, the *almost* smile.

"This is not going to work," Meredith said simply, her long, elegant fingers resting calmly on the soft leather clutch in her lap. "It isn't right."

"The hospital, you mean? The doctor says I should be able to go home in a few weeks. He—"

"No, Samantha. Not the hospital. You. And Christopher. I tried. I honestly tried. For my son's sake. But I just cannot accept this marriage."

Samantha sat bolt upright. Pain shot across her abdomen. "You're not serious."

"I'm deadly serious. You are not the right woman for my son."

"Isn't that for Chris to decide?"

"Perhaps. Perhaps not."

"I love your son, Meredith. You can't just wish me away."

"Are you so sure of that?" Meredith arched a perfectly tweezed brow, her smile widening.

Samantha watched, transfixed, as the slender fingers, no longer elegant but predatory, reached inside the leather bag.

45

He didn't take a chance with the elevator, couldn't risk that someone might recognize him from the picture in the paper, even though the thing was years old. He headed for the stairs and looked quickly around, but no one was watching him. Lucky for him, too, that the ditzy dame at the reception desk looked as if she'd never watched the news or read a paper in her life. Without blinking she gave him Sam's room number and by the time she told him that visiting hours would be over in ten minutes, she was talking to his back.

He took the stairs slowly, keeping his head down. His heart thudded as he approached the doors at the top of each landing, half-expecting the cops to crash through and cuff him. At the landing to the third floor, he stopped to rest, pissed that he wasn't in better shape. Then again, he was pissed at so many things, many he still didn't understand. This was the worst, not knowing, not getting it. At least he knew one thing he had to do, and that was to force Sam to listen. Force was one thing he did know a lot about.

He regained his breath and started up the stairs again, and with each footstep came the chant in his head.

She will listen. I'll make her listen. She's gotta listen.

As he neared the sixth-floor landing, a crawly feeling came over him—the snake was down his shirt again. He tried to shake it off, tried to figure out why, but he didn't have time.

There was a glimpse of white, then an arm shot forward. Instinctively, his hand went for his chest and it collided with the handle of a knife. The blade, though, was invisible, buried somewhere under his jacket. He looked up, past the white coat now splattered with red, and stared at the face.

In that last moment, Frank felt a peculiar sense of satisfaction. He had put the pieces together. He finally got it.

46

TERESA DELACRUZ NEEDED to drop thirty pounds. Her love affair with fast food was becoming an all-out orgy. Drive-through windows en route to and from work poised like snipers ready to attack her disappearing waistline. She couldn't remember the last meal she'd eaten that wasn't resting on her lap in a box or bag; it had to have been six months ago. June. The last time she'd been on a date was in June, too.

Now she was a member of the Elasticized Waistband Brigade, and her nursing smocks too closely resembled maternity wear. The weight-loss group she joined encouraged goal-setting. Last week she had successfully gone the entire seven nights without any junk food while watching television. This week's resolution was twofold: up the veggie intake to five a day and increase physical activity.

The vegetable thing she could do, but exercise was one thing Teresa hated. She didn't like sweating, nor did she enjoy the heart-pounding feeling of breathlessness that accompanied the free aerobic class she'd taken when her neighborhood health club was recruiting new members. So the concessions she made to becoming fit were to park her car in a remote corner of the hospital's lot, and to take the stairs instead of the elevator.

It had been a long day, and she was eager to get home even though it meant watching *Law and Order* reruns alone and munching on celery instead of potato chips. Her crepe soles made little mouse squeaks on the tile as she headed toward the door leading to the stairs. The shoes were on their last life. There wasn't much arch support left. Of course Teresa knew if she were a few pounds or thirty lighter, her feet wouldn't hurt so much, but that was no consolation tonight. On the plus side, she was going down the stairs, not climbing up.

At first, the door to the stairwell hardly budged. It wasn't locked, more like something was blocking it from the other side. Teresa was tempted to give up and go back to the elevator, but the rounded silhouette she'd seen earlier in the washroom mirror kept her shoving at the door. A few more firm nudges widened the gap enough for Teresa to see the cause of the obstruction: a man's body, lying in a puddle of congealed, brownish blood.

"She wanted to pay you?" Tom's voice at the other end of the phone was aghast. "What did you do? What did you say?"

Samantha knew it was late, but Meredith Paxton's visit had left her so on edge that she couldn't sleep, even though before the woman's visit she had wanted nothing more. She had awakened Tom, but at his insistence, she had long since gotten over feeling guilty for leaning on her friend at all hours. "I told her no dice, of course."

"I knew the woman was no good. Sometimes you can just tell, you know? How did she react?"

"She was perfectly awful. Threatened to disown Chris, leave him with no inheritance if he married me."

"Jesus. Is it a ton of money, Samantha? Would Chris care?"

"I don't know how many zeroes, exactly, but quite a few. And while I don't think Chris cares much about it, Meredith says he would always resent me if I made him give up what was rightfully his. Nice mess, huh? Here I thought she was starting to like me, but it was all show."

"Didn't I tell you she was trouble?" Tom said again. "So what are you going to do? Tell Chris?"

"And be the cause of a family feud? Can I really live with myself if I force Chris to choose between me and his inheritance?"

"Well, if you're not going to take the cash and run, and you're not going to tell Chris . . ."

She sighed. "I know. What other options are there? Keep trying to get Meredith to like me? Or just keep on seeing Chris and pretend nothing has happened. Maybe that'll force Meredith's hand so she'll have to follow through on her threat and Chris will see his mother for what she is."

"A manipulative bitch."

"Is burying one's head in the sand still frowned upon?"

"Not tonight, it's not," Tom said kindly. "You've got to get well. Making important decisions that will affect the rest of your life shouldn't be handled from a hospital bed. Doc Lundstrom's advice? Get some sleep and forget about the old bat."

"I don't know if that's possible. There's a lot of commotion coming from down the hall, but I'll try."

"It'll all work out, Samantha," Tom said. "If you and Chris were meant to be together, it'll all work out. By the way, I'm almost over my cold. I'll be in to visit soon. Night."

"Thanks, Tom. For everything."

She hung up, no further ahead than when she'd called her friend, but grateful as always for his empathetic ear. She looked over at the bouquet of pink lilies, props for a doting future mother-in-law role that Meredith was playing. The water in the vase had turned murky, the elaborate dotted blooms beginning to fade. Though Samantha's eyes grew heavy, her brain wrestled for solutions to this latest problem. Regardless of her eventual decision, someone was going to get hurt.

How much easier it would have been if I'd died in the accident. And cheaper, too. Was that how Meredith saw it?

She was suddenly struck by the black humor of it all. Frank Ventresca, who'd never made a success of anything in his miserable life, couldn't even succeed in killing her.

You messed up again, Frank. What else is new?

Though Samantha tried to take Tom's advice and forget about Meredith, her visit, and the woman's nasty little checkbook, she couldn't, and soon, her old nemesis insomnia was back. She was plagued well into the night with troubling thoughts and an inexplicable creeping dread that coiled around her and squeezed. Minutes later, footsteps sounded in the hall outside her room, and someone gently closed her door. The commotion down the hall was constant now, the cacophony of voices making sleep impossible.

What was going on?

47

SHE'D FALLEN ASLEEP WITH the reading light on. Now the bedside clock read 2:30. Outside, huge flakes of snow punctuated the blackness, some so large Samantha could see their six points clearly from where she lay. In her mind, she pictured downtown Boston decorated for Christmas, a photographer's delight with wreaths, bells, colored lights, and nativity scenes at every turn. She was desperate to be home, and wished fervently that she could prepare for the season by decorating her own apartment. She wanted to shop for presents, help the student council trim the tree in the school's entrance hall, pore through cookbooks with Beatrice and spend a Saturday making cookies. Those things, she was certain, would heal her, and quickly.

No way in hell, her doctor had said three times now.

She looked up. The water-veined ceiling had developed some new lines, and with some creative leeway, Samantha could make out the rudimentary tracing of a long, bony claw, its five jagged tentacles fanning out ominously over her bed.

For her imagination to be working overtime like this proved that she was bored silly.

Though still feeling sluggish and washed-out, Samantha knew there was no point in trying to sleep. There was whispering outside her door, unusual in a place that was generally morgue-quiet at night. Then, from the hallway, a narrow shaft of pale yellow light stretched across the foot of her bed. Someone had cracked open her door. More whispering.

"You can come in," she said quietly. "I'm awake."

It was a doctor, a young woman Samantha had never seen before. Her hands were jammed into the pockets of her lab coat.

"Mrs. Quinlan, I'm Dr. Knapp. Have you managed to sleep at all tonight?"

"I dozed for a while, I think, but it's been so noisy. What's going on?"

"We've had a . . . a bit of a problem. There's a police officer in the hallway who'd like to ask you a few questions. Are you up to it?"

"Police?"

"I'll let the officer explain."

Sergeant Minardi's olive skin, black hair, and naturally red lips gave her the look of an exotic cover girl.

"Mrs. Quinlan," the doctor said after introductions were made, "if you get tired, or don't feel you're up to this, the sergeant will understand." She shot the officer a warning look and added, "Not too long, please."

Sergeant Minardi pulled up a chair and sat down. Samantha raised the back of her bed, wondering what could have happened and whether the other patients on the floor were being awakened for questioning as well.

"Mrs. Quinlan, you had issued a restraining order against a Mr. Frank Ventresca, is that right?"

"Yes."

"He was stalking you, harassing your son?"

"He seemed to show up everywhere. And there were phone calls, flowers . . . he even phoned me here. What's all this about?"

"He knew you were in the hospital?" Minardi asked.

"My son inadvertently let it slip when Frank called the house. I think Frank rigged my car somehow, did something to the brakes. That's how I ended up like this."

Again she heard the slushy quality of her speech, the words laboring through a mouthful of fur. The sergeant, too, was eyeing her strangely.

"Frank's a mechanic," Samantha added stupidly.

For what felt like the hundredth time, she was asked to recount her history with Frank. Robotically she retold the story, her alien voice sounding like a poor-quality recording. The sergeant met Samantha's eyes openly, not with embarrassment, or curiosity, or unspoken accusation and blame, but with a quiet understanding and compassion.

You've been there, Samantha knew instinctively. *It takes one to know one.*

Eventually it was Minardi's turn to speak. "We're still checking your car, Mrs. Quinlan. Curiously, we didn't find a single trace of Frank Ventresca anywhere on the vehicle. Not inside it, not underneath it. Not a single hair, not a single print."

"He wore a hat, gloves," Samantha protested. She remembered Chris's warning and said, "Who knows what tricks he's learned after fifteen years in jail? And after my accident, he disappeared. Left his job, his apartment. Would an innocent person do that? Just disappear?"

"We found him, Mrs. Quinlan. Earlier tonight."

"You did? Well then, this should be interesting. I can imagine the wild stories he concoc— Where was he?"

"Actually, he was here. Seems he was on his way to see you."

"And you stopped him? How did you know he'd—?"

"Not us, Mrs. Quinlan. Frank Ventresca met up with someone else in the stairwell, just down the hall from here . . ."

Samantha heard the hesitancy in the sergeant's voice.

"You haven't got him, have you," Samantha said, her faint hope dwindling. "He escaped. He's given everybody the slip. Again."

There was a long pause, the hospital corridors once again silent as a tomb.

The sergeant pursed her lips. At length she breathed deeply and said, "Frank Ventresca has escaped, Mrs. Quinlan. Permanently. A few hours ago, someone killed him."

48

FRANK VENTRESCA. DEAD. She couldn't believe it.

Samantha repeated the three words often. *Frank is dead.* They made no more sense to her now than they had when she first heard them. Who would want to kill Frank?

A dozen scenarios flickered through her mind. A prison crony, someone Frank had wronged while in jail, seemed likeliest. Drug deal gone wrong, perhaps. She thought of the black pills she'd found in Matthew's locker just over a month ago. Could there be a connection?

At 5:30 Dr. Knapp poked her head in and asked Samantha if she was all right. Did she want a sedative? Samantha refused. Yes, she wanted a decent few hours' sleep, but not if it meant more of that groggy, drugged-out feeling that seemed to be with her constantly now. She would let her body find its own rhythm.

More disturbing than the idea of Frank's slain body lying not more than a hundred feet away was the thought of what might have happened had he lived. Another few minutes, a few silent footsteps, and he would have been in her room. For what? Would she have had to endure that hot stale breath, those grimy hands, his guttural cry of release while he raped her again? Or was he at the hospital for another reason—to kill her?

She uttered the phrase aloud. "Frank is dead." There should be some relief, some peace, she thought. His death should mean an end to the nightmares, and to those times when Chris's touch, no matter how gentle, would cause an involuntary shudder of fear. She wouldn't need to be afraid for Matthew's safety any longer either. Frank would pay no more surprise visits to the arcade, bring no more pizzas to the house.

The man from Mars was dead, but Samantha took no comfort in it. She had wished Frank gone, but not this way. Someone had killed him, and she needed to know why.

She was glad now she'd refused the sedative. Her mind was besieged by fragmented sentences, jumbled syllables coming as rapid as machine-gun fire. If she could just slow them down, take control and rein them in, perhaps somewhere in the flotsam, something might hold together and make sense. She forced one deep breath, another, then closed her eyes and waited.

Soon a voice came. It was Matthew's.

If Frank ever tries to hurt you again, I'll kill him.

When the blackness outside her window transformed into a pearl gray dawn, Samantha called home. Matthew was just waking up.

"Are you coming to the hospital today?"

She heard a big yawn. "Sure, Mom. Why?"

She found herself stalling. "In the end-table drawer, beside the couch—my notebook is there. Can you bring it with you? You know the one?"

"Coil-bound? Red?"

"Yes. Are you eating all right?"

"Better than ever. Mr. L.'s taking me for breakfast this morning. Maybe he'll spring for steak and eggs."

"I suddenly feel very unneeded."

"Ah, come on, Mom," Matthew said, sounding more alert, "no one defrosts a TV dinner like you."

"I miss you too," she kidded. "And don't forget the damn book."

Then, choosing her words carefully, Samantha told Matthew what had happened to Frank. She didn't know what reaction she was expecting, but Matthew had plenty to say.

"He was vermin, Mom. The lowest of the low. If he was dirt on the bottom of my shoes, I'd burn the shoes."

"Matthew—"

"I'm serious, Mom. Now he can't hurt you anymore, and he won't be trying to play Daddy with me."

"But he was murdered, Matthew. Stabbed. I don't wish that on anyone. Not even Frank."

Her son's final words before hanging up sent an icy blade of fear through her.

"I guess that's where we're different, Mom. Me? I'm glad he's dead."

49

THE DAY WAS ENDLESS, the hospital bed a cage, and Samantha was trapped in it. She was down to her last three crossword puzzles and she had twenty-four pages left in a second-hand Agatha Christie paperback before she would discover the truth about the strange goings-on at Bertram's Hotel. Her mind flipped between thinking of a seven-letter word for "leafstalk" and racing to solve the clues before Miss Marple, but concentration on either diversion eluded her. The hard-of-hearing patient across the hall had his TV cranked up full blast, so Samantha was treated first to a sitcom's canned laughter, then the gunfire and horse whinnies of a Saturday-afternoon western.

Her lack of concentration couldn't be blamed solely on her neighbor's television. Samantha wanted her notebook, more than anything hoping that somewhere in the aimless wandering of pen on paper, something she'd written in the last months would leap off the page and provide her with some answers.

Lunch came and went, a forgettable puréed soup of undetermined origin and something called fish Creole, which no self-respecting Creole would eat. Samantha's sweet tooth was no longer satisfied with mixed fruit, yogurt, and ice cream. Somewhere out there was a world of cheesecake, cream puffs, and chocolate, and all she wanted was her fair share.

By the time Matthew showed up in the late afternoon, Samantha was ready to lunge at him, her broken leg be damned. He set her spiral-bound book on the bedside table, hesitated a moment, then planted an awkward kiss on her cheek.

"Can't stay long, Mom. Mr. L.'s waiting downstairs. Gave me a ride over, but he's still coughing so he didn't come up. Sent you this, though." Matthew handed her a large Starbucks cup, still warm to the touch. "One tall espresso roast."

"Yes!" cried Samantha. "I knew I had a guardian angel."

"I smuggled it past the caffeine police," Matthew said, inclining his head toward the door. He held up gloved hands and whispered, "But if you get nailed for it, you're on your own. My prints aren't on that cup."

"Your loyalty is touching. Tell Tom thanks, and that I'm nominating him for sainthood. And what's with that cold of his? It's sure hanging on. He should start popping the echinacea."

"I'll tell him. Mom? You feeling okay?"

"I will be after I drink this coffee." She pulled back the plastic tab on the lid and took a sip.

"You look . . . tired."

"Well, after everything last night— I'm fine. Really. Maybe you better run, if Tom's waiting."

Any other time she would have been reluctant to see Matthew leave, but the sight of her notebook was mesmerizing her like the swaying pendulum of a clock.

Matthew checked his watch. "I've got a little time yet. I got the impression Mr. L. wanted a few minutes with one of the nurses he spotted in the coffee shop."

Samantha smiled. "That's our Tom." Then she grew serious.

"Matthew? What you said last night. About Frank?"

For a moment, Matthew stared at the floor. A rosy flush spread across his cheeks. "Yeah, I know," he said, looking back up at her. "I've been thinking about it, too. And maybe it wasn't a nice thing to say, but I can't help it, Mom. Frank is dead and I'm not sorry. With him gone, our problems are over. Finished."

Chris's visit later that night was brief as well. Samantha had been riffling through her notebook when he arrived, and the sight of him brought Meredith's visit back full force. This was the man she was supposed to leave. The one she wasn't good enough for.

His kiss landed softly on her mouth and paused there. The faint woodsy smell of his aftershave made her want to burrow closer. How long had it been since she had nestled in the crook of his arm, shared whispers in the dark? She knew she could never leave him, that come what may, Meredith Paxton was in for a fight.

"I bear gifts. Well, one, anyway." It was a bottle of her favorite perfume, Ralph Lauren's Romance. "Maybe you'll feel more like your former self if you spray a little on." He hoisted himself onto the edge of the bed and kissed the hollow of her throat. "And if it doesn't work for you, it'll at least do wonders for me. God, I miss you."

"Likewise," she said, giggling at how his lips tickled. She shoved him away playfully. "But you're the wrong kind of doctor. I want someone to tell me I'm ready to go home. Matthew's birthday is on Wednesday. I need to get a present."

He eyed her curiously. "I don't think you're quite ready to go home, Samantha."

She didn't blame him for staring. She knew she wouldn't win any beauty contests. The gauze had been removed late in the afternoon and now a blazing purple goose egg with a few greenish patches decorated her forehead over her right eye. "You've got yourself a real bargain, haven't you, Dr. Paxton? A little makeup, a wheelchair, and I'll be a most memorable bride. Maybe our wedding guests can sign my cast."

There was a glimmer of a smile, but the puzzled stare persisted. "Samantha, are you feeling all right?"

Actually, she wasn't. Something she'd eaten for supper wasn't agreeing with her. It had been another nondescript meal—Chinese beef and broccoli with steamed white rice, tomato soup, chocolate pudding. Her neck was achy, and though she knew the temperature in the room was comfortable, she was sweating and her skin was clammy. Earlier she had turned off her reading lamp, but the overhead fixture was still on, and the light from it was piercing her eyes. "I've been better," she admitted, then added, "I'm sorry."

He took both her hands. "What on earth for?"

"To put it plainly, I'm bad luck. Maybe you deserve better. Any second thoughts? Now's your chance." Again she heard her syllables run together. Was she that tired?

"It'll take a lot more than your purple face and a crazy old ex-con to get rid of me. Besides, Frank is . . . gone now, so it's smooth sailing for us."

Here's another one who thinks so, Samantha mused. Why couldn't she be so sure?

"Maybe I should call for a nurse," Chris said. "Your pupils are dilated and you seem, well, kind of stoned."

"No, Chris, it's okay. I always seem to get this way at night. I must be overtired. And I was up most of last night, with the noise, then the police . . . Maybe I just need to rest."

He released her hands. "I'll leave you, then. Be by tomorrow." He slid off the bed and kissed her again, looking for a long time into her eyes. "Take care, my girl," he said. "I love you."

"Love you too," she murmured. "And Chris? Can you turn off the light on your way out?"

With the room now bathed in darkness, her light-sensitive eyes felt somewhat better. She tucked the blankets under her chin, the perspiration-soaked sheets and pajamas making her shiver. *I've felt better* was an understatement, she knew. Samantha was sick, but she wouldn't call for a nurse. She wanted to go home. Getting the hospital staff up in arms over a flu bug she'd probably picked up from some kid at school via Matthew wouldn't put her any closer to her apartment and Chris in time for the holidays.

She would rest up today and tomorrow. By Monday, she would be as good as new.

50

MATTHEW'S FIRST CLASS OF the day was music and he was tempted to not show up, except Mr. L. would probably tell his mom and get her all worried. Even worse, he might drive over to Mrs. Bea's during a spare period and discover Matthew wasn't sick at all. So he reported to class, took his clarinet case from the shelf in the storage room, and headed to his usual seat in the front row on stage, managing a smile for Kelly, who smiled back. The band warmed up with "Hello, Dolly!" but Matthew's mind wasn't on the music. Twice he'd missed playing the F sharp and the atypical mistake drew a stern look from Tom.

After class Matthew beetled down the aisle of the auditorium before Tom could ask any questions. He grabbed his jacket and gloves from his locker and headed home. This would be the first time he had ever skipped school, and he didn't feel good about it. Still, it had to be done, and if there were consequences, he would just have to deal with them later.

Running most of the way, Matthew was breathless by the time he reached Mrs. Bea's front gate. He flipped the metal latch, careful not to make noise, and he closed it quietly too. That was the funny thing about Mrs. Bea—she complained her hearing wasn't what it used to be, yet Matthew knew she could hear how many times he hit the Snooze button on his alarm in the morning. He tiptoed up the back stairs. The new lock Tom had installed was a foreboding tempered-steel contraption, but as Matthew inserted his key, he thought a pro could probably get past it in three minutes, max. When he got inside, he didn't hear Mrs. Bea calling to him, nor did the phone ring, so he concluded his return home had gone unnoticed.

In his bedroom, tucked under some folders in his desk drawer, were the photocopied pages from his mother's journal.

Because their apartment was so small, there weren't many places to run, hide, or be alone, so mother and son adopted strict rules about privacy. The parameters were clear—here's where you keep your stuff, here's where I keep my stuff. Hands off.

Yet here he was, intent on prying again into his mother's private thoughts, and he couldn't afford to waste valuable time feeling ashamed. He had been up most of the night, uneasy about what he had learned but unable to pinpoint why. Yet there was something in these pages he needed to know. He was sure of it. Once more, he began to read.

He skimmed information about his mother's dates with Chris, but he was interested in what was written about Coach Ehrhart and Mr. Petrella. Both men were making life hell for her at work, with Ehrhart growling at her on a daily basis. Matthew didn't have Ehrhart for phys. ed., but some of his friends did, and their complaints were all the same. Mean as a snake. An asshole. A sadist. Jeff Filion, who sized up people pretty accurately, was sure Ehrhart was wired on something. Still, wired or not, the coach wouldn't come after his mom just because she suggested one of his athletes needed to dry out somewhere. He couldn't be that much of a wingnut. Likewise, he wouldn't go to such extremes just to stick up for his friend Petrella.

What about that middle-aged hormone? Petrella, according to the journal, had once made a pass at his mom. Now the guy was out of a job, his marriage was a bust, and he was just dumb enough to think that none of it was his fault. Easier to blame someone else. Like Matthew's mom. He'd threatened her, too.

. . . people's lives falling apart. Don't you feel responsible? How'd you like someone poking around in your business?

Words uttered by a man on the edge. Or had he already slipped over it?

Another page of the journal was dated the day after Derek Townsend's suicide. The space was almost equally divided between the events in the cafeteria and the locker search afterwards, during which the appearance of ten black pills ripped a hole in the trust his mother once had in him. One sentence, written in his mother's neat, feminine hand, stood out above the others.

Is Matthew lying?

It still hurt, that lapse in trust, but Matthew had to get past it. His mom needed him now. He was sure of it. The answer to everything was right in front of him, on these photocopied pages. If only he could make the connection.

51

THE FOLLOWING MORNING, Samantha felt marginally better. Her neck was less stiff, and the sun's rays streaming through the window weren't punishing her eyes. A nurse had helped her into a fresh pair of pajamas and washed her hair. She'd eaten a substantial breakfast—cereal, orange juice, a buttered English muffin, a hard-boiled egg, decaf tea—but she still felt a long way from being her old self.

You seem . . . kind of stoned.

Perhaps Chris hadn't chosen the most diplomatic words, but his assessment was bang-on. Samantha felt permanently hungover, the car accident turning into the bender to end all benders. Her doctor assured her there had been no serious trauma to the head, so why wasn't she feeling better?

Another nurse came for Samantha's breakfast tray, made small talk about the cold weather and said she was glad to see Samantha was eating.

"Figure if I score points for good behavior, I can go home," Samantha said.

The look the nurse gave her said it all.

"Yeah, I know. No way in hell."

Samantha adjusted her pillows, clicked on her reading lamp, and began leafing through the pages again, her written record of the events of the past few months no more enlightening now than they'd been last night.

Perhaps a different approach. She dated the top of a fresh page and, centered in capitals, she printed WHO TAMPERED WITH MY CAR? Underneath, at the margin, she wrote OPPORTUNITY.

She had racked up the car last Monday, the same day that Derek's father had paid her a surprise visit at school. He had been distraught and more than a little tipsy, leaning against the Toyota. How had he known which car was hers? Was it even conceivable that, in broad daylight, he could have shimmied under the chassis to commit sabotage?

Risky, but she supposed it was possible. The staff parking lot was behind the school, shielded on three sides by the U-formation of the five-story building. Samantha remembered Ehrhart's complaints about the wiseass who twice this year alone had let the air out of his tires. As yet, the culprit hadn't been caught, nor had the person who'd put sugar in Halloran's gas tank. The teachers' cars, invisible from the street, were easy targets, and that day, Samantha had parked up against the building, the hulking structure enshrouding her car in shadow. It had been blustery, so anyone going to a car would be hurrying, eyes squinting through the blowing snow and focused on his own vehicle, not on anything else.

She thought Townsend's first name was John, if her memory of Derek's file was accurate, so she wrote that down beside OPPORTUNITY. Almost immediately, she added three question marks, thinking about the other events before and after her accident.

The drugs showed up in Matthew's locker the day Derek died. Not Townsend's doing. And the dead dog in Chatham? How could she reasonably connect John Townsend to that?

Maybe she was coming at this all wrong; maybe her accident and the other occurrences weren't related at all. Determined to keep an open mind, she put brackets around the question marks.

At once she was struck by another possibility: Tony Puglia. He knew about cars and had worked on hers. She tried to imagine saucer-eyed, lovesick Tony, perhaps angry about being rebuffed by her, his emotions mounting until he felt compelled to teach her a lesson she wouldn't forget. In these modern times, if a woman plotted murder to ensure a spot for her daughter on the cheerleading squad, then the scenario with Tony as villain didn't seem so far-fetched. His contrite visit to the hospital—a ruse?

Samantha began writing Tony's name under John Townsend's, but midway through she stopped. Tony's voice echoed in her brain.

Mr. Petrella checked the work himself.

52

LATER THAT AFTERNOON, Samantha received a visit from Sergeant Minardi. She was wearing a whopping marquise-cut diamond ring on her left hand. Since the policewoman had last spoken to her, she had found the time to get engaged. Samantha offered her congratulations.

"When's the big day?"

"Valentine's Day."

Around the same time she and Chris were getting married.

There were a few pleasantries about weddings and Minardi complained about a guest list that was already at 250 and steadily climbing. Then she said, "Down to business. We've gone over your car, Mrs. Quinlan. Figured out why you had no brake fluid. Someone opened up your rear bleeder screw."

It may as well have been Swahili.

"Pretty clever, too. See, there's lot of ways you can get a car's brakes to malfunction. Pinch off a brake line and the brakes will overheat. Removing the copper washer between the flex hose and the caliper will get you into some serious trouble, too. But those methods require time, and the perpetrator would need to get under the car." Minardi showed a hint of a smile. "My brother's a mechanic," she explained. "Some of his knowledge rubbed off on his little sister."

"And this—what was done to my car—"

"Simple. All someone needed was a wrench and twenty seconds. Person bends over, pretends to tie his shoe, reaches around to the inside of your back tire, and loosens the bleeder screw one turn. Could have been a day or two before your accident, maybe a week, but gradually your brake fluid drains away."

"Wouldn't I have noticed? My brakes felt fine."

"Then all of a sudden, you hit 'em once, twice, then nothing, right?"

Samantha nodded. "But Frank is dead, Sergeant Minardi. Who killed him?"

The sergeant shrugged. "Another con's our best guess right now."

"This . . . bleeder screw. If it's not a complicated thing to tamper with—"

"A fourteen-year-old with an A average could do it."

Tony Puglia?

"So a person wouldn't necessarily need to be a licensed mechanic."

Jim Petrella. He taught tenth-grade auto. Bert Halloran, Hank Ehrhart. They tinkered with cars on weekends.

"What are you getting at, Mrs. Quinlan?"

She opened the can of worms. "I don't think Frank Ventresca is the one who tampered with my car."

It would have been simpler, *neater,* if the perpetrator had been Frank. He *could* have done it, sure. He had the know-how. He had phoned her, stalked her. He was *the type.* He could have found the opportunity to plant drugs in Matthew's locker as well, set up a family crisis to prove how much a boy needed a dad. His real dad.

He was also the type to creep into her apartment, rummage through her things, tear up the picture of Scott, and steal her underwear. He could have followed her and Chris to Chatham, too, but that, to Samantha, was where the premise of Frank as suspect fell apart.

Samantha had reread her journal several times, passing over it until she was cross-eyed. And she could still hear Frank's voice. *Memberhappy.* Then in a moment of blessed clarity, it came to her. Happy. *Remember* Happy. He had once told her a story about his cherished puppy and how, in a fit of drunken revenge, his father had abandoned it. His voice had caught when he'd told her.

Frank could not have killed Buster. She knew that in her heart. So who had? And why? Was the dead dog unrelated to the other events? Had Frank committed the other acts but not killed the dog?

No. Everything had to tie together. She just wasn't seeing how.

She swung wide, steering at all her information from a new angle. Frank was dead, killed while on his way to see her. Had he come to harm her, finishing what the car accident hadn't accomplished? What if the opposite were true?

He had been coming to warn her. He knew something. Was it possible? In the weeks that he had followed her, Frank had seen something, something that didn't add up. In the end, maybe he understood, but too late.

Was that it, Frank?

Samantha wondered what she had stumbled on to. She had sent Sergeant Minardi off with stories of her unsettling encounter with John Townsend and the strange visit from Tony Puglia. She recounted the threats made by Hank Ehrhart and the disintegration of Jim Petrella's life. Now she regretted her haste, realizing there were many levels of hate. Whoever had killed Frank had crossed way over the line. What had begun as an effort to scuttle a relationship had quickly escalated into a vindictive campaign of terror, then murder.

Someone's bad news? Samantha was still alive. But it wouldn't be for long. With Frank out of the way, the killer would try again, and this time, nothing would be left to chance. Frank, the sinner but also the savior, was dead, killed up close and personal. Samantha could expect the same.

When Samantha had read the journal entries after Matthew's visit, she reasoned that if she could only learn the why, then she would know the who. Yet again, she tried to keep her mind open to other possibilities, but when she studied the events in their entirety, she could arrive at one reason for everything that had transpired.

Which left only one who.

53

MATTHEW WAS RELIEVED when Chris answered the phone on the second ring. "We've got to talk."

"Just got in the door," Chris huffed. "What's up?"

"I'm worried about Mom. Did you see her yesterday?"

"Yes, but not for very long. Why?"

"How'd she seem to you?"

"A little out of it, I guess."

"Out of it as in tired? Or out of it as in drugged?"

"To be honest, I told her she looked a little stoned. She seemed to have some trouble pronouncing a few words clearly."

"She's like a robot, Chris."

"True. But she's been through a lot, Matthew. Come to think of it, I should have peeked at her chart, seen what kind of painkillers they're giving her. Maybe they're just too strong."

"I don't know. I think there's something else. I've been reading her notebook, the one she uses kind of like a journal and—"

"You what?"

"Yeah, I know. When Mom finds out, she'll ground me until I'm thirty-seven, but I was looking for something—"

"So you read your mother's journal? You couldn't just ask her?"

"Chris, forget about the journal a second, will you? I didn't find what I was looking for, but it got me thinking. Lots of weird things have been happening to Mom, a few of them I didn't even know about, and yeah, Frank's grubby hands were in on some of it, but there's more. I've heard some stuff, and something's not right. We've got to talk," he repeated, a desperate plea in his voice.

"Okay, Matthew. I know you wouldn't go through your mom's notes unless something was really bothering you. Tell you what—have you had dinner?"

"No."

"Then I'll swing by, we'll go find some seafood, and you can tell me what's on your mind. Then we'll go visit your mom. Give me twenty minutes."

"Thanks, Chris."

Samantha punched in Chris's number and got no answer. Ten minutes later there was a busy signal, then again no answer. She left a message. "I hope this means you're on your way here. I really need to talk to you."

As soon as she hung up she regretted what she'd said. How could she tell Chris what she suspected?

Sergeant Minardi was off duty, Samantha was told when she tried to reach her. Was there a message? "Just give her this name for me," Samantha said, "and ask her to please check it out."

Her evening meal was half-eaten. The minestrone soup would be cold now and the white sauce on her pasta had congealed into tapioca lumps. Somehow amid her ever-growing anxiety, Samantha managed to consume a buttered roll and a bowl of vanilla pudding, though she couldn't remember the taste of either.

"Shame on you. I'm going to have to summon Nurse Ratched with her cattle prod."

Tom stood at the foot of her bed, looking well rested and healthy. He was pointing at her food tray.

"Am I ever glad to see you! Come here." Samantha opened her arms wide. "I need one of your super-duper hugs."

He came toward her, setting the paper bag he was carrying carefully on the bedside table. Arms around her, he said, "What gives? Not happy here?" He patted her back. "I can see the food's not a big hit, but you scarfed down whatever was for dessert. Typical, Quinlan. Anyway, maybe this'll cheer you up." He reached into the bag and removed a plastic take-out container.

It was a full six inches high and so dark it was nearly black. Death by Chocolate, her favorite dessert, surrounded by a puddle of raspberry coulis.

"From Benito's?"

"Where else? Thought a little decadence from your favorite bakery was in order. You've been through hell."

"And I look like hell, too. Go ahead and say it. Everyone is staring at me like I've got leprosy."

"Leprosy? Nah. Just one big purple splotch on your head. But I hardly noticed."

Normally she would have laughed but now she couldn't muster a smirk.

"Thanks for the cake," she said simply.

"Something's definitely amiss here," Tom said, pulling up a chair near the bed. "By now the Samantha I know would have half that dessert devoured. What's going on?"

"Oh, Tom, you're going to think I'm nuts. Believe me, I've thought so myself these past few hours. But—"

"Come on, spill it. We've shared a few nutty stories over the years."

"I think Chris's mother is trying to kill me."

54

TOM LUNDSTROM THUDDED onto the chair. "Kill you? God, Samantha, I knew the old dame was no good, especially after she tried to buy you off, but murder—that's a big leap. Where are you coming from on this?"

"Bear with me. I'll try to explain. First, you'll agree that Meredith Paxton does not want me to marry Chris."

"That's obvious."

"And what better way to squash a relationship than to undermine it, to make my being with Chris fraught with so many complications that eventually one of us would bail out."

"Which she did how?" Tom leaned forward, his expression one of both curiosity and sympathy.

"She started by putting drugs in Matthew's locker."

"What?"

"At first I suspected Matthew might really be on drugs, but the more time went on, I knew it couldn't be true. Then, when I began to think about why the pills might be planted, only a few things made sense. One, that someone was trying to paint Matthew as a kid with a problem and me as a lousy mother, or two, that marrying a woman with a druggie son was just not an attractive package for the likes of Christopher Paxton, heir to a fortune.

"Oh, I tried to imagine Petrella doing such a thing, and he could have, but it made more sense for it to be Meredith. Paxton Pharmaceuticals manufactures the pills that I found, and Meredith was in the school that same day."

"But if that were true, Samantha, it didn't work. Your relationship with Chris didn't suffer."

"That's right. So, on to the next thing. The dog. Meredith didn't want Chris and me to get closer—"

"But to kill a dog? Just to throw water on a romance? That's pretty vicious, and if I can share some old-fashioned thinking, not exactly a woman's style."

"I know. It was supposed to look like Frank did it, like he was terrorizing us."

Tom rubbed his furrowed brow, then drew a knee up to his chin, resting his foot on the chair. "What about the obvious instead? What if Frank really did kill the dog?"

"No. Frank loved animals. As twisted as the man was, that's one thing he would not have done."

Frank had entered her apartment, had torn Scott's picture, and had taken her underwear as a souvenir, of that she was certain. Frank was a thirty-eight-year-old Tony Puglia. He had delusions about her, about love, without the slightest idea of how to cope with having either. Dangerous? Potentially. But a killer? She didn't think so.

"Okay," Tom conceded, "I'll ride along with your theory a while longer. What else makes you think the old gal wants to do you in?"

"My car accident."

"Wait a minute. You're not going to tell me old lady Paxton

messed with your car, are you? That type wouldn't know how to pump her own gas."

"That's what makes it so perfect. The tampering points directly at Frank and away from her. Plus, Meredith wouldn't have to do it herself. She's got a driver, some loyal old goat who's been with her for decades, shuttles her around in bad weather and on long trips. He was waiting in her Mercedes when we came out of the boutique that night."

"Risky," Tom said. "Opens up a whole blackmail thing. Chris's mother would have to pay big to keep the guy's mouth shut."

"She's good for the money, Tom. Besides, she'd see it as cheaper in the long run." Samantha looked at Tom's face, still skeptical. "All these months, she's been playing the part of devoted future mother-in-law, making sure she was seen with me at the club, in restaurants, in her favorite dress shop . . . and there was a wedding dress she made me try on. She told me how beautiful I looked in it, but the whole time, she was mocking me. The dress was hideous. There was her command performance at school, too, taking my bloody clothes to the cleaners so you could see what a caring person she was. If you hadn't been there, she wouldn't have thought twice about letting me walk around in those clothes."

She waited for Tom's reaction, but he remained quiet, still hugging his knee to his chest, his chin propped on top of his knee while he gazed at some vague spot on the wall behind her. "Something's not right," he said after a long while. "It's the order." He lowered his leg to the floor.

"What do you mean?"

"Crimes usually escalate in severity. Least they do in the books I read. I think Meredith Paxton would have tried to buy you off first, then failing that, would have made an attempt on your life, not the other way around."

"She's trying to get rid of me any way she can. She's desperate. She even said so. 'Desperate people can be driven to desperate acts.' Her words, Tom."

"The old lady really said that? I'll be damned. Still, if she's that desperate to have already wanted you dead, then she wouldn't have settled afterwards for just wanting you out of her son's life. There's no reason I can think of for the old bat to have tried to pay you off. Not if she's intending to kill you. She wouldn't show her hand, announcing she's the enemy by signing a check."

"Maybe, after the car accident, she got cold feet. Realizes murder isn't that easy . . ."

Tom sighed. "Possible, I guess. Still— Never mind. Don't know about you, but I think better after I've had something to eat." He pulled a Delicious apple from his jacket pocket and buffed it on his pant leg.

Samantha reached for the dessert Tom had brought and cracked open the lid.

"One thing you haven't explained, my friend," Tom said, crunching his apple, "is who killed Ventresca?"

"It had to be Meredith. The only way this all makes sense is if I've had two stalkers. Frank had been following me, and somewhere along the way, he noticed something. Maybe the frequent appearance of a black Mercedes, I don't know. Maybe he drove out to Chatham, saw who put Buster on the porch. When he put it all together, he came to tell me and Meredith had to stop him."

Tom munched rhythmically on his apple, staring now at the snow swirling outside the window. Samantha picked up the fork from her supper tray, dragged a piece of the cake through the raspberry purée. She had been deprived for too long. This was better than she remembered.

"Be Christmas soon," Tom said, still preoccupied with the view to the outside. There was a tinge of sadness in his voice. "Your favorite time of year, right?"

The apple was bitten to its skinny core, and Tom pitched it into the wastebasket. "Buy a fella a drink?"

"Help yourself," she said, waving to the plastic water jug on the cluttered bedside table.

She heard him pouring water, taking long gulps, then refilling the glass. His thirst was matched by her gluttony. She devoured the chocolate cake and dipped her finger into the remains of the raspberry sauce. As she finished, she felt Tom bump against the side of her bed.

"Sorry," he muttered, returning to the chair. "Been a long day."

When he was silent once more, Samantha said, "What is it, Tom? You're so deep in thought."

"This theory of yours. You could be right, of course. It's just that—"

She saw him starting to gaze off into the distance again. "What?"

"Well, I've got another idea, but you won't like it."

"Let's have it."

He hesitated. "You may never speak to me again."

"Tom, for God's sake."

"Okay, but remember, I'd never do or say anything to hurt you. I am worried, though. Let's just suppose that everything does lead back to Frank. He put the pills in Matthew's locker, he killed the dog, he rigged your brakes. You've never had two stalkers, only one, a dangerous one, who's had fifteen years to become angrier, more vindictive."

"But someone killed him. Who?"

"Could be an outside chance that Frank met up with someone connected to the prison, but I think it's more likely that Frank was killed by someone trying to protect you from him."

A thick band of tension constricted her chest. She went clammy with fear. "What are you saying?"

Tom reached across the blanket for her hand. "Better face it, friend. Could be that Frank was killed by none other than your fiancé."

55

THE INSIDE OF CHRIS'S SAAB was showroom-spotless, and as Matthew buckled his seat belt, he noticed the car still had a brand-new smell.

Chris had on a tan suede bomber jacket, black cords, and a turtleneck, and Matthew thought he looked cool. Jeff Filion, currently on a '40s gangster kick, would say, "Da guy's got class." Matthew liked Chris, a lot in fact, and thought he would make a great dad. He was easy to talk to and always showed an interest in what Matthew was up to, whether it was music, or schoolwork, or his crush on Kelly. He was a good friend, too, especially when Matthew called him about the pills in his locker. Chris really believed the drugs had been planted there, and had given him some good advice, too. "Give your mom a little space," he'd said. "She'll come around."

Chris was right. She had, and Matthew's trust in Chris climbed another notch.

A few of Matthew's friends had single moms who were dating and they were eager to share horror stories over lunch in the cafeteria, but he couldn't join in. Matthew wasn't creeped out by the thought of Chris and his mom together. In fact, he liked seeing the two of them hanging out. They spent a lot of time laughing and teasing each other, like they'd known each other forever. Because they were comfortable as a couple, Matthew was comfortable too, and he never felt he was cramping their style by being around. Yeah, he gave Chris a lot of points. Chris made his mom happy.

"Where we off to?" he asked.

Chris checked his side mirror and pulled away from the curb. "If you feel like seafood, I know a great place up the coast a little. Are you game?"

It seemed strange to be going so far for fish, particularly when Boston had so many good seafood restaurants, but Matthew shrugged and said, "Why not?"

Once Chris merged onto northbound 1A, he turned down the radio. "I guess you better tell me about your mom's journal and what you think you found."

Chris wanted details about Ehrhart and Petrella and what they'd been up to at school, so Matthew filled him in. Chris was especially interested in Jim Petrella, who had once made a move on Samantha.

"I didn't really get much out of the journal," Matthew said guiltily, "except for two things that kind of bug me."

Chris looked over at him, an eyebrow raised. "Which are?"

"Someone tore up a picture of my dad. Uh, Scott. Mom always kept it in the end-table drawer under a bunch of stuff. One day she went in there and found the thing ripped in half. I think she figured I'd done it, after I found out about Frank and all that, but I didn't, Chris. I'd never mess with Mom's things."

"Like you'd never read her journal?"

Matthew sighed. "Okay, so I'm not too credible right now. There's something else, though, and I know you won't think I did this."

Chris signaled and pulled out to pass. When he maneuvered the Saab safely back into its lane, he said, "Let's hear it."

"Well, it's kind of gross to say, but some of Mom's best underwear is missing."

"What?"

"I'm not kidding. You know how careful Mom is with her money. Well, she splurged on this fancy underwear. She wrote in her journal that she felt guilty about it but— Uh, then there was some personal stuff. Anyway, she wore it once and then she couldn't find it."

"And from this you conclude . . ."

"That the same creep who came into the apartment and tore up the photograph also took the underwear."

"Which sounds like Ventresca."

"Yeah, I thought so too, at first."

"But not now?"

"I think there's more going on here, Chris. Besides, Frank's not able to defend himself anymore, is he? Pretty convenient, wouldn't you say?"

Chris signaled again and turned off the highway. There was a trace of a smile at the corner of his mouth. Matthew thought he must sound like a real idiot, playing Hardy Boy and expounding wild theories to someone as smart as Chris, but then Chris surprised him again, his face stony. "Tell me what you think is going on, Matthew."

He was about to do just that when he took a good look outside. They had passed a few strip malls and some houses and now there didn't seem to be too much around. "Hey, Chris," he said, "where exactly is this restaurant?"

56

SWEAT POURED FREELY and she felt nauseated, the impact of Tom's words too much to bear. Samantha flung back her blanket. Despite the signs of a blustery winter beyond the frosty pane of glass, she wished she could open the window. The air inside was cloying, suffocating, toxic.

"Tom, what you're suggesting—it's just not possible."

"I know that I've upset you, but don't you see? The reason you're upset is because, deep down, you know it *is* possible."

"Chris couldn't kill anyone. Not even Frank."

"You believe his mother is evil, capable of all sorts of machinations. Why not the son?"

"Because I've been with Chris. For over a year. He's the gentlest, kindest man on the planet."

I could kill the bastard with my own hands. Chris's words. Uttered on the night she'd told him about the rape. But he hadn't meant it. Not literally.

"Chris didn't do it," she said, her tone emphatic.

Tom blinked, blinked again, and said nothing. He had found a new spot to stare at, this time at the floor between his shoes.

"I've called the police."

He looked up.

"I left Sergeant Minardi a message to check out Meredith Paxton. That's how much I believe she's guilty." She sat straight up. Her neck was stiff again, and the pain was radiating forward in staccato jabs. She kneaded the tender muscles from her scalp to her shoulders but the pain persisted. A nasty headache was building. Too much tension, too much time lying in a cramped position, and now, she hated to admit it, there was too much of Tom. She wished he would go home.

"Tom, I'm not feeling very well—"

"The police will get to the bottom of everything," he said. "Just answer this one thing. If Meredith Paxton or her driver loosened your bleeder screw on the night of your accident, why did you lose all your brake fluid so fast?"

"I don't know." She sighed, fed up with thinking and too sick to care anymore. "Maybe they didn't do it that night. Maybe they tampered with my car in the school parking lot. Or late at night while my car was parked at home."

Why hadn't she thought of that? The car couldn't have been tampered with that night. It had to have been earlier. Easy enough if all it took was a wrench and twenty seconds, as Sergeant Minardi claimed.

A steel vise squeezed the back of her neck. Intense pain shot to her temples. Samantha knew something was wrong. She was sopping wet. Sweat puddled under her arms, behind her knees, between her thighs. The smell of perspiration was rife around her. Her heart beat a manic tattoo. A migraine? From the chocolate?

Tom no longer stared at the walls and floor. He fixed his gaze on her but said nothing.

"Tom," she gasped, "I feel like shit. I think I might throw up. Can you buzz—"

She froze. Tom remained relaxed in the chair. His face was

devoid of concern, devoid of any emotion. He made no move to summon a nurse.

"Tom?"

An eyebrow rose.

She struggled to process her thoughts but couldn't. It was all too horrible, and the stabbing pain in her head was out of control.

"I never said a thing to you about the bleeder screw," she said at last.

He snapped his fingers. "That's right! You didn't."

It wasn't possible. Yet, looking at Tom now, she knew it was true. He was calm, his forehead unlined. His hands rested comfortably on his knees. There was no tension at the corners of his mouth.

"Poison?" she gasped, still not wanting to believe. "In the cake?"

Tom Lundstrom slowly shook his head. "Your cake was perfectly fine, Samantha. Not a thing in it. But anyone taking MAO inhibitors knows you can't mix them with anything containing tyramine. Cheese, alcohol, even your jumbo cup of Starbucks could cause a reaction. And that triple-chocolate cake combined with the raspberries? You could have a real problem there. Death by Chocolate. Great name."

"But I don't take MAO inhibitors . . ."

"Sure you do," he crooned. "Ever since you've been in here. Sixty milligrams of Nardil. From my own stash. The supper trays aren't exactly guarded. Clever, huh?"

Tom's antidepressants. He'd once told her he had to be careful what he ate. No aged foods. No beer, Chianti, cheese. Chocolate in limited amounts only.

She placed a palm over her heart, as if somehow that might quell its rapid beating. What was happening to her? And could she keep Tom talking while she reached for the nurse's buzzer?

"I don't underst—"

"You don't understand? Oh, but you should. Don't twins have an uncanny perception of what the other is thinking? That's how you described us, wasn't it? I'm your twin brother, the one who comes around to take your kid to ball games, fix your plumbing, fill out your tax return, help you shop for a used car. For fifteen years we've been closer than lots of married couples."

"That's right, Tom, we have." She spoke in a whisper, afraid to move her lips, afraid to move anything in case the slightest motion would send her thudding heart through her ribcage.

"Then you get engaged, and what was I supposed to do? Just stand back and let it happen? It should have been me. Everyone at school said so. When the pills were found in Matthew's locker, you should have come to me. We always handled things together before. I waited for you, but you didn't come."

Oh God, Tom.

Desperate people can be driven to desperate acts.

"Funny," he said, draping an arm across the back of the chair, "you got a lot of it right. That dog. Really wrecked your weekend, didn't it?"

She knew if she made it through this, she would ache all over again for that dog. She would probably ache for Frank, too, whom she never wished dead.

Gingerly, she adjusted her position, feigned loosening stiff joints as she allowed her hand to flop alongside the mattress. The buzzer had to be dangling here somewhere.

"Too bad about Ventresca," Tom said, his words a macabre lullaby. "He spotted me in Chatham that night, leaving the Paxton house. Of course, he didn't remember who I was or what I'd been doing, but he pieced it together eventually and knew I'd set up the car job to look as if he did it. He was coming here the other night to warn you, problem being, the stupid jerk followed me and tried to threaten me like the big blowhard he was. Announced straight out that he was going to tell you everything. I told him to go ahead, that you'd never believe him.

"Stood to reason that since the police were looking for him, he couldn't exactly waltz into the elevator, could he? So I waited in the stairwell, wearing a lab coat I borrowed from the school play's costumes, and Frank and I . . . had a brief encounter."

"Then," she gasped, "I did have two stalkers."

Tom smiled. "For quite a while. But you can't compare me to Ventresca. He deluded himself into thinking the two of you had a relationship. But you and I really did."

"Then why all this? And the brakes?"

He waved his hand philosophically. "Love and hate. Such strong emotions, aren't they? And not so far apart as people may think. I guess when I was reduced to twin brother status, I crossed that fine line."

From inside his jacket Tom removed a length of shimmery black fabric. Her missing lingerie. He pressed the silken cloth to his face and breathed deeply.

Sickened, Samantha averted her eyes. She could not find the buzzer. She remembered Tom bumping against the bed. He'd hidden it then, tucked it somewhere during his pretense of being thirsty.

A nurse would not come. Samantha had asked them to leave her supper tray behind, saying that she might be hungry later. Now the nursing staff would be eating their own meals, tending to paperwork, sharing gossip. Someone would peek in later, but not until at least eleven. How long would it take her to die?

Tom read her next thought, and before she could scream, he yanked the scarf from around his neck and gagged her tightly with it. She heard the snick of a knife before she saw the blade. "Touch that scarf and I'll cut you," he whispered, the blade close to the hollow of her throat.

He used her lingerie to bind her hands in front, then he scudded about the room as if in the midst of spring cleaning. He closed the door and drew the drapes. She thought she heard him humming. She had scant seconds to fumble for the closest thing to a weapon within her grasp—her dinner fork. She closed her hands over it and pulled it to her.

Tom returned to his seat and prepared to watch her die. "How's your head, Samantha? Probably hurts like a son of a bitch. Worst headache you've ever had in your life, I'll bet."

She nodded, her mouth crammed with damp wool. She felt tears welling in her eyes but she fought them off.

"Hypertensive crisis it's called in the medical textbooks," Tom said. "More commonly, 'the cheese reaction.' Basically, there will be a dramatic spike in your blood pressure. Then poof! A brain hemorrhage, maybe a heart attack, and bye-bye.

"I tell you, it's ironic. Been taking those pills for years, watching my diet, but I never could shake the depression, the boredom. Now guess what? I haven't had a pill in two weeks, and I've never felt better. I'm damn near euphoric. Sometimes it's just best to get to the source of the problem and wipe it out, don't you think?"

Sweat pooled beneath her breasts, ran in rivulets under her cast. Her throat was parched and she tried to swallow but there was no saliva. A man she had known for half her life wanted her dead and if she didn't do something soon, he would succeed.

"You know, I can't really complain, Samantha. There have only been two people in my life that I've hated, and you're the second one."

He leaned back in the chair, his smile broadening to a grin. "I can see that you're thinking. Good for you. I've always thought you were smart. Have you figured it out?"

57

THEIR WATER GLASSES HAD been refilled three times but the food still hadn't arrived. "What's the holdup?" Matthew asked, tearing into his second dinner roll. "Can't they get the lobster to die?"

Chris inclined his head toward a long table in the middle of the restaurant. Twenty-odd men in dark suits were animatedly conversing in Japanese. "Bet they got their order in before ours and it's screwed up the kitchen. Sorry, bud. Every time I recommend a place to someone, it goes to hell. Let's hope the food, when it comes, is as good as I remember it."

The restaurant had plenty of polished teak, fish netting, and seashells. Assorted marine paraphernalia crowded on shelves high on the walls, along with yachting trophies and well-worn books on sailing. A gargantuan papier-mâché mermaid dangled from the ceiling, turning and swaying in the fluctuating air currents.

Chris and Matthew sat by a wall of curved glass in a section of the restaurant that cantilevered out onto Massachusetts Bay. For the last forty minutes, fueled by bread and water, Matthew told Chris what he knew.

"Things haven't been the same. Not since you and Mom got engaged."

"What do you mean, haven't been the same?"

"Oh, it's been subtle, but the message was clear."

"Matthew, your mom's known Tom Lundstrom for ages. They've been friends since high school. Wasn't he best man at your mom's wedding?"

Matthew nodded.

"It's only natural he's going to feel protective toward her. And you. I'm the newcomer, right? Bidding for a large chunk of your mom's time. Tom's bound to feel a little . . . well, left out for a while. Just so you know, I'm okay with their friendship, Matthew. Your mom depended on Tom for a lot of years."

"That's just it. Suppose Mr. L. feels Mom owes him something?"

"Conjecture, Matthew."

Their waitress breezed by the table with a tray of multihued drinks in tall glasses. "Won't be too much longer, guys," she said. "Can I bring you some more bread?"

"Just our meal, please. It's been forty-five—"

She was already gone.

"Chris, maybe I can't prove any of this, but all I know is, ever since you gave Mom that ring, Mr. L.'s been treating me different. He's been . . . *possessive.* Telling me I can talk to him anytime, you know, if something's bothering me."

"Sounds like he's just being a nice guy."

"No, it's more than that." Matthew's voice climbed higher. "He's been making like I *should* have something bothering me. And he's been laying on the substitute dad crap heavy, too, wanting to plan a camping trip, spend more time together."

"Matthew, that's just Tom's way of saying he doesn't want to lose the relationship you have. Maybe he feels you've been slipping away a little."

"Yeah, but there's been stuff about you, too." Matthew looked away.

They were interrupted again, this time by the manager, a robust seafaring type with a full gray beard and wind-burned cheeks. There was another apology, a promise of complimentary desserts and his assurance that their meals would be up shortly and well worth the wait. On cue, Matthew's stomach growled.

"I'll be putting ketchup on my napkin in a minute," Chris muttered. "What stuff about me?"

Matthew hesitated. "Like when Mr. L. fixed our loose railing. He said, 'Chris is too busy to do this, I guess.' It's the same spiel every time. Mr. L.'s good to us. You, not so good."

"Okay, I'll concede he's a tad jealous so he's undermining—"

"Jealous? What if it's more than that? What if he's obsessed?"

Obsession seemed to be the buzzword these days and Matthew knew it. Newspaper and magazine articles screamed headlines with the theme of the moment. *Obsessed Fan Found in Celebrity's Home. Mother of Four Bludgeoned by Obsessed Jilted Lover.* Just as a hypochondriac imagines himself having every ailment he's read about, so too was Matthew eager to apply the latest media label to a family friend. At least, that's probably how Chris saw it.

"Chris, the underwear thing. And my dad's picture. What if Mr. L. was responsible? He was putting a new lock on our back door. What's to say he didn't have a key copied for the old lock? It would have been easy. Borrow Mrs. Bea's key, come fix our railing, run to the hardware store for a few nails and get a key made at the same time. He could have walked right in, anytime he wanted. And for someone who's already handy around the house, doesn't it stand to reason that he could be handy with cars, too?"

Chris drained his water in one continuous swallow and plunked his glass on the table. "Matthew," he said after a time, "you've come up with a lot of could-bes. But remember, Frank could have done all those things too."

"But Frank's dead. He didn't kill himself. If Frank was willing to wait fifteen years to get together with Mom, what's to say Mr. L. hasn't been doing the same thing?"

Chris sprung to his feet. "Come on."

"What's up?"

"We're leaving."

"Here comes our food!"

Chris reached inside his jacket and peeled off three twenty-dollar bills and slapped them into Matthew's hand. "Tell the waitress to pack it all up. We'll eat in the car. I'll bring it around."

"We're going to the hospital, aren't we." Matthew was standing now, too.

"You'll feel better, right? Seeing your mom? And so will I."

58

FOR PLEADING NOT GUILTY to witchcraft and for refusing to stand trial during the Salem hysteria of 1692, Giles Corey was subjected to unspeakable torture. For two agonizing days he endured while stone weights were piled on a wooden plank atop his body before his chest finally caved in and he succumbed to eternal sleep.

Pressed to death.

Samantha felt she would die the same way, so excruciating was the pain in her chest. The weight of a dozen anvils bore down upon her, and she struggled for breath. Her scalp, her brain, her eyes, she was certain, would rip from her skull, leaving nothing but an empty, anonymous shell.

In the throes of her suffering, Tom sat coolly, eyeing her in that same detached way he'd earlier examined the floor. He was composed, restful, serene. He was also settling in for her final moments; he removed his coat. His white button-down shirt was starched and pressed. Ralph Lauren's horse and polo player froze mid-play over the left breast. She and Matthew had bought the shirt for him last Christmas.

"Scott was a tremendous athlete," he said, his breathing slow and even. "He was headed for the bigs, that's for sure. He got the scholarship, he got the glory, and he got the girl. Nobody pays much attention to the number-two guy. The *almost* guy. The one who *couldn't quite.*"

She was drenched, the perspiration cooling her body to Arctic degrees, but the tremor that shuddered through her had no root in physiology. She was terrified. She sensed what was to come and she didn't want to hear it.

"These star athletes, they all want to go for the gold. Swifter, higher, stronger, and all that. Give them a challenge, they'll conquer it. A new horizon, they'll sail to it. Trouble is, they don't admit to having any limitations. They don't know when to call it a day and go home.

"That was golden boy Scott's problem. Great athlete, shitty glider pilot. He was sloppy, a novice who couldn't make it to the next level. Now, me? Harness me in a hang glider and I had it all over him. I rode those thermals like a pro, did 360s, soared the ridges with the best of them. Bugged the shit out of him. He tried to keep up, but he never could. It was really easy to plant the seed."

Through eyes that felt bulged beyond the sockets that held them, she stared at Tom, her high-school chum, the man she trusted leaving her son with on so many occasions. She looked for evidence that he had changed, thinking she should see the menace, the evil somewhere on his face. She saw good old Tom, familiar Tom. She saw her best friend.

"'Nothing like gliding at Torrey,' I told him. 'Make a great place for your honeymoon. All that sun, the beaches, the mountains. Who doesn't want to go to California?'"

She remembered the day Scott had suggested it. He had been so eager, and yes, she wanted to see where the movie stars lived.

"'You'll catch some great air,' I said. 'Just bring me back a picture of you making your turns with those cliffs behind you.' He wasn't going to refuse. He couldn't. Especially when I bet him two hundred bucks that he would chicken out. I threw out the hook and he bit.

"One of the first rules you learn in flight training: no relatives or friends on the ground with cameras. Cameras make you do stupid things in the air. Well, Scott proved that to be true. With a little help from his loving wife."

He didn't sabotage the hang glider. He didn't fire a shot into the sail. Yet, from across the country, Tom, at age eighteen, had killed Scott.

He was getting to his feet. "End coming soon, Samantha. You're showing all the symptoms of hypertensive crisis. Yes, my doctor warned me all about it when I started the medication, told me to call Emergency immediately if I noticed any signs like the ones you've got." He drew near, placed a large hand over her breast. "Tachycardia," he announced, smiling. "Oh, sorry, I didn't mean to take liberties. Did Frank grab at you like that, once upon a time under that nasty old lilac tree? Or did he dispense with the above-the-waist foreplay and make straight for the—"

Her hand shot forward and she heard a sickening *schtuck*. There was a millisecond of dreadful silence as Tom's eyes locked with hers. Then came a terrible moan, an endless bestial cry, followed by a rush of footsteps in the corridor. Tom's hand closed over hers as he withdrew the dinner fork. It was over, she thought. She hadn't killed him and now he would use the weapon against her.

Warm sticky blood covered her hands and soaked through the pristine white of Tom's shirt. He clutched at the wound, and Samantha turned her head to the side and retched. The scarf was too tight. She would choke on her own vomit.

She was dizzy, weak, and beginning to hallucinate. In the hazy distance she thought she heard a duet of voices. "In here! Quick!"

59

IN THE CORNER OF THE ROOM stood an artificial Christmas tree. It was tall, slender, and beautifully decorated with large gold ornaments and a lavish garland of ribbon. It was the first thing Samantha saw when she regained consciousness. She was aware, too, that the pair of voices had added a baritone. Chris and Matthew were near the window talking to Dr. Buchanan. She heard unintelligible murmuring, then clearer fragments of conversation.

" . . . gave her Procardia . . . very lucky." The doctor.

"But she'll be all right?" Chris. So good to hear his voice.

And Matthew's. "She's got to be. That's all there is to it."

"Hey," she said, her voice tremulous. "I'm over here. Anybody want to talk to me?"

Downy kisses dusted her forehead and cheeks, and there was a rush of so-good-to-see-yous along with declarations of love, relief, and gratitude to God. There were hugs, too, but they were cautious.

"I'm not that fragile, am I?" she asked when Chris's tentative embrace ended too quickly.

"You're not exactly ready for the Boston marathon," Dr. Buchanan said. "But these two fans of yours told me you're quite a trooper and I can see they're right." He looked at Chris and Matthew. "Not too long now." He patted Samantha's blanketed foot and left.

"You both look so tired," Samantha said. Chris's eyes were ringed black, Matthew's slightly less so.

"You're no Mrs. Universe either." Chris took her hand. "Honestly, Matthew, you'd think she could have run a comb through her hair—"

"A little lipstick, at least—"

"Too late," she said, her voice still breathy and weak. "I've got the ring. I'm letting myself go."

Across the hall, a television blared on. A children's choir was singing "Angels We Have Heard on High" on a morning news show. Matthew went to close the door.

"You spent all night decorating that tree?" Samantha asked. "It's gorgeous."

"Don't look at me. That's woman's work. Mom did it. Thought it would cheer you up."

"Your mother?" The tree did bear Meredith's designer touches. An attempt to atone? Or simply another devoted-mother-in-law performance. "I'm surprised." Then she added, "Especially after her last visit."

"Why? What happened?"

"I think you should ask her yourself."

Chris looked at her quizzically. "I'll do that."

Matthew was beside her. "Mom, how are you feeling?" He wagged a finger. "The truth, young lady."

She smiled. "A little like I've been steam-rollered and my body's still trying to resume its normal shape."

Her headache had abated to a dull throb and the tightness

across her chest had eased. A pair of crutches and months of therapy waited for her. She wasn't going to complain.

There was still a question left unasked and the unpleasantness of it hung in the air like a dense layer of yellow smog. "What about . . . Tom?"

She could scarcely utter the name and knew that once in her apartment, she would purge the place of anything he had ever given her—fifteen years' worth of mugs, picture frames, books, plants. During all those years, the ghost of Frank haunted her from the shadows. Now she had another ghost, another horror to endure.

"He's been arrested, Mom."

"Doctors patched him up."

She remembered the awful sound, the tines of the fork piercing tough flesh, the grotesque mixture of chocolate and blood. The sour taste of nausea rose in her throat and she swallowed hard.

Death by chocolate.

It could have ended so differently.

"What brought the two of you to my room last night? I wasn't expecting a visit from either of you."

"You can thank your son for that." Chris clapped Matthew on the back and kept his arm across his shoulder. "Meet Matthew Spillane, clarinetist by day, teen detective by night. He had the goods on Tom, wouldn't stop yakking until I believed him."

"But how—?"

"Not now, Mom. It's a long story and we're all pretty tired."

She nodded, reaching for Matthew's hand. They were a circle of three.

"Let's see what we've got here," she said, her voice growing thick with fatigue. "One smarty-pants teenager, one guy with Cruella De Ville for a mother, and me, who seems to always have a jailbird somewhere in my life."

"Yeah, we're a fine trio, all right," Chris said.

"At least we ain't dull," Matthew added in his best '40s gumshoe.

Samantha looked at the two of them, Chris with his outer gentleness and inner strength, and Matthew with his intellect, his humor, and his dreams for the future. "I think we're what you'd call a normal, modern family."

ACKNOWLEDGMENTS

TO MAKE SURE I GOT things right (or close to it), I leaned (not too heavily, I hope) on the following fine folks:

Superintendent Mike Shea, Division One, Hamilton Police Service

Detective Constable Steve Martin, Halton Regional Traffic Unit

Jim Westiuk, Jim's Service Centre

Karl Dinzl, Skysailing Ontario Hanggliding and Paragliding School

Gabriel Jebb, Torrey Pines Gliderport

Greta Peso and Walter Harmidarow: astute readers, talented writers, great friends . . .

Bryan Prince: tireless, enthusiastic supporter . . .

. . . and as always, I can count on Al: through thick and thin, you're the greatest.

ABOUT THE AUTHOR

CATHY VASAS-BROWN lives in Southern Ontario with her husband, Al, and their four cats—Watson, Holmes, Spike, and (Sir) Arthur. She is the author of *Every Wickedness,* which was nominated for an Arthur Ellis Award for best first crime novel.